(In the East E

CW00383307

FAMIL

By Kim Hunter

Other Works by Kim Hunter

EAST END HONOUR

WHATEVER IT TAKES

TRAFFICKED

BELL LANE LONDON E1

EAST END LEGACY

EAST END A FAMILY OF STEEL

PHILLIMORE PLACE

EAST END LOTTERY

FAMILY BUSINESS

A DANGEROUS MIND

Web site
www.kimhunterauthor.com

Dedication

In loving memory of Charlie
1937-2016
Dad I miss you more than words could ever say!

FOREWORD

This year has been the toughest of my life and for me just
to finish this novel has been a mammoth task. The
emotions a person experiences at the loss of a loved one
are the worst in the world but it has allowed me to draw
on my inner feelings and hopefully this will show in the
depth of my writing. We are never ready to let a loved
one go even if we know deep down that it is their time.
The feeling of total devastation is at times overwhelming
and almost too much to bare. To all those people who are
suffering and experiencing such a loss, my heart reaches
out to you.

Kim Hunter x

QUOTE

"There is nothing like wounded affection for giving poignancy to anger."

Elizabeth Gaskell (1810-1865)

CHAPTER ONE

December 26th 1959

'Bird Dog' by the Everly brothers was playing loudly on the radio as Wilf Nicholson thickly lathered his hair with brylcreem. Still living at home with his mother and father in a two up two down end of terrace on Buxton Street in Shoreditch and after working for Hayes funeral directors over in Hackney for the last six years, going for a night out was the only thing that kept Wilf sane. For someone from such a poor background, his high hopes and dreams of a career in the city had been about as achievable as a trip to the moon. On the day that he left school it was a matter of taking the first position that came up and that had turned out to be for Vernon Hayes. He hated the job, he hated living in this piddling little house and if he was honest, he hated his parents as well. They had never achieved anything and in his eyes seemed content to always be poor, well Wilf had bigger plans and he was going to make sure they came to fruition. Pulling on his jacket, he did one final inspection in the mirror, the flannel suit was new and Wilf turned in all directions to admire himself. He knew he was handsome and tonight, in his eyes at least, knew he looked sharp. Happy with the image staring back at him he slowly made his way downstairs. The annual Christmas bonus, albeit paltry, still sat behind the clock on the mantelpiece and opening the envelope he stuffed the contents into his trouser pocket.

"You going out tonight son?"

"No dad, I thought I would get dressed up just to sit here with you two."

Nora Nicholson rolled her eyes upwards and sighed. Her son was always rude to his father and she hated it. John, her husband of thirty years, had always worked hard for them and had given his only child everything he could but it was never enough and sometimes Nora felt like slapping her son but of course she never did. Wilf was the apple of his father's eye and John had been far too lenient with him, maybe that was where the problem stemmed from, still it was too late to change him now so getting up from her chair, Nora walked over and gave her son the once over before kissing him tenderly on the cheek.

"Very smart, very smart indeed."

Wilf wiped his face with the back of his hand and grimaced as he did so.

"Alright mum, that's enough or you'll mess my hair up." Picking up his front door key from the mantel piece he checked his hair again in the mirror before turning to his mother.

"Don't wait up!"

Without another word Wilf was out of the house in seconds. The Rivoli ballroom was having its grand opening tonight and Wilf Nicholson had managed to get a ticket. Not one to have any close friends he was always happy to go out alone. He didn't like the idea of having to buy other people drinks, well not unless it was a woman and there was the chance of a leg over at the end of the night. It was a long bus trip over to south London as Wilf didn't have the cash to pay for a taxi but he was so excited that for once he didn't grumble. The Rivoli was originally a picture palace but had recently been purchased by Lenny Tomlin and turned into a dancehall. Anyone who was anyone would be there tonight and as the bus neared his stop Wilf could feel the excitement building to a crescendo in the pit of his stomach. Climbing the three steps up to the double doors Wilf again checked his reflection in the glass before stepping inside. 'Mack the knife' was blearing out and Wilf began to snap his fingers as he walked towards the main room. Red velvet flock wallpaper covered the walls and chandeliers and glitter balls hung from the ceiling. It was all a feast for the eyes and Wilf had never seen anything like it. Moving to the right hand side bar that ran the whole length of the room he scanned everything in detail. Leather clad booths were arranged similar to a rail carriage and he thought that when the lights dimmed it would be a perfect place to get up close and personal with a girl. If there was one thing Wilf Nicholson loved more than himself it was women and he wasn't fussy how they came. His work colleagues told him he was nothing better than a male whore when he bragged about his weekend conquests on a Monday morning. Sometimes it was the truth but most of the time when he'd been unlucky and had been forced to resort to masturbation, his imagination had run wild and the stories he'd repeated were crude and about as depraved as his mind would allow. Walking up to the bar and after ordering a pint he scanned the room again and his eyes soon fell upon a group of four young girls. Running a hand through his hair and after adjusting his tie Wilf picked up his drink and made his way over. Lena Salmon was at the Rivoli with two of her friends and much to her annoyance, her wall flower of an older sister, Daisy. Lena was tall and slim with a figure to die for and with her peroxide blonde hair she stood out above all the other women in the room. Wilf introduced himself and to begin with Lena seemed interested, that was until he told her he worked for a firm of undertakers. The distaste on her face was noticeable to

3

all but she wasn't bothered. In a strange way Lena
Salmon was exactly the same as Wilf Nicholson, she
wanted the finer things in life and that included a husband
with a very good career and money to spare.
The three women instantly hit the maple sprung floor and
Daisy was left standing alone with the self obsessed
young man. She was so nervous that she stared at the
ground in embarrassment. Wilf wasn't happy at Lena's
brush off but after taking a moment to study the young
woman he reasoned that she wasn't too bad to look at and
besides, anything was better than another hand shandy
and a pack of lies for Monday morning.
"You want a drink darling?"
Daisy thought for a second and then remembered what
she'd heard her sister and the others talking about earlier.
"I'll have a dry martini please."
"Oh no you won't, I ain't bleeding loaded you know.
You'll have an orange juice and like it."
Wilf didn't usually speak to women that abruptly but he
had a feeling this one was as inexperienced as they came.
He took a couple of steps towards the bar and then turned
back to face her.
"You coming or what?"
Daisy smiled and shuffled forward, he wasn't what you'd
call romantic but she couldn't deny that he was good
looking and in all honesty boys never usually showed any
interest in her. The couple stood awkwardly together for
the rest of the evening as Wilf talked nonstop about
himself and filled Daisy's head with lies. When the last
song was announced Wilf grabbed her hand and led her
out onto the dance floor. As they smooched he began to
kiss her neck and starting to feel uncomfortable she
scanned the room but there was no sign of her sister and
the others. Daisy suddenly realised that they had already

left and she was now alone with this boring idiot. Her Dad would go mad when she arrived home on her own and she was sure that Lena would get the blame but then again it would serve her sister right. Daisy hadn't even wanted to go out tonight but her father was always trying to bring her out of her shell and had insisted that she went along with Lena. Daisy was shy to say the least, and the evening out was now turning into a nightmare.

"What's up?"

His voice startled Daisy and as she looked up he could see tears beginning to form in her eyes.

"I think my sister and her friends have already left."

"Don't worry about that darling; I'll make sure you get home safe and sound. Scout's honour."

Daisy breathed a sigh of relief and when the music ended she collected her jacket from the cloakroom. It was cold outside so when Wilf placed his arm around her shoulder she didn't resist.

"Where do you live sweetheart?"

"Elsiemaud Road, it's not far."

Wilf didn't know the area that well but well enough to know that to get to Elsiemaud Road you had to pass Brockley cemetery. In the darkness Daisy didn't see the sickly grin as it spread across his face. They walked along but didn't chat and as they reached the entrance to the cemetery he suddenly grabbed Daisy's arm and pulled her inside.

"No don't!"

"Oh come on girl, I only want a bit of a kiss and a cuddle."

Daisy again tried to stop him pulling her but Wilf was strong and she was no match for him. Finally she relented as she reasoned that it wouldn't hurt for a couple of minutes so long as no one saw them and told her father.

"Alright but only for a minute. My Dad will go bleeding light if I'm home late."

Before she knew what was happening Wilf had marched her across the grassy walkway and backed her up against a grave stone.

"Oh don't Wilf please! My dress will get all dirty."

Wilf Nicholson ignored her plea and within seconds his hand was up Daisy's skirt and he began to feel her body. The feeling was new to her and she couldn't deny that she liked it but a nagging image of her father made her try and fight him off. It was useless and when his fingers found themselves inside her knickers and he began to explore her she couldn't help but respond. As he pulled down hard Daisy felt her underwear drop to the floor and he soon began to force his knee forward pushing her legs apart.

"No no please I mustn't."

"Come on sweet cheeks, you know you want to."

"No no I don't!"

"Shush baby, it will be alright I promise. Just trust me sweetheart, you'll love it once you get going."

Laying her down onto the ground he climbed on top of Daisy and as he entered her and felt her whole body tense, he knew it was her first time. By anyone's standards Wilf Nicholson had more than an average size penis. He was the kind of bloke that would get it out without a moment's hesitation and he had a habit, much to his works mate's disgust, of showing off how big he was at any given opportunity. Daisy whimpered in pain and the sound only heightened his pleasure knowing that no one had been there before him. It was all over in a matter of minutes and when he at last rolled off of her Daisy scrambled to her feet and pulled up her underwear.

Standing up Wilf lit a cigarette and pecked her on the cheek. His breath was rancid and she now couldn't understand why she had been so attracted to him in the first place.

"Thanks for that darling. You can make your own way home from here cant you?"

It was a rhetorical question and he didn't wait for a reply. As Daisy stood and watched him walk away with a spring in his step tears streamed down her cheeks. Had she been raped? She didn't think so and besides no one would believe her if she said he had forced himself on her, after all, what was she doing with a strange man in the dead of night in a cemetery? Slowly she made her way home and creeping up the stairs she lay down on her bed fully clothed. She could still smell him and the tears came thick and fast until she cried herself to sleep.

It was now over two months since that fateful night and she hadn't clapped eyes on Wilf Nicholson, nor had she clapped eyes on her period and she knew that she had to confide in someone before it was too late. One Sunday morning and after she had thrown up in the outside toilet for the umpteenth time, Daisy climbed the stairs and knocked on her sisters bedroom door. Not waiting for an invitation she turned the handle and went inside.

"Lena, Lena I need to talk to you."

Lena Salmon suddenly sat bolt upright in bed, her hair was in rollers and her face was still covered in night cream. She screwed up her face as she spoke and at the same time wiped the sleep from her eyes.

"Well it's nice of you to wait for an invite I must say. What do you want Daisy?"

Daisy took a seat on the bottom of the bed and when she suddenly began to cry Lena instantly changed her tone. Placing a hand on her sister's shoulder she softly spoke.

7

"Come on now love, it can't be as bad as all that?"

"It is, Oh Lena, I think I'm pregnant."

"You're what? Whose is it?"

Daisy swallowed hard before she answered, shame filled her to breaking point but she knew it was useless to try and say anything other than the truth.

"You remember that night we went down the Rivoli, that bloke who was all over you but you weren't having any of it? Well, he ended up walking me home because you'd left me and well, one thing led to another and I didn't want to but he...."

"Bloody Nora! Dad's going to blame me for this I just know he is. Did that bloke force himself on you, because if he did well you could...."

Daisy placed her hand in the air in an attempt to silence her sister.

"If you're asking did he rape me? Then the answer is no, I could have walked away but I didn't."

"Have you told him?"

"I ain't seen hide or hair since that night, oh Lena, I don't even know where he lives."

For once Lena was silent. Deep in thought she bit down hard on her highly polished thumb nail as she wracked her brains. Suddenly she stopped and looked in her sister's direction as she recalled the conversation she'd had with the man.

"I know where we can find him and tomorrow we'll take the day off work but no telling mum or dad about this until later ok?"

Daisy wasn't happy about the deceit but neither was she happy about being pregnant. She wasn't looking forward to seeing Wilf again but deep down she knew she had little choice in the matter. The following day the sisters set off for work as usual but when they reached the tube

8

station they boarded a train to Hackney. Hayes funeral directors stood at the end of Hoxton Street and as they neared the building that would ultimately seal her fate, Daisy began to shake uncontrollably which didn't go unnoticed by her sister. Stopping dead in her tracks Lena grabbed Daisy's hands and stared deep into her eyes. "Sweetheart you have to pull yourself together, we have to get this sorted before we can even think of telling mum and dad."

Daisy nodded her head and as Lena pushed hard on the front door a bell instantly rang out. A grey haired man walked through from the back room in a smooth silent manner which was typical for the business he was in. He smiled at the two women to reveal a set of yellowing teeth that appeared to be far too big for his mouth. In a calm low voice he bowed his head as he addressed the women.

"Good morning and how may I help you ladies?"

"Well I'm hoping you can Mr. It seems one of your employees forced himself upon my sister and now she's in the family way!"

Vernon Hayes was instantly embarrassed and he knew or at least he thought he knew, exactly who the women were referring to. Wilf Nicholson's antics were legendary and he was the only man capable of this wicked evil deed. If any of the locals got wind of this shameful situation, well it certainly wouldn't be good for business.

"Please come through to my office ladies. I'm sure we can sort this out without too much fuss."

Lena marched through to the back with Daisy following in hot pursuit. In the rear workshop they both came face to face with Wilf and Lena was in no mood to hold her tongue or speak quietly about her accusation.

"That's him, he's the one that got our Daisy up the duff!"

Wilf's face suddenly went crimson when he recalled who the two women were. He knew that to try and deny it would be futile and would also show him in a cowardly light. Walking over he reluctantly took Daisy's hand in his.

"Is this true?"

Daisy Salmon nodded her head and lowered her gaze at the same time, just as she always did when she was frightened, embarrassed or didn't have a clue what to say next. Wilf suddenly took a step backwards and as he did he bumped into his boss.

"I think you and I need to have a word in private Wilf. Go into my office and close the door, I will join you in a moment."

Ten minutes later and the two men returned to where Daisy and a rather impatient Lena were still standing. Wilf had been told in no uncertain terms that he must do the right thing and marry the poor girl, that or he wouldn't have a job come Monday, he was also warned that no one else on the manor would employ him either. At the end of the day Wilf had called at Daisy's house and asked Mr Salmon for his daughters hand in marriage. By the end of that week Daisy had been introduced and warmly welcomed into the fold by Wilf's parents. A date was set for two weeks time but for the next fourteen days and while he was still a free man Wilf Nicholson made the most of his time. Meeting up with as many women as he could, he was rough with them and never gave away his name. With each encounter he imagined that the whore beneath him was Daisy and he swore to God that he would make the little bitch that had trapped him; suffer for the rest of her life.

CHAPTER TWO

TWO YEARS LATER

Being allocated the flat on Roy Street was a dream come
true and after many months of living with Wilf's parents,
the couple finally moved into their very own home.
While living with her in-laws, Daisy's married life had
been happy, well maybe not happy but at least content,
even if her husband did have an insatiable appetite for
sex. Now after the first week of running her own house
everything changed for Daisy Nicholson and not in a
good way. Struggling up the stone steps, in one arm she
carried little Stella and in the other she held onto the
handle of the pram. Reaching the top she placed her
daughter back into the carriage and pushed it along the
landing. Alice Partridge who lived next door had just
stepped outside when she saw her neighbour and her
heart went out to the poor little kid, well at least that was
how she saw her, just a kid not much older than Alice's
own girls. Daisy always looked so weary and
downtrodden and Alice had heard the nightly ranting that
came from the flat. Wilf Nicholson was a pig to his wife
but the poor little girl never once answered him back.
"Hello love, been down the market have you?"
"Hello Mrs Partridge, yes just to get a few veg. My Wilf
has to have fresh everyday or there are murders. Not so
easy with this one and another on the way though."
"How far gone are you now sweetheart?"
"Six months but it feels like a lifetime, I ain't been
sleeping at all lately."
Daisy gently rubbed her stomach.
"This little bugger does nothing but kick me, I swear he's

11

going to be a footballer some day. Listen to me, dreaming again but I really would love a little boy Mrs Partridge."

Alice gently touched Daisy on the arm as she walked away.

"You take care of yourself, have a cuppa and put your feet up for a bit love."

Daisy placed her key into the lock and wished that she could do just that but there was so much left to do and if she hadn't completed her chores by the time he came home then there would be hell to pay. She didn't mind so much for herself but Wilf was so volatile she was always worried that he might start on Stella.

"Come on sweetheart, let's get you inside."

After laying Stella down for a nap, Daisy set about tackling the housework. An hour later she had pulled out the copper and was heating the water to do a wash. Wilf's shirts had to be pristine and he insisted on a fresh one in the morning and again at night before he went out for the evening. Lugging the laundry basket down to the outside square she hung out the washing and made her way back up to the flat to begin the evening meal. When a knock came at the front door, Daisy was in the middle of making a meat pie and sighing to herself she wiped her floured hands down the front of her apron. Her sad expression instantly changed when she saw who her visitor was.

"Lena!!!"

"Hello Sis, I was in the area and thought I'd pay you a surprise visit."

As usual Lena Salmon was done up to the nines and had her trademark Siamese cat tucked safely under one arm. Her peroxide hair was styled in the latest fashion and Daisy couldn't help but admire the beautiful dress that her sister was wearing.

"I see he still hasn't decorated then?"

"Don't start Lena, Wilf works long hours and...."

"And he's a complete bastard is what you should be saying."

Lena Salmon still wasn't married and probably never would be but she did have a trendy flat on Portobello road that was financed by Cyril Kramer, a portly middle aged banker that granted Lena her every desire. Always one for wanting the high life, Lena had decided after seeing her sister get tied down to a total bully of a husband, that she would never get caught in the same way. It would be far better to exploit men and her ample assets meant she was able to milk many poor suckers for her own gain and right at this moment that sucker happened to be Cyril Kramer.

"Is he treating you any better?"

The look on Daisy's face said all that needed to be said and Lena proceeded to place her hand into her shopping basket. She had a crafty grin on her face as she pulled out a can of Spillers cat food.

"Put this in his pie darling."

"Lena! I couldn't possibly."

The idea did make Daisy laugh and she didn't protest any further when her sister placed the can onto the draining board.

"Just in case honey! When that bastard is playing you up you just might change your mind and at least you can smile knowing what he's really shovelling into that spiteful gob of his!"

By the time her husband arrived home Stella had been bathed and was in bed, a full gravy dinner was waiting to be dished up and the clean shirts were hanging in the wardrobe. Glancing down at her ankles she could see they were badly swollen and she thought back to Alice's kind words, but there wouldn't be a hope of putting her feet up until after he'd gone out for the night. In silence Wilf sat down at the small dining table in the front room and after Daisy had dished up the meal and placed her own back into the oven she set about running him a bath. Ten minutes later and he appeared in the doorway.

"Have you looked in that fucking mirror lately? You're a fat heffer Daisy; how the fuck did I get lumbered with you?"

After the day she'd had Daisy for once couldn't hold her tongue.

"If you hadn't forced yourself on me then you wouldn't have got lumbered and besides Wilf Nicholson, you ain't that much of a bleeding catch either."

His fist seemed to come out of nowhere and Daisy screamed as she clutched at her stomach. She was desperate to protect the life growing inside her but when he lunged for a second time and knocked her backwards into the hot water she didn't stand a chance. Wilf grabbed her by the scruff of the neck and threw her into the hall and at the same time radio's in all the flats along the landing suddenly seemed to increase their volume. No one ever poked their noses into anyone's business but for once Daisy prayed that someone would. Wilf marched out of the kitchen and Daisy crawled along the hallway to the toilet. The blood came thick and fast as soon as she sat down and with tears streaming down her face; she said a silent prayer in the hope that her baby would be saved. Daisy remained in the toilet until she heard the front door slam and then standing up and wincing with every step, she walked back to the kitchen. Mild cramps had begun and she hoped above hope that they would soon start to subside. As usual her husband hadn't even bothered to empty his own bathwater but for once she was grateful. Tentatively stepping in she allowed her whole body to submerge but there was nothing comforting about the warm water as it caressed her body. She must have remained there for over an hour because when she opened her eyes she could feel and see that not only was the water cold but it was crimson red in colour. When she at last got dressed, wiped out the tub and replaced the big heavy lid, there was a knock at the door.

"Daisy, Daisy love, are you in there sweetheart? It's me Alice Partridge."

Opening up Daisy fell into the woman's arms just as her waters broke and she sobbed until there were no more tears left in her.

"Oh lord above, whatever has he done to you now?"

"The baby, I think I'm losing the baby!"

Alice couldn't believe what she was hearing, it went against everything she believed in when a man laid a hand on a woman but to do it to a woman carrying a child was, well she didn't have any words for it. Alice was old school and had lived in the East End her entire life. There were plenty out there who would beat Wilf Nicholson to within an inch of his life if they got wind of this and Alice was tempted to tell but she knew that if she did then the only one to really suffer would be dear sweet Daisy. Holding the young woman around the waist Alice helped her back into the hallway.

"Sweetheart you've got to leave that bastard before he bleeding well kills you."

"I can't Mrs Partridge; I mean where would I go with a little one? It's not acceptable to walk out on your marriage no matter how bad it is, so I know there's no way my family would help me."

15

Daisy doubled over in pain again and Alice knew it was time to call for help.

"You need looking at young woman and I ain't taking no for an answer. I'll get my Burt to go to the telephone box and call the midwife."

"Oh God Alice the pain! I can't take this pain!"

Alice Partridge applied a cold flannel to the poor girl's brow but it was of little use and she prayed that help would arrive soon as Daisy thrashed about the bed in agony. Thirty minutes later and there was a knock on the front door. Daisy glanced at the wall clock but breathed a sigh of relief with the realisation that her husband wouldn't be back for at least a couple of hours or if she was really lucky he wouldn't return until the morning. She never questioned him about where he went and the smell of cheap perfume was always overpowering on his clothes but at times she welcomed it if it meant he left her alone. Alice Partridge let the midwife in, a local woman named Mrs Mumbecroft, and hearing them speak in hushed tones, Daisy knew that her neighbour was revealing that she was a victim of domestic abuse. It wasn't mentioned during the examination but when the midwife had finished she turned to Daisy and her face was grave.

"I'm sorry Mrs Nicholson but your baby is dead. You are so far gone that the only option is to deliver it as normal. It will be very painful I'm afraid but I can give you something to speed up the labour. I'm sorry but that's about as much help as I am able to offer you."

Daisy burst into tears and as soon as Mrs Mumbecroft had administered the injection the contractions hit her like a wave, over and over again. This time it was far worse than it had been with Stella and each one made her feel as if her stomach was being ripped open. She wanted

16

to shout out, tell them all to go to hell and leave her alone but the pain was so bad that all she could do was bite down on the bed sheet with every fresh onslaught of pain. Every time she pushed Daisy felt like a piece of her was dying, being torn from her body and without her consent. Two hours later and after being told to give one last push her baby finally emerged. His complexion was pink and his tiny rosebud lips were perfect and all Daisy wanted to do was cradle him in her arms and shower him with love but she didn't get the chance. Cutting the cord Mrs Mumbecroft then scooped up the poor little mite, wrapped his tiny body in some old news papers and then handed him over to Alice.

"There is a cardboard box in the hallway, put it in there and I'll dispose of it later."

Daisy wanted to scream, it it! He wasn't an it. Why were they talking about her baby as if he was a piece of rubbish to be tossed away, his very existence to be brushed under the carpet as if his little life had no meaning? Daisy didn't have the strength left in her to cry let alone scream but her whole body was aching for her dead baby. When the midwife pushed down hard on her stomach to help release the afterbirth Daisy screamed out in agony again. It took three further attempts before it came away but at long last the trauma of giving birth was finally over. When Daisy had been cleaned up and the sheets changed Mrs Mumbecroft took a seat on the bed beside her patient. The normally stern looking woman gave a thin smile as she began to speak.

"I do not wish to discuss your marriage or pry into what goes on in your home Mrs Nicholson, but I will tell you that if this ever happens again there is a strong possibility that you won't be able to bear anymore children. Do you understand what I'm saying?"

Daisy nodded her head but didn't speak as she felt too ashamed. Alice and Mrs Mumbecroft walked from the bedroom and after a short while Daisy heard the front door close as the midwife left. Miraculously Stella had slept through all of the noise and her mother's screaming and for that Daisy was grateful. When Alice was sure that the young woman was alright she quietly slipped out of the flat so that Daisy could get some much needed sleep but that wasn't about to happen as at three am Wilf Nicholson fell through the front door. He was drunk and smelled of sex but then that was nothing new. Hauling herself out of bed Daisy guided him along the hallway and after undressing him, led him over to the bed. He tried to kiss her but when he lent forward and began to wobble about Daisy gently pushed him down onto the mattress and within seconds he was snoring loudly. Grabbing a blanket she slowly made her way back into the front room to sleep on the couch.

The following morning and totally unaware of the previous night's events Wilf sat down at the tiny dining table and waited impatiently for his breakfast. He had a raging headache and was in no mood for conversation, if that lazy bitch of a wife didn't hurry up then he was going to teach her a lesson. Before he had time to call out Daisy carried through a plate full of eggs and bacon and setting it down stared at her husband. She felt nothing but hatred for the man and wished with all her heart that he would just drop down dead right where he was sitting.

"In case you're interested, I lost the baby last night." Wilf continued to tuck into his food but with a mouthful of egg and just like a pig, he sprayed out pieces of food as he spoke.

"Can't you do anything fucking right? Well we'll just

18

have to make sure you get up the duff again. Get
yourself ready for when I come home tonight."

"Did you hear any of what I just fucking said?"

"Don't fucking start girl or you'll get a bleeding back
hander!"

"But I'm bleeding!"

"Nothing that won't wash now get out of my sight so I
can eat my breakfast in peace. You're always fucking
whining woman and it does my fucking head in!"

"For God's sake! I lost our child last night and it was all
because of you and what you did!"

Wilf suddenly stood up and she knew that she had
overstepped the mark and if she didn't shut up she was in
for another beating and this time he might just finish her
off. That thought alone silenced Daisy when she realised
that poor little Stella would be left all alone. Daisy
bowed her head and doing as she'd been told, made her
way into the kitchen to begin washing up.

Three years later and Daisy was once again
pregnant but this time and just like the last, it wasn't
easy. With Stella she had sailed through the nine months
without any problems but this pregnancy had been
dreadful. Her morning sickness had begun at three
months and now almost at the end of her term, she was
still being sick on a daily basis. Wilf was still just as
selfish but luckily when she had informed him that she
was in the family way again the beatings had stopped.
Stella was growing into a lovely child and couldn't wait
for the new baby to arrive, she was very close to her
mother but where her father was concerned she hated him
with a vengeance. As yet he hadn't laid a hand on her but
she would lay awake at nights and listen to all that he put
her mother through. Not yet aware of what sex was, she
still knew that the noises coming from her parents'

bedroom most nights weren't good noises. Sometimes she held her hands tightly over her ears until they stopped and most mornings she would notice a new bruise on her mother's face or arms. The flat had to be quite at all times when her dad was at home but once he left for work it would be filled with laughter and music. Daisy loved to dance and even now with her belly almost fit to burst she would swing Stella around as they moved to the latest tunes. After what felt like a lifetime to Stella her little brother finally arrived and she was in awe of him. He was so tiny and when her mother allowed her to help feed and bathe him Stella made a secret promise that she would protect him always. Things in the flat seemed to improve but Stella couldn't be off noticing that little Dougie was the apple of his father's eye. It didn't matter how well she did at school or how much she helped around the house, Stella Nicholson was all but ignored by her father. When Dougie started school things seemed to go from bad to worse, the boy had no interest in football or woodwork and all he wanted to do was play with the little girls and their dolls. At first Wilf ignored his son's behaviour but when others began to laugh and make snide remarks within earshot he decided to take matters into his own hands. One day after a severe beating while Daisy was out shopping, he swore Dougie to secrecy but his bruises gave the game away and for once Daisy stood up to her husband.

"If you ever lay a bleeding hand on him again I'll swing for you Wilf, if God is my witness I'll bleeding well swing for you. You can batter me all you want but you will not hurt my children. Do you hear me? As God is my judge I will stab you while you sleep and don't think I won't!"

He studied his wife for a moment, usually he would have

given her a back hander just for speaking out of turn but there was something different this time, something in her eyes that told him she was deadly serious. Wilf Nicholson grabbed his hat and with a mocking laugh left the flat. The depth of her anger must have registered as from then on he left the children alone, or at least he did until Stella became a teenager. Years passed and somehow Daisy and her children muddled through and managed to live with the hand that god had dealt them. They were never happier than when it was just the kids and Daisy even though they were poor and sometimes underfed. At times just living was hard but in a strange way they were still so grateful for the life that they had.

CHAPTER THREE
2014

Wilfred Nicholson slammed the door to the flat and headed off along the open air landing. He could smell the disinfectant on the wet concrete and he wrinkled his nose in distaste. Wilf had resided at the flat on Roy Road in Bethnal Green for the last fifty three years and it was hard to comprehend where all that time had gone. Now nearing eighty, Wilf still viewed himself as a young man and not as the old codger that everyone else saw. He had always been a wide boy and had only married Daisy because he'd got her pregnant after just a single liaison. There was no way that he would have been able to stay in the East End in the late fifties unless he'd done the honourable thing and married the girl. It was always a sore point and he had made his wife suffer for getting up the duff for the whole of their married life. That said it hadn't stopped him dipping his wick whenever he got the chance which had been many times over the years. Poor old Daisy was a gentle woman who would never say boo to a goose let alone stand up to her husband even though she knew he had carried on with other women and he had never bothered a jot whether she'd found out or not. On the day she married Wilf, Daisy Nicholson had believed she was in love and that she would get the happy ever after, how wrong she was. The only reprieve from his violent temper and vicious mouth had been when she'd given him a son but it hadn't lasted long and when the boy turned out to be effeminate Wilf had blamed it on Daisy. Their first child, conceived out of wedlock, had been a girl and Wilf had never given Stella the time of day as a youngster but when she turned fifteen he had violently raped her while his wife was out at bingo and his son was next door with Alice Partridge. When he had finished his assault Wilf fell asleep on the couch, only to be woken a few minutes later with the feel of cold steel touching his throat.

"Ever lay a hand on me again you cunt and I will slice your fucking balls off and stuff them into your mouth!" The look in her eyes was enough to tell him that his daughter was deadly serious in her threat and from that day forward they barely exchanged a word. Daisy couldn't be off noticing the tension whenever the pair of them were in the same room but she had decided not to confront either of them for fear of making the situation even worse than it already was. Whatever her husband had done and she was in no doubt that he was the one at fault, it was best to let sleeping dogs lie. Wilf Nicholson never forgot that threat and now here he was all these years later relying on the woman for his daily meals, laundry and the provision of care for his ailing wife. His dream of being supported by his son had come crashing down around Wilf's ears early in nineteen seventy eighty. Dougie had just turned thirteen when one day and out of the blue when they were all halfway through their Sunday lunch, he had thought it was an appropriate time to announce to everyone that he was gay. Wilf hit the roof, food flew in all directions and after he had upended the table he had thrown his son out of the flat with only the clothes he stood up in. Daisy had pleaded with her husband but her words had fallen on deaf ears and from that day on, everyone was banned from even mentioning the boys name which broke Daisy and Stella's hearts but as always they had to obey or face the wrath of a man who ruled his home not out of any kind of love but purely by fear.

Reaching the ground floor court yard Wilf Nicholson

straightened his tie and adjusted his trademark trilby hat. Even in his final years, where his dress was concerned the man was smart to the point of obsession and each evening Stella still laid out a freshly starched shirt for her father to wear. She was now no longer frightened of him, hadn't been since she was fifteen, well at least not physically but his tongue could still cut you like a razor and to argue with the old man just wasn't worth the hassle. Reaching the end of the road Wilf turned onto Roman Road and continued on towards the heart of Bethnal Green. Most would have completed the half mile journey in a few minutes but at his age it took Wilf twenty five. He didn't worry, there was nothing waiting for him at home, well not as far as he was concerned. Daisy hadn't been up to having sex for several years now and Wilf still had needs even if it was often a case of the mind being willing but the body wasn't able. So many nights over the years Stella had lain awake listening to her father abusing her mother. Daisy's cries were enough to break her daughter's heart but she knew that she had no right to interfere in a couple's marriage even if they were her parents.

Entering the 'The Old George' Wilf smiled when he saw Charmaine was on duty. Tall, raven haired and buxom, Charmaine Pearson was definitely his favourite. The pub had been Wilf's regular for years and when it had unexpectedly closed for refurbishment in two thousand and thirteen he had been more than a little disgruntled but since the re-launch he was as happy as a pig in shit, something he was proud to tell anyone that cared to ask. The place might well be trying to establish itself as a gastro pub but to Wilf Nicholson, it would always be 'The Old George'. He wasn't against the new menu as he didn't ever eat in the pub and the rebranding had forced a few of his old pals to drink elsewhere but the young busty barmaids more than made up for that and Wilf was starting to come in earlier and earlier. Every night it was the same; he would stand on the bare trendy floorboards and wait for a welcoming chorus from the barmaids.

"Hi there Wilfy babe."

"Hi darling man."

"Hello there sweet Wilfy."

Glancing along the bar and only after he made sure there were no more greetings to receive would he venture over to one of the stools and take a seat. Wilf raised his shoulders as if he were a preening peacock. He didn't see the sniggers as the girls laughed at the silly old fool behind his back. To Wilf, he was still the same old babe magnet he'd been before Daisy had trapped him and tonight, despite his age, he wanted to fill his boots. The other girls knew better than to serve him and Wilf Nicholson waited patiently until Charmaine was free to get him his drink of choice. The pub was busy and it was a further five minutes before Charmaine reached her number one fan but not once did he complain. At home Wilf Nicholson was a tyrant to his wife and daughter but sitting here in front of the young woman he was a pussy cat.

"What can I get you sweetheart?"

Charmaine leaned over and her low cut dress revealed her ample bosom. Wilf moved forward so that only the barmaid could hear his words.

"My usual and I wouldn't mind copping a quick feel of your tits as well. What say we meet round the back of this place when your shift is over and we can get those pink nosed puppies out for an inspection?"

Normally Charmaine Pearson could handle the rudest of punters with her sharp wit but today had been a bad day and it was also the first time Wilf had out right propositioned her. For a few seconds she studied the old man and there was something in his eyes that she just didn't like something that told her in no uncertain terms he'd meant every single word he'd just said and it wasn't just playful banter.

"Where the fuck do you get off talking to me like that? I ain't no brass you know."

Wilf realised he had over stepped the mark big time but he still didn't apologise. In his mind if she flaunted her assets night after night then she was just what she'd said she wasn't, a whore. When Charmaine's loud voice echoed round the pub the bar was now deathly silent as the other punters waited with baited breath to see what would follow but with Wilf's next sentence they all burst into laughter.

"Your loss sweetheart, all I can say is that once you've experienced the Wilf you wouldn't have looked elsewhere. I won't ask twice love so let that be a lesson learned."

Wilf Nicholson now turned his back on the bewildered barmaid. He was embarrassed but no one would have known it by his demeanour. When Charmaine walked off in the direction of the kitchen everyone continued as before. Wilf sipped at his drink and scanned the room, old Reba Hanson was in tonight but trying to get a shag out of her would be like trying to get blood out of a stone, in other words not a hope in hell. Reba Hanson was in her early seventies and years earlier had been known as a good time girl, in all probability she was as up for it today as she'd always been, just not with Wilf Nicholson, she couldn't stand the arrogant arsehole of a man. Suddenly the Landlord appeared from out of the back kitchen and marched behind the bar.

"Wilf Nicholson, I want you out of my pub now!"
Again everyone stopped talking and looked in the direction of the bar.

"What's all this about Dick, has that little tart been telling tales. It ain't my fault if she's fucking frigid. If your girls insist on having their tits on show for the world and his bleeding wife to see then they shouldn't start moaning when someone wants to cop a feel."

Dick Kendal tried to grab Wilf from the other side of the bar but he wasn't fast enough and as quick as a flash the old man slipped off of the stool and was heading towards the pubs front door.

"I've had enough of you over the years, what with complaints about you getting your cock out and your foul mouth."

"Fuck off you tosser and stick your bleeding pub up your arse, your beers shit anyway. Everybody knows you water it down you slimy bastard!"

The pubs front door slammed shut before the Landlord could say anything further but he did notice several of the regulars looking at their pints and eyeing him suspiciously. Strolling in the direction of home, Wilf was more than a little pissed off with the fact that the place would now be out of bounds, well at least for the next few weeks. Reaching Bonner Street Wilf was just about to turn into Roy Street; he even had his block of flats in sight when a sharp pain surged through his upper body. Falling against the wall of the newsagent's corner shop his entire chest felt like it had a ton weight pressing down onto it and when he touched his brow he could feel a clammy sweat starting but at the same time he was shivering with cold. His body suddenly jerked and sliding down the wall he landed on the cold pavement as his heart stopped and he took his final breath. Thirty

27

minutes later and Vani Chaudry was returning home to his shop after spending the evening visiting his sister. A Bhangra song was blearing out of the radio and Vani was happily bobbing about in his seat to the beat of the music. As soon as he turned into Bonner Street he saw Wilf's body and instantly switched off the radio. Screeching his van to a halt he ran over to help but Vani realised instantly that it was far too late. He knew who it was straight away; the Nicholson's were regulars in his shop and newspapers were delivered to the family's flat daily. Removing his phone Vani dialled the emergency services and within a couple of minutes a squad car arrived on the scene. Constable Steve Perry was about to feel for a pulse but stopped when his fingers made contact with Wilf's skin. The old man was already cold and it would take a miracle to bring him back to life. Radioing in he informed the ambulance that there was no need to break the speed limit. His partner Ivan Link removed a blanket from the boot of the car and covered the corpse. Standing on either side of Wilf Nicholson the constables silently waited for the body to be collected. Vani had been into his shop to find out the address of the Nicholson's flat and after scrawling it down onto a scrap of paper he handed it to PC Perry.

"Should make things a little easier officer."

"Did you know the man well?"

"No not really, he used to come in now and again but it was mostly his daughter I saw. Nice woman but from what gossip I've heard, the same can't be said for that old codger."

"You shouldn't listen to gossip Mr?"

"Chaudry, Vani Chaudry."

"You shouldn't listen to gossip Mr Chaudry it never does anyone any good and in my experience, it can also cause a whole lot of problems."

"I agree constable but it's difficult not to, especially here in the East End. Can I get either of you a cup of tea?" Steve Perry was just about to accept the offer when an ambulance turned up. A few checks were carried out on the body and then it was loaded into the ambulance. The policemen and Vani were left standing on the pavement and things now felt a bit awkward.

"If there's nothing else constables I think I'll go indoors."

"That's fine Sir but we will need to take a statement at some point. My colleague or I will call in tomorrow what time would be convenient?"

Vani scratched his head for a few moments trying to remember if he had any appointments.

"Any time after ten, it's a bit manic first thing what with all the paperboys but once they are on their way it gets quiet for a while."

PC's Perry and Link then drove along to the Flats on Roy Street. After climbing the concrete stairwell and walking along the open air landing they reached the Nicholson residence at the end of the block. Stella had just been in to check on her mum and was about to switch off the hall light and turn in herself when she heard a knock on the front door. It didn't alarm her as it wasn't that late and her brood were always calling round no matter what time of the day or night it was, especially if they wanted something and that was more often than not. Opening the door just a fraction Stella peered outside and her heart was instantly in her mouth when she saw the boys in blue. The door was flung open and she rapidly began to speak.

"Oh no, oh please tell me it ain't one of my kids?"

"Mrs?"

"Nicholson and its Miss, I live here with my parents."

"May we come inside for a moment Miss Nicholson?"
"Yeah of course. Come on through but try not to make too much noise as my old mum is asleep in the next room.

Stella walked in the direction of the front room and the officers entered the flat and followed her. Suddenly Daisy called out in a very feeble voice.

"Stella! Stella! What's all the noise about, what's going on?"

"It's alright Mum, nothing to worry about you just go back to sleep love."

Inside the small front room and once Stella had closed the door she again began to speak but now there was an even more frantic tone to her voice.

"Now are you going to tell me what all this is about or are you just going to wait until I go off my bleeding nut with worry?"

"I'm afraid we have some bad news, a short while ago a gentleman collapsed and died in the street and we believe it was a Mr Wilfred Nicholson."

"Oh thank god, for a minute I thought you were going to say something had happened to one of my kids?"

"I take it that Mr Nicholson is your father?"

"Well he's my biological father but that's about all the old cunt is!"

Steve and Ivan looked at each other and couldn't believe what they had just heard. The woman must be in shock to say such a thing but with Stella's next sentence they were left in no doubt that she had meant every word.

"Don't sound good does it but he was a total and utter wanker. For the whole of my mother's married life that bastard has terrorised her and me come to that, at least he did when I was younger. As far as I'm concerned its good riddance to bad rubbish and I hope he rots in hell."

PC Pearson gently touched Stella's arm and gave a caring smile.

"I'm sorry to hear that Miss Nicholson. Now I will need someone to identify the deceased tomorrow."

"Well it certainly won't be me; I ain't wasting another second of my time on that old wanker. I'll get my boy to do it if that's alright?"

Flabbergasted at her words the policemen could only nod their heads and after making sure there was nothing more Stella needed they said goodnight and left the flat. As she closed the front door Stella leaned back against the paintwork and after sighing heavily she then smiled. Tomorrow her and her mother's lives would change forever and it was definitely going to be for the better.

CHAPTER FOUR

ONE WEEK LATER

Stella walked across the communal square at the rear of the flats and as she did so she stared up at the building. It was ugly, cold and grey, and Stella had hated living here for as long as she could remember. She wasn't sure exactly how old the flats were but reasoned that they had to have been built before the war or at the very latest just after. There were four separate buildings with three floors and two open concrete landings spanning the whole length of each. In the eighties many of the residents had used their right to buy and had either renovated the properties or sold them on at a huge profit a few years later. Number twenty three wasn't one of them, Stella's father had never been interested in owning his own home and the council had done little to improve their living conditions. Inside were three bedrooms, a small front room, a toilet and a tiny kitchen. The bath tub, as with so many local authority buildings of that period, was situated in the kitchen and covered over by a large piece of board that had to be removed every time anyone needed to wash but which also doubled up as extra work surface when the bath was not in use.

Stella Nicholson had never married but had still given birth to four children. The first being Stevie at the end of nineteen seventy eight when she was just eighteen. Tony Miller was a young boy with high flying dreams and who had only been interested in Stella for one thing. By the time she realised her predicament it was too late and Tony had instantly disappeared from the area. Her father had gone crazy when he found out, it was history repeating itself but there was little he could do and the mention of adoption was soon forgotten when Stella and her mother flatly refused to even discuss the option. Three years later Stella gave birth to her second child. Veronica or Ronnie as everyone called her was the result of a one night stand. As with the first pregnancy Wilf had again hit the roof and had wanted to throw his daughter out onto the street along with her bastards but he was persuaded not to by Daisy. It was probably only the third or fourth time in the whole of her marriage that Daisy had stood up to her husband and on each occasion she had received a severe beating for questioning him but it still hadn't stopped her. Family was all that Daisy Nicholson cared about and her kids would always come before any man or his needs. Raising two children as a single parent was really hard, there was never any spare money and Stella now had to obey her father's every command. Wilf hadn't wanted any more mouths to feed so he always made sure that his daughter didn't have much free time and had banned her from leaving the flat after dark but it didn't stop Jane appearing six years later. Stella hadn't meant for it to happen but one day when her parents were out and the kids were at school, a council worker called round to repair a leaky tap. Stella was so lonely and after she'd made the man a cup of tea and they had innocently chatted away about nothing in particular, one thing led to another and it had resulted in another little girl, Jane. This time Wilf hadn't even commented, he also didn't give the baby a second look but then that was nothing unusual as he'd ignored Stevie and Ronnie since the day they'd been born. Finally when Stevie turned seventeen Raymond came kicking and screaming into the world. By then Stella was almost thirty six years old and she swore to herself that he would definitely be her last child. Keeping to her word was easy as Raymond turned out to be a little monster and his mother knew that if he had been born first, she would never have had any others. The years seemed to fly by and Stella Nicholson soon found herself on the wrong side of fifty but she always reasoned that life was what you made it and she still had a whole lot of living left to do.

Hauling the heavy shopping bags up the stairs Stella tried to block out the screaming and shouting that seemed to surround her on a daily basis. There were hoards of kids running up and down the landings and a domestic could always be heard happening somewhere in one of the flats. Sometimes it got so bad that the Old Bill were called but no one ever got involved, there were some nasty pieces of work living in the blocks and if you knew what was good for you, you kept your nose out of other people's business. Home was at last in sight and Stella continued to struggle with the bags until she reached the flat. Placing her key into the lock she called out.

"Mum I'm back, you alright Mum?"

There was no reply and Stella could feel the panic begin to rise from the pit of her stomach. Dropping the bags onto the floor she ran through to her mother's room but Daisy was nowhere to be seen.

"Mum! Mum! Where are you sweetheart?"

Pushing open the lavatory door Stella found her mother sitting on the toilet holding a small bowl.

"Oh Mum, whatever are you doing, you gave me such a bleeding scare."

Daisy looked up with doe like eyes that instantly melted her daughter's heart. Looking closer Stella could see that the bowl held her father's false teeth.

"Don't you think we should bin those Mum?"

"But they're good teeth!"

Leaning up against the doorframe Stella couldn't help but smile at her mother.

"I know sweetie but they're no use to anyone else, why don't you give them to me for safe keeping."

Daisy reluctantly handed over the dentures and after Stella had placed them into her coat pocket she helped her mother to get up and then walked her through to the bedroom.

"Why don't you have a little lay down Mum and I'll fetch you a nice cuppa."

Daisy nodded her head and a few minutes later Stella collected the shopping bags and began to put the groceries away. When the kettle had boiled she made herself a coffee but didn't bother with a drink for her mother as she knew Daisy would now be sound asleep. Walking into the front room she took a seat on the old worn out sofa and scanned her surroundings. The wallpaper was ancient and she wracked her brains trying to recall if it had ever been redecorated but nothing came to mind. The furniture was old but comfy and at least Stella was grateful that the flat was warm. As her eyes looked up at the photographs that lined the mantelpiece she began to evaluate her life and it didn't amount to much. The only thing she'd ever achieved, the only thing she was proud of, was her four children. Her first born Stevie, despite his father being a complete and utter wanker had turned out to be a hard worker who ran two very successful shops in the East End. His wife Jo was lovely and had given Stella three beautiful grandchildren. Stella's daughter Veronica hadn't been so lucky when it came to money but she was happily married and had again given Stella grandchildren. Then there was Jane, the thought of her brought a smile to Stella's lips.

35

Jane was a different kettle of fish altogether. Married to Roger, an accountant, they made one very snooty couple. Jane had a good job in social services and Roger was on his way to a partnership, there were no children but her daughter, after a rocky start, now seemed happy enough so Stella couldn't complain. Lastly there was the boy Raymond, now he was one of a kind and Stella was grateful that they broke the mould after he emerged. At nineteen years old he was as slippery as a fish and as cunning as a fox. You couldn't leave him alone in a room with anything of value, not if you wanted to see it again. Drugs had been Raymond's downfall but still Stella couldn't turn her back on him, much to the disgust of her other children. Whenever he paid her a visit Stella would slip him twenty quid, if only to ease her own conscience with the knowledge that he at least had the means to put food in his mouth though she very much doubted that the money would be spent in the supermarket. A tear dropped onto her hand and she instantly wiped it away. Stella had always been a strong woman and she knew the worst wasn't over yet. As much as the family had spent their whole lives in a council flat, her father had been a man of money. Just after her parents were married he'd inherited two shops from a long lost uncle, or that's what he had told his wife but the truth had surfaced one Christmas when Wilf was liberally lubricated with brandy. While working for Hayes the undertakers he had been put in charge of preparing the bodies of people who were unidentified. On one such occasion Wilf had gone through the pockets of an old man and found a set of keys to a locker at Waterloo station. Placing them into his own pocket he had waited six months to see if anyone came forward and when they didn't he took a trip to the station.

The locker contained a small leather suitcase and inside was five hundred pounds, quite a windfall in those days but the real items of value were the deeds to two shops, one on Roman Road and the other right opposite Liverpool Street station. After paying a visit to the boarded up buildings Wilf then sought out the advice of a solicitor. Using the story that the old man had given him the deeds he inquired if they were legal. After a quick investigation Wilf was informed that as far as the law was concerned the properties were his. Not one to take chances or to invest his own cash, for years the rental income they had brought in each month had been meagre but since Stevie had gone into business fifteen years ago and took over the properties he had paid his grandfather a handsome sum each month. The two shops were now worth a staggering amount of money but Stella was already worrying what her father's Will would reveal. Draining the last of the liquid from her mug she was about to check on her mother when the front door opened and her youngest son appeared.

"Hello boy, I've been trying to get in contact with you for over a week, did Ronnie manage to speak to you about your grandad?"

"Sorry Mum but you know what I'm like when I go off the radar. I saw Ronnie yesterday and fucking good riddance to the cunt is all I can say. How's Nan?"

"Alright, actually I think she's relieved but you know your Nan, don't say a lot at the best of times. Would you like something to eat love?"

Raymond walked into the kitchen and opening up the cupboards scanned the shelves to see what was on offer. When he turned up his nose at her larder Stella gently pushed her son out of the way.

"Pass me the pan; I'll fry you up some nice bacon and

eggs. You go and check on your Nan but make sure you're quiet, I can't do with her waking up just yet."
A few seconds later Raymond reappeared.
"She's fine Mum, dribbling in her sleep as usual. Do you know when the funeral is?"
"Not yet love, there will have to be an autopsy but I would imagine we will be able to bury the old sod within the next two weeks, the sooner the better as far as I'm concerned. Did Ronnie tell you about tomorrow?"
As Stella handed her youngest son the plate of food she saw him gently shake his head and knew that he was hurt. None of her other children ever included him in things; oh Stella realised it was his own fault as the family could never trust him but never the less it didn't sit well. Raymond might be a thief and a drug addict but at the end of the day he was still her son and she wouldn't turn her back on him even if the others did.
"I expect it just slipped her mind love. Everyone is coming over for Sunday tea, I wanted to do a big roast but what with all the grandkids there's just too many of us now, so I'm just doing a small buffet."
"You don't really want me here mum and I definitely know the other fuckers won't want to see me."
Stella gently touched his arm.
"Don't say that Ray, you're my son and I love you. I don't care what your brother and sisters think, I do want you here and that's all that matters, besides if the truth be told I'm really not looking forward to it myself. Come on; let's go through to the front room before your food gets cold."
Stella took a seat on the sofa beside her son who was precariously balancing the plate on his knees. It had always been the same, he needed to be close to her and he didn't even contemplate taking a seat at the small dining

table. Raymond tucked in and it looked like he hadn't eaten for several days, that realisation hurt Stella deeply. The conversation didn't resume until the plate was empty and when Ray turned to his mother Stella tenderly wiped away the egg yolk from his chin.

"So what's up Mum?"

"Nothing love, why do you say that?"

"Well, you normally like nothing more than having all of the family around yet you said you weren't looking forward to it?"

Stella Nicholson slowly scratched her head and nodded in agreement at the same time.

"I'm dreading them asking about grandad's will and believe you me it's going to be the main topic of conversation I can assure you. I don't blame Stevie, it's his livelihood at stake but you know what Jane and Roger are like. She's my own flesh and blood, but your sister can be one greedy and manipulative cow when she has a mind."

The conversation was brought to a halt when Daisy appeared in the doorway. Her white hair was dishevelled and Stella could see that the side of the old woman's dress was tucked into her knickers. Getting up from the sofa she gently led her mother into the kitchen.

"Come on sweetheart, let's get you sorted out and then we'll have a nice cup of rosie."

Daisy Nicholson only smiled. The woman was approaching her eightieth year and her lack of conversation wasn't down to any type of dementia but purely the fact that she was mentally and physically worn out. Years of a demanding husband had chipped away at her bit by bit. She was emotionally drained and all that Daisy wanted was to be left alone in peace and quiet. Suddenly Stella remembered that her purse was in the front room and that her mother's pension money was also inside. Raising her eyes up to the heavens and exhaling a deep lungful of oxygen she prayed that Raymond hadn't cleaned her out totally. About to lead Daisy back into the front room she stopped when she fleetingly saw her son pass the doorway.

"I need to get off now Mum, see you tomorrow."

With that Raymond Nicholson slammed the door closed and Stella went to see if she had any cash left. Sitting her mother down in the small armchair in the corner Stella then removed her purse from the mantle and hesitantly snapped it open. Strangely there was only twenty pounds missing and to Stella that was fine because she always gave him twenty when he called round anyway. To her it was a good sign, a sign of respect; after all he could have taken well over a hundred.

"So?"

"So what?"

"Has the little sod cleaned us out?"

"No Mum he hasn't and his name is Raymond as you well know. Right, just let me go and fetch the tea then you and me need to have a little chat about things before the others get here tomorrow."

Setting her mother's china cup down onto the small table beside her chair Stella took a sip of her own drink before she spoke.

"So what do you want to do about Dad's funeral, burial or cremation?"

Daisy Nicholson's next sentence had her daughter lost for words for several seconds.

"You can leave the old fucker on top as far as I'm concerned."

"Mum!"

"Don't Mum me, that bastard treated me like a dog, no,

worse than a dog. You know me Stella and I ain't no
hypocrite, nor am I about to shed a load of bleeding
crocodile tears for the benefit of others. I've prayed for
years for this to happen. I don't know about you but I
feel like having a party and dancing on his bleeding
grave."

Stella burst out laughing, she couldn't help herself. It had
been years since she had seen her mother so feisty and
she liked it. Looking closely into Daisy's eyes Stella saw
a glint and leaning forward she placed a kiss onto the old
woman's cheek.

"What was that for?"

"No reason, just because I love you. We're going to be
alright Mum ain't we?"

"Of course we are you soppy sod, now am I getting a
sandwich because my stomach thinks my throats been
bleeding cut."

"Alright, give me a minute and I'll fetch you some grub.
I really don't know where you manage to put all that food
mother, really I don't."

CHAPTER FIVE

Stella had been up with the larks. The family were not due to arrive until four o'clock that afternoon but they were a hungry gutted bunch and Stella knew there would be a lot of food to prepare if she wanted them to all leave her home satisfied. Thankfully Daisy wasn't awake yet and Stella was glad because it took at least an hour each morning to get her mother washed and dressed and today Stella needed as much time as she could to prepare the food. Placing a saucepan of water on to boil for the eggs she was shocked when she glanced into the hall and saw her mother approaching and already fully dressed.

"Morning Mum, I didn't think you'd be up for ages."

"Well good job I am, with that hoard of yours coming round later there's a lot to do. Now where do you want me to start?"

Stella couldn't believe the transformation as Daisy rolled up her sleeves and began to butter bread. The film Benjamin Button entered Stella's mind but she knew that her dear old mum just felt free from the shackles of marriage and it had given the old woman an energy that she hadn't seen for years. Stella switched on the radio and as Bill Haley began to belt out 'Rock around the clock' mother and daughter started to dance before bursting into a fit of giggles. Finally when Stella had composed herself she turned to her mother with a wide grin on her face.

"I've missed this, the last time I can really remember you dancing with me like this, well I must have been about six years old."

Lifting her mother's chin Stella saw the pools of tears and as one dropped onto Daisy's cheek Stella gently wiped it away.

"I'm sorry sweetheart I didn't mean to upset you."
Daisy grabbed her daughters hand and lifting it to her
mouth tenderly kissed it several times.

"You have nothing to be sorry about. If anyone should
be sorry it's me, sorry for all those years that I didn't
stand up to that evil fucker. All those years when he
made you and your kid's lives a living hell and I just
stood by and didn't say a word."

"Yes you did Mum, I remember when I had Stevie and he
wanted to throw us out but you wouldn't let him. You
were there when I needed you the most and I can't ask for
more. We both know what a cruel man he was and the
walls in this place ain't that bleeding thick Mum. I heard
all the horrible things he used to make you do."

Daisy placed her index finger onto Stella's lips as she
slowly shook her head.

"Let's not waste another breath on the fucker, now what
do we need to do next?"

The two women worked hard and by three o'clock the
bath top was full to over flowing with all manner of
foods. Stella stood back to admire the spread and at the
same time wiped the back of her hand across her
forehead.

"Bloody hell, I ain't sweated like this for ages. I'll just
go and freshen up Mum and then we can have five
minutes sit down and a nice cuppa before they all get
here and world war three breaks out."

       At five to four that afternoon Stella heard the
front door open and she rolled her eyes upwards as if to
silently say 'here we go'. Raymond was the first to arrive
and walking into the kitchen he greedily eyed the food.
About to reach out and grab a sausage roll he pulled away
sharply when his mother slapped his wrist.

43

"Oh no you don't, you can wait until the others get here. Go and keep your Nan company in the front room." Raymond did as he was told but there was little conversation as he had nothing in common with the old woman. Daisy on the other hand didn't like her grandson much. She would never let her daughter know how she felt but there was just something about the boy. Oh he came over all nice but there was something devious about him, maybe it was just a case of he was too much like his grandfather. Stella filled the kettle up with water, got out the mugs and rinsed the wine glasses. She was tempted to open a bottle of red but knew if she did she wouldn't be able to stop and being drunk around her grandchildren was a definite no no. Stevie and his brood were the next to arrive and Stella could instantly see that Bianca, Stevie junior and little Wilf didn't want to be there. Heading into the front room none of the kids gave her a second glance as they were all glued to their mobiles but Stevie and his wife Jo walked over to Stella and both kissed her warmly.

"How are you doing Mum?"

"Oh you know me Son, mustn't grumble. Before you go in I'll warn you that Raymond's here."

"What the fuck is he ......"

"You can stop right there Stevie! You are all my children and Ray is as welcome in this house as you and yours are. Please, just for today, can we all try and get along love?" Stevie tenderly touched his mother's cheek and smiled. He had always been and always would be so proud of his dear old mum. Struggle was an understatement regarding all that she had been through yet she always had a kind word and a cheery smile for everyone. If you had a problem then Stella was the only person you wanted to go to, she never turned her back and was as loyal as they

44

came.

"If that's what you want sweetheart but he hadn't better step out of line. Jo, keep your handbag with you because the crafty little cunt will have your purse away in the blink of an eye."

Stella was just about to tell her eldest off when the door opened and her two daughters and their partners walked in. Stella loved Ronnie's husband Sam, he worked so hard on the bins and never complained. On the other hand Jane's old man Roger hardly ever spoke a word to anyone. Her daughter said he was just a shy man but Stella saw it as just plain rude.

"Hello you lot, where are the kids Ronnie?"

"Hi Mum, well little Robbie's got a football match that he couldn't get out of and the other two had the chance of some spare tickets for the party in the park. I knew you wouldn't mind them not being here and besides, it means we will all be able to sit down for once."

When all of the family except for Stella were seated in the tiny front room, though several of them had been forced to make do with the floor, Stella came in and placed a large tray of glasses onto the coffee table. Sam grinned, he was partial to a tipple on a Sunday afternoon and for once Ronnie wouldn't be able to complain.

"What's all this about then mum?"

Stella glanced around the room at her family and smiled at each of them in turn.

"Me and Mum thought it would be nice to have a toast, not in your grandad's memory but in thanks that the old fucker has finally gone! It's only prosecco but it'll do for that old bastard. I wasn't going to waste your Nan's pension money on the real McCoy!"

The room was instantly in uproar with laughter, well all apart from Jane and Roger who thought the statement had been made without taste and Stella should be showing more respect. Stevie noticed his sister's expression and between bouts of giggles he leaned over and whispered in her ear.

"For fucks sake Sis, for once take that broomstick out of your arse and relax."

"I don't know what you mean Steven!"

"Are you now saying that you liked the old sod? Think you'll get a bigger slice of the Will do you?"

Stevie Nicholson could instantly see his sister stiffen up but Jane didn't fall for her brother's bait and only tutted loudly. Stella knew each and every one of her children like the back of her hand and when she began to feel that the tension was building between her son and daughter she suddenly stood up.

"Right you unruly lot, me and your Nan have worked bloody hard on that food so if you'd all like to form an orderly queue, I now declare the buffet open."

Everyone filed into the kitchen except for Stevie and Ray. Raymond Nicholson had been sitting next to his niece Bianca and his right hand was now almost touching the young girl's clutch bag. Stevie stood up and walking over to his younger brother, kicked out at Raymond's outstretched leg.

"Ow!!!"

"Touch that you thieving little cunt and you'll get a fucking clump."

"But I wasn't going ......"

Stevie cut his brother off dead, he'd heard so many excuses over the years and there wasn't a thing that Ray could now say that his brother would believe.

"Look you little tosser, none of us would give you the time of fucking day if it wasn't for Mum! So just make the most of it while she's still here because come the day

when she isn't, you will be out on your fucking ear."
With that Stevie went to get some food with the rest of
his family. Alone in the front room Raymond wiped a
tear from the corner of his eye. God knew he couldn't
help the way that he was, at times he even hated himself
and at this present moment in time he would have given
anything just to be a part of the family again. The only
trouble with Raymond was the fact that as soon as the
urge to take drugs started to rear its ugly head again, all
good intentions would go out of the window and he
would be exactly as his brother described. Knowing this
hurt him desperately but life was a bitch and then it was
over so getting to his feet he decided it would at least be
best to get some grub in his belly before the gathering
came to an end. When they had all filled themselves with
Stella and Daisy's amazing food, Stella knew it was now
time to tackle a difficult subject. Placing her plate and
glass down onto the coffee table she addressed them all.
"Right, I know you all have a load of questions that
you've been desperately waiting to ask so you'll now get
a chance to speak, but please, only one of you at a time."
Facing Stevie, Stella knew that for obvious reasons he
would be the one who was most concerned so she asked
him to begin.
"I don't want any arguments so this is the fairest way.
Stevie you're first love."
"Ok Mum fair enough, so what's in the old man's Will?"
"I haven't got a clue love."
"But Mum I need...."
"Sorry Stevie but I can't go into this until the Will is
read, Ronnie you're next sweetheart."
Ronnie Stevens looked at her husband and shrugged her
shoulders. Neither of them was interested in the money
and their only concern was for Stella and Daisy.

"Can you both stay in the flat; I mean I know it was in grandad's name?"

Right at the moment Stella felt nothing but love for her girl and she could feel tears as they started to build in her eyes. Breathing in deep she looked at her daughter lovingly and for just a second they were truly connected.

"Its fine babe thanks, I've already been down the council and we're tenants in right, so in answer to your question, Nan and me will be fine."

Stella turned to Jane and the woman then looked to her husband for guidance. Totally out of character Roger began to speak and the whole room was mesmerised. It wasn't down to what he was saying but just the fact that he was speaking at all.

"Stella, Daisy, Jane has told me that Mr Nicholson owned a couple of properties that in today's market are both worth a considerable amount of money. Now I, or rather the company I work for, would be more than happy to realise the true value and offer them on the open market on your behalf."

Stevie was instantly on his feet and words couldn't begin to describe the serious look on his face. Jo knew from past experience that when her husband looked like this there was no telling where it would all end, she just hoped that he'd hold his anger inside while he was in his mother's house, sadly he couldn't or wouldn't.

"Listen here you money grabbing little cunt! Those shops are mine do you hear, I've sweated my bollocks off for years to make them the success they are today and if you think that you and that snobby bitch I have the misfortune to call my sister, are going to pull the rug from under my feet then you can fucking think again pal."

"Look Stevie, I was only trying to give the benefit of my

48

financial expertise. I really don't want to step on anyone's........."

"Listen here you piece of shit I don't give a flying fuck what......"

Stella couldn't believe what was happening and getting up from the sofa, her voice was raised as she spoke.

"That is enough do you hear me! I am well aware that some of you are only here to find out what was in Wilf's Will so let me say this for the final time! Me and Mum ain't got a fucking clue so you'll just have to wait until after the funeral. Lord above knows we've all suffered at the hands of that old man and I had hoped that just for once we could get along and have a nice time but it seems to me that some of you are cut from the same cloth as your grandfather and that alone saddens me. Now if you don't mind I would appreciate it if you all fucked off home right now."

One by one they left but Jo was the last and turning to face her mother-in-law Stella could see her daughter in laws sadness.

"I am so sorry its ended up like this Stella but please don't look at Stevie in a bad light. He has worked so hard over the last few years to build those shops up and the thought that he might lose it all is more than he can take. Surely you can understand that?"

Stella tenderly embraced the woman.

"Of course I can you silly mare but Jo I really don't know anything. The old man left strict instructions that nothing should be revealed until after the funeral. Tell Stevie I love him and that I understand completely but he will just have to be patient like the rest of us."

When the front door was at last closed and Stella had placed the chain on the lock she turned to face her mother.

49

"Fuck me Mum, whatever's going to happen?"

"I haven't got a clue love, hopefully the old git will have left everything to me but if he hasn't and it causes rows then there ain't much you can do about it. Now stop worrying about things you have no bleeding control over. Go and put the kettle on I'm parched."

Stella walked into the kitchen with her shoulders slumped, this could end up tearing her family apart but then maybe that's exactly what the old man had been planning all along. Stella knew her mother was right in what she'd said but it didn't make the situation any better by hearing it. Her father was a mean nasty man and if he knew the upset he was causing he would be doubled over with laughter, well she would make sure that whatever happened nothing would divide her family, nothing!"

CHAPTER SIX

The house on Roundwood Avenue was palatial. Massive white columns adorned the double front doors and the driveway swept around in a large circle with separate entrance and exit gates. Eight bedrooms, a triple garage housing a Lamborghini, games room, personal gym and the obligatory indoor swimming pool, made it one of the most desirable properties in Essex. Up in the vast master suite Stevie Nicholson admired himself in the full length bedroom mirror. His handmade shirt fitted perfectly and the creases in his trousers were razor sharp. Gucci loafers topped off the outfit and he knew that today's clobber had set him back almost a grand and that he would receive many admiring glances when he arrived at work. Happy with what he saw Stevie then sauntered down the large sweeping staircase and entered the massive kitchen. The house was his pride and joy and it had taken years of hard graft before he'd been able to afford to move out to Brentwood. The mock Georgian facade of the house made him feel like royalty every time he pulled into the drive and when he stepped inside the marble hallway the vision of opulence always brought a smile to his face. The eldest of the Nicholson kids, Stevie had married his childhood sweetheart Jo eighteen years earlier. Jo was the complete opposite to her husband, oh she kept herself fit and was always well turned out but the money had never really mattered to her. Her children were all that counted and they all knew she would do anything for them, but that said, they were not the easiest bunch to deal with at times as they had been given far too much by their father regardless of her protests. Jo's morals and principles were old school and family was definitely all that she cared about but sometimes when she was alone in the impressive house her husband loved so dearly; she would often reminisce about their first few years of married life together when they had shared a small flat with her mother in the East End of London. Back then they didn't have two penny's to rub together but Jo had recently begun to realise that she was far happier then. Jo Nicholson loved her husband with all her heart, always had and always would but at times she didn't like him. When the twins had arrived within their first year of marriage Jo had seen an instant change in Stevie. She couldn't argue that he had worked hard to support them all but when he began to walk rough shod over others to get what he wanted Jo wasn't happy. His mother worshiped her son and wasn't aware of this flaw in her eldest child's character and Jo wasn't going to be the one to tell Stella. The woman was a fantastic mother in law and Jo would never do anything to hurt her.

"Morning babes!"

Stevie placed a kiss on his wife's cheek and then gently slapped her behind before taking a seat at the table with his two eldest children. Jo remained where she was but continued to talk to her husband with her back to him.

"You feeling a bit better today babe."

"Not really but there ain't much I can do about it is there, where's little Wilf?"

Bianca was in the middle of filing her nails when she suddenly looked up with a frown on her face and answered before her mother had time to reply.

"Still in his pit as usual. How come me and SJ always have to get up but that little wanker gets away with murder?"

"Watch your fucking language B, I ain't paid out god

knows how many thousands on your education so that you can talk like a fucking fish wife."

"But it ain't fair Dad!"

Stevie didn't continue with the conversation and picking up his paper he began to read the headlines while Jo carried on frying the bacon. She rolled her eyes upwards, why oh why did the day always have to kick off with a row but then her daughter was picked out of her father's arse or so her mother in law was always fond of saying and as much as she didn't want too, Jo had to agree with the woman. Stevie junior or SJ as he was known to his friends and family was much quieter but he would always go along with whatever his sister wanted just to keep her happy. There was only ten minutes between them but how he obeyed her every word anyone would have thought that she was years older. Walking over to the table Jo placed a plate in front of each of them. The eggs and bacon were cooked to perfection but not one of them had the good manners to thank her. Putting another plate onto a tray she headed into the hall and then made her way upstairs. Stopping outside little Wilf's room Jo coughed loudly before she turned the door handle and walked inside. Her youngest son had been named after his grandfather and at only sixteen years old he could be a real handful if he had a mind to. No one had liked the name Stevie had picked for his boy as in reality they had known that it was chosen only to keep the old man happy. In the past Jo had wished her husband had a normal job even if that meant the family being short of cash; at least they wouldn't be beholden to anyone. She knew her daughter wouldn't agree with her as the girl loved money almost as much as her father. Bianca also had a mean streak and Jo hated it when she called her little brother a wanker but then in all honesty sometimes she was forced to agree, especially when it came down to washing her son's sheets.

"Leave it alone Wilf or it'll drop off."

Propping himself up in bed Wilf's face turned crimson as he waited for his mother to place the tray onto his lap.

"I wasn't doing anything mum."

"No of course you weren't son and the Pope ain't catholic either, now eat your breakfast before it gets cold."

Jo bent down and picked up the discarded clothes from her son's bedroom floor. Sighing loudly she walked into his en suite and placed them into the laundry bin.

"You could at least pick up your pants son, I wasn't put on this earth to fetch and carry after you!"

Jo Nicholson was well aware that she would have done just as well to save her breath because when it came down to instilling any discipline in the house, it was as if she was invisible. The only one who was able to crack the whip was Stevie and at times even he was ignored. Checking the bedrooms before she went downstairs Jo again sighed heavily, SJ's was pretty tidy but when she poked her head into Bianca's it looked like a bomb had gone off. Clothes covered the floor, makeup was spilt on the expensive dressing table and there were used plates and cutlery along with empty discarded cans of red bull just visible from under the bed. Suddenly she snapped and marching along the landing Jo descended the stairs two at a time and was back in the kitchen in seconds. Striding over to the table she stood staring daggers at Bianca until the girl looked up from her breakfast.

"What!"

"You might well say what young lady. I have just been into your room and it looks like a bleeding pigsty."

"You have no right going into my room in the first place mother. How I chose to live is up to me."

54

Suddenly Jo wanted to slap her daughter and as Stevie studied his wife he knew exactly what she was thinking. Normally she was a calm woman and it took a lot to rile her so B's room must really be in a hell of a state. Stevie gently covered his wife's hand with his own and nodded his head slowly.

"Right! Tonight when you get back from work Bianca you can tidy your room."

"I will not! For Christ sake I'm eighteen years old and you can't tell me what to do anymore. Besides I'm meeting Gracie and the others tonight. We're going for a few cocktails and then to see a film at the Empire over in Basildon so I won't even be home for dinner."

"Firstly young lady, you are not eighteen for another month so you shouldn't even be drinking."

"Give me a break, everyone does it."

Suddenly Stevie lost it and he slammed his palm down onto the dining table in frustration.

"While you are still living under our roof there are rules, rules you all break on a regular basis and its going to stop. Secondly I might not be able to fucking force you into staying in but I can stop your bleeding wages. If you ain't back here by six to tidy your room there won't be any money in you pay packet come Friday, let's just see how long you manage without any cash."

Stevie was already out of his seat and picking up his car keys.

"You can't do that Dad!"

"Just watch me."

Kissing his wife on the cheek Stevie Nicholson walked into the hall and called back over his shoulder as he did so.

"You two can find your own way into work today, try using one of your two cars in the drive, cars I might add that were paid for by me."

With that the front door slammed and Bianca and SJ
stared at their mother in disbelief. Jo had to turn away in
a desperate attempt not to smile. These pair had pushed
and pushed for months and finally Stevie had snapped.
Well as far as Jo was concerned it was long overdue. As
usual the traffic was bad and it took Stevie forty five
minutes to cover the twenty five miles to the Roman
Road shop and it wasn't until he pulled into the small
parking space at the rear that he finally calmed down.
His kids would be working the Liverpool Street shop
today and he decided to give it an hour and then check
with his manager to see if they had arrived, god help
them if they hadn't. The Roman Road shop was one of
the biggest in the area and had been the first to be opened
by Stevie several years earlier. As he walked around to
the front he stared up at the sign and as much as it always
made his heart swell with pride, today he felt the
foreboding doom that now weighed heavily on his
shoulders. Tapping on the front door he only had to wait
a few seconds before Tammy Carter opened up. Tammy
had been with him since day one and he trusted her above
all others, even above his manager Ivan Sedgwick.

"Morning Tam, everything alright?"

"Sure is Stevie, the new stock arrived last night, Ivan and
the girls are putting it out as we speak."

A couple of months earlier Stevie had decided to hold a
spectacular once a week where he would purchase one
off loss leaders to get customers into the shop. As
everything in the place was priced up at a pound he
needed a lot of footfall to earn a good living. In the first
few weeks he had been down several thousand profit
wise but it hadn't taken the locals long to learn the
system and now every Monday the place was earning a

fortune.

"Remind me what it is this week Tam?"

"Big brand toilet rolls, should be nearly four quid a packet but here?"

"Just a quid, everything just a quid!"

They both laughed as they went down the aisle to the rear of the store. Customers had to wind down three sections before they got to the loss leader, therefore it was common sense that they would purchase other items on their way and this they did in abundance. Reaching the display Stevie first spoke to his manager.

"Looking good Ivan my son."

"Thanks Mr Nicholson and might I say on behalf of myself and the rest of the staff, we were saddened to hear about the loss of your grandfather."

Stevie only nodded his head, he didn't want to talk about his family with his staff and besides they didn't even know the old bastard. Facing the girls he then spoke to each of them in turn. Tracey was the newest member of the team and Stevie was well aware that she was raising two children alone and that it was a continual struggle. She reminded him so much of his dear old Mum that he would often shove an extra tenner into her wage packet at the end of the week. Next was Lou, a middle aged housewife who had worked at the pound shop for the last five years, she was a shy timid woman and never really said much, unlike Barbara Morton who at sixty seven should really have been retired and Stevie knew fine well that she didn't have to work, well at least not for financial reasons. Barbara was lonely, her husband was in residential care and never having had a family of her own the woman needed to be around other people. All in all they were a happy band of workers that was unless Bianca and SJ happened to be in the store. Stevie liked his kids to experience work in both shops so they would do a week here and then a week at the Liverpool Street branch. Tammy Carter could just about put up with SJ, at least when he was on his own but as soon as his sister appeared everything would change. The girl thought she was above working in a place like this and would talk down to customers and staff alike. Several times Tammy had wanted to give the girl a back hander but she needed her job and as much as her boss made her feel a valued member of the team, at the end of the day blood would always be thicker than water.

"I'll be in the office if anyone needs me."

Climbing the stairs Stevie entered the small area of storeroom that he had cordoned off to do his daily business from. There was only a desk, chair, telephone and a computer but they were all he needed to run his little empire. Dialling the other shop he waited for his call to be answered.

"Good morning Quid Land, how can I help?"

Sarah Jones had recently been hired as a manager. To begin with Stevie had been reluctant as the girl was fresh out of university but she seemed to be settling in well so he was prepared to give her the benefit of the doubt, at least while her three month trial was still ongoing.

"Hi Sarah its Stevie, have my two wayward kids arrived yet?"

"Yes Mr Nicholson about ten minutes ago."

"Right, I want you to get them both cleaning out the stock room. I know they hate that so if they give you any lip, tell them it's on my orders."

"Yes Mr Nicholson."

With that the line went dead; Sarah wasn't very happy about telling Bianca what she had to do as the girl was unpleasant at the best of times. That said it wouldn't stop her carrying out her boss's wishes, she needed her job too much to ever go against him.

Stevie sat back in his chair with a smile on his face but it didn't last long when thoughts of his grandfathers Will again entered his mind. Deciding that he really needed to pay another visit to his mothers he slipped out of the shop and made the short distance over to his old family home on foot. Walking across the square he glanced all around and remembered back to his childhood and growing up here. The area had always been poor but back then people still all knew one another and took pride in where they lived. Not now, now it was full of foreigners and litter and most didn't even know the names of their neighbours. Over the last couple of years Stevie Nicholson had begged his mother to leave, even offering to buy her a nice place in one of the up and coming areas but Stella wouldn't hear of it. She hated the flat and most of the memories it held but as she had told him on more than one occasion, it was still her home. Knocking once and then turning the door handle he stepped inside and called out to his mother. When there was no answer he walked into the front room.

"Hello Nan, is Mum about?"

"No she ain't boy, nipped out over an hour ago and didn't say where she was going."

Stevie was disappointed but decided not to stay and wait because if his mum was down the market and had bumped into any of her friends she could be gone for quite a while.

"Tell her I'll pop back later Nan alright?"

"Ok love, now best you be on your way because you're interfering with my telly programmes."

"Oh God forgive me!"

Stevie was still smiling as he closed the front door and

59

headed back in the direction of his shop.   The women in his life were all real characters, some things about them were fantastic and some not so nice but when it came down to it, he wouldn't have them any other way and God help anyone that said a bad word against them.

CHAPTER SEVEN

While Stevie was enquiring as to his mother's whereabouts, Stella had boarded a tube and was heading to Soho. Over the years she hadn't kept in contact with any of her brother's old friends but after knocking on a couple of doors earlier that morning she had finally found one of them who knew where Dougie was now living. Getting on a train at Bethnal Green Stella was soon disembarking at Piccadilly Circus. Turning into Great Windmill Street she walked the entire length and when she reached the end Brewer Street ran horizontal across. Deciding to turn left first, she nervously continued to walk along. The area was strange to her as she'd never had any reason to come here and like many others she expected it to be dirty with street girls standing on every corner. It turned out to be the exact opposite and Stella was pleasantly surprised. Soho was clean and upmarket and its appearance wasn't scary at all, although she was in no doubt that its sinister side probably came to life after dark. Her eyes scanned both sides of the road in search of Delphine's Bar and restaurant and she prayed that Lee Wood's, the man that had given her the address, actually had his facts right. It was still only just after ten and the area was very quiet. There were a handful of people milling about but none of them looked very friendly or approachable. So many years had passed without any contact that she didn't even know if she would recognise her brother. She hadn't got a clue if he had changed physically or what sort of lifestyle he was leading but just the very mention of Soho had made her mind go into overdrive regarding what he was doing for a living. When Stella reached the end of the street she turned around and headed in the opposite direction.

Just when she thought that no such bar existed she came to a large building with a high gloss black facade. Looking upwards she saw the name 'Delphine's' in giant gold letters. Shielding her eyes with her hand Stella peered through one of the huge front windows and spied a woman inside who was sweeping the floor. Tapping gently on the glass made the woman jump and as she waved Stella away she mouthed the words 'we're shut'. Not one to be brushed off easily especially as she'd gone out of her way to leave her own manor, something she hadn't done in years, Stella tapped again only this time it was with a little more force. She could see the woman shake her head in annoyance as she walked to the door and after hearing a large bolt as it slid over its catch, the door finally opened.

"Are you fucking thick or what? I said we're closed!"
As the door began to close again Stella placed the palm of her hand onto the wood and pushed forward. The cleaner opened up but this time her face was full of fury.
"Are you all the ticket love, because I said we're closed or are you fucking deaf as well as thick?"
"I would appreciate it if you weren't so bleeding rude and no I am neither deaf nor a brick short of a load. I'm looking for my brother and I was given this address."
Now the cleaner was intrigued. Macy Langham had been the char lady at Delphine's for the last six years and she liked to think that she was sharp enough that not a lot normally got by her. At fifty eight years of age she was well past her prime and when she had no longer been able to sell herself on the streets Dougie Nicholson had taken pity on Macy and given her a job.
"And just who might that be if you don't mind me asking?"
"Dougie, Dougie Nicholson."

Suddenly the door flew wide open and much to Stella's surprise the petite woman embraced her in a kind of bear hug.

"Why the fuck didn't you say so, Dougie is my hero and if you're his family then anything I can do to help you is a pleasure."

"Is he here?"

"Nah, him and James are down the market but they won't be long love. Come on in and I'll put the kettle on. I didn't think the boss had any family so it's nice to meet you."

Stella followed Macy into the vast bar area and as she did so she struggled to take in how classy the place was. Prejudging the area she had assumed it would be seedy and grubby but nothing could be further from the truth. The furnishings were all covered in soft cream leather and a brass hand and foot rail on the mahogany topped bar gleamed under the crystal lighting.

"Nice ain't it? Dougie deserves it mind, he's worked his bleeding socks off for years to get a place like this. You met his husband?"

Stella swallowed hard. True she knew her brother was gay but him being married hadn't even crossed her mind. The world had indeed changed a lot in the last few years but marriage? Well it was certainly a bit of a shock, albeit a nice one. Suddenly she had an image of her father hearing that little snippet of news and she couldn't suppress the laughter that instantly spilled from her mouth. Macy Langham's eyes narrowed at the thought of someone mocking her boss.

"Ain't nothing fucking funny about it Mrs, Dougie worships his partner even if James is a bit of a, well never mind about that, forget I said anything."

"But you didn't."

"Didn't what?"

"Say anything."

Stella placed a hand onto Macy's arm.

"Please you've got it all wrong, I wasn't laughing regarding what you said only of the thought I had regarding our late father but that's a private matter I would rather not go into."

Macy shrugged her shoulders and headed towards the back to make them both a hot drink. Just as she reached the doorway she glanced over her shoulder and gave Stella a look that said 'don't touch anything'. Again Stella wanted to laugh, her brother lived in a strange world indeed and she was interested to learn more about it. Ten minutes later and the cleaner reappeared with two steaming mugs and placing them down onto one of the tables she beckoned for Stella to join her.

"So how come Dougie's never mentioned you?"

"It's a long story and a private one at that. What time did you say they would be back?"

"I didn't but it won't be too much longer."

Macy eyed Stella suspiciously but Stella ignored the woman.

"So Mrs?"

"Macy."

"So Macy, are you going to fill me in on Dougie's husband only I don't want to look a fool when my brother introduces his partner."

The woman's words were music to Macy Langham's ears, as much as Macy loved her boss and she did without question, she was also one of Soho's biggest gossips.

"James? If I'm honest I can't stand the sight of the little fagot, don't get me wrong, it's not that I'm homophobic or anything but I just can't stand it when people are out for all they can get and that one is as greedy as they

64

come. You see he's a lot younger than the boss so Dougie gives him everything he asks for. Just lately the greedy bastard has been asking for more and more. I don't have to tell you that this place is a goldmine, I could see by the look on your face when you came in that you were impressed but nobody has bottomless pockets. James always wants Dougie to buy him stuff and sooner or later the fucking money, well it's bound to dry up and god above only knows what will happen then."

About to ask more Stella was stopped when the front door opened and two men entered the bar. The first was no more than thirty, thin and his facial features were very feminine. With an immaculately cut full head of hair Stella could see that he would have had no problem passing as a woman if he had a mind to. The second man was taller and thicker set, his hair was receding a little but nothing stopped her recognising Douglas Nicholson from Roy Street Bethnal Green. When he saw her Dougie let the shopping bags drop to the floor. For a few seconds they studied each other's faces and then almost running Dougie swept her up into his arms.

"Oh my God! Oh Stella my beautiful lovely Stella it's so good to see you after all these years."

Stella could feel the onset of tears but this time she didn't force them away and she laughed wildly when her brother began to twirl around with her in his arms. The emotional moment was halted when a loud cough was heard. They both turned to see a not so happy James Nicholson as he stood leaning up against one of the supporting pillars with his arms arrogantly folded across his chest. His head was tilted to one side and his lips were pursed as he tried to make a silent statement. There was no smile on his face and Stella could see that he wasn't happy about being left out. Dougie instantly released his sister and walking over to his husband, placed a hand tenderly on the man's shoulder.

"Sorry love, where are my manners. James I'd like to introduce you to my big sister Stella."

"Charmed I'm sure!"

James then collected up the bags and without another word minced off in the direction of the kitchen.

"Take no notice of him, he doesn't like being left out but he'll soon calm down. Come on let's take a seat and you can tell me all that's happened over the years. Macy babe, fetch a couple of fresh coffees would you darling?"

Macy Langham did just as she'd been asked and Stella was sure that a few minutes later she could feel her ears burning at what she could only imagine was being said in the back kitchen.

"So Sis, what's been happening with you, god I've missed you girl. You don't know how many times I've thought about you and mum over the years. How come it's taken thirty five of them for you to get in touch with me?"

Dougie's face was now serious and she could tell that he was hurting and probably had been for years.

Momentarily she felt guilty but then realised that he had been just as capable of getting in touch as she was.

"Oh I don't know Dougie; I suppose life got in the way. I stayed living with mum and dad so it wouldn't have been easy."

"You never married?"

"Unlike you? No I didn't but it didn't stop me having four kids and all by different fathers I might add."

Dougie Nicholson began to laugh; his sister was always able to bring a smile to his face. It had been the same even when they were small and at times, especially when the old man was being mean, it was all that had kept him going. For a few seconds the bar was silent as they both quietly reminisced and then Stella leaned forward and gently took hold of her brother's hand.

"I'm so glad I've found you, but I do have an ulterior motive for being here."

"I don't doubt that so why don't you just spit it out and let's see where we go from there."

Stella took in a deep breath and after accepting that there was no easy way of saying things she just blurted it out. "The old man is dead."

There was no response or reaction from Dougie but did she really think there would be, did she want someone, anyone, to be sorry about Wilf's death just to ease her own guilt?

"So?"

"So what? I couldn't give a shit about that old cunt or have you conveniently forgotten how he threw me out at just thirteen years old. None of you ever bothered to find out if I was alive or dead. I slept on the streets for weeks Stella and came within a hairs breath of becoming a rent boy just to survive. It could all have gone so horribly wrong, especially back then when it wasn't nearly as safe out on the streets as it is today. "

"What happened?"

"I was one of the lucky ones; a club owner took pity on me and let me sleep on his office floor in return for running a few errands. It wasn't ideal but at least I had a roof over my head. When it was at last legal for me to work behind the bar Graham, he was the club owner, well he gave me a job. I worked my butt off over the years and I don't mean literally, the rest so they say is history and now I have a partner, my own restaurant and doing very nicely thank you."

"That Macy woman told me you were married! When

67

did that happen?"

"Two years ago. James can be hard work at times, very demanding and I know he has a roving eye and hasn't always been loyal to me but I totally adore him Stella. It wasn't until we met that I really knew the meaning of true love."

"Well good for you."

Stella didn't mean what she'd just said, she hated anyone that was unfaithful whether they were gay or straight but she knew better than to voice her opinion, especially so soon after meeting up again. Their brother sister relationship had to be slowly rebuilt and she didn't want to jeopardise it by saying something out of turn.

"So tell me about your brood then."

"Well there's my eldest Stevie, I had him only months after you left. He married young and now has three kids, well I say kids but they're nearly grown up now, teenagers with attitude, except for little Wilf."

"You are joking me?"

Stella couldn't stop herself from laughing.

"I know it ain't good but I think my Stevie was trying to keep in dads good books seeing as he rents the shops from him. So then there's Veronica, thirty three, and who we all call Ronnie. She's married and also has three kids. Jane was next, now she my dear brother really would make you laugh. She married an accountant called Roger, no kids and neither of them thinks that their shit stinks. The others just put up with Jane and her snobby ways, I suppose that's what families do ain't it? Lastly there's my boy Raymond who's nearly twenty. There isn't much I can say about him, at least not anything good. He's a bit of a tearaway and dabbles in drugs but what can I do about it Dougie, at the end of the day he's still my son."

68

"Don't sound like you've had it easy girl?"

"I can't complain we've always had food and a roof over our heads. Look Dougie the reason I came here was to see if you will come to the funeral? They will be reading the Will after, not that I would imagine we've been included but I would like you to be there all the same, if only for mum's sake."

"How is the old girl Stella?"

Stella could see the concern etched all over his face and she knew that the only reason he hadn't asked after his mother yet was because he was frightened of the answer, frightened that she might have already died.

"Frail but then I suppose that's to be expected at her age. That old cunt led her one hell of a life and it only got worse after you left."

"I can imagine."

"I must say though, since the old man snuffed it she has found a new lease of life. There's no one to tell her what to do and I think she finally feels free. I didn't tell her I was coming here today as I didn't want to build up her hopes. Oh Dougie you don't know how much she's missed you and how it broke her heart when you left. So what do you say, will you come?"

The conversation was interrupted when James and Macy re-entered and as Stella studied the younger man more closely, she really couldn't deny that he was strikingly beautiful. Walking over he held out his hand and smiling revealed a stunning set of bright white teeth that Stella knew must have set her brother back a few thousand pounds.

"Nice to meet you at last Stella and I can only apologise for my rudeness earlier it was all just a bit of a shock."

"Don't worry about it love, compared to some of the greetings I've received over the years that was nothing.

Anyway I best be getting back, mum will be wanting her dinner soon."

Stella stood up to leave and Dougie tightly embraced her. Handing over a business card he didn't want to let go of her hand, it had been so good to see her again and he didn't want this special moment to end.

"My numbers on there, give me a call when you know the date and time."

"I will, nice to meet you James. Bye Macy."

Dougie Nicholson walked his sister to the door and after another embrace he watched as she headed off down the road. Stella had aged and he knew that it wasn't just the years that had given her the lines. To raise four children alone and in a hostile environment must have been horrendous at times. Hopefully now that they had been reunited he would be able to ease her burden a bit, if only financially. Dougie had a spring in his step when he walked back into the bar. It wasn't everyday that you woke up next to your husband and only family member and then just three hours later you find out that your family is now huge and that they want you to be a part of their lives again. Walking over to James, Dougie was all smiles until his husband spoke and the man's words knocked the wind out of Dougie's sails.

"So how much did the old cow want?"

"Sorry?"

"Well she hasn't turned up here after all these years just to ask after your health now has she?"

"She didn't want anything other than to tell me that my father had died. Sometimes James you really are a total bitch! I'm going upstairs for a nap; wake me if we get busy."

James knew he had overstepped the mark so he didn't attempt to add any further insult or comment in any way.

He wasn't usually short for words but apologising was definitely out of the question, the word 'sorry' just wasn't in his vocabulary. He'd spent the last week trying to wangle a new pair of designer shoes and upsetting his sugar daddy wasn't the best way to get them. When his husband came back down again James would be all sweetness and light, if there was one thing he was good at it was twisting Dougie Nicholson around his little finger.

CHAPTER EIGHT

A week later the funeral had been arranged and the flowers booked. Stella had decided to hold the wake at The Old George but it had taken some persuading to get the Landlord to agree. She hadn't previously been privy to what had occurred at the pub on the night of her father's death but Stella wasn't surprised in the least when all was revealed. To begin with the Landlord, Dick Kendal, had flatly refused but when there was mention of him providing a buffet the pound signs soon registered and he couldn't do enough to accommodate her request. Considering how they all felt about Wilf Nicholson most of the family were surprised that there would even be a wake but Stella had lived by East End traditions for the whole of her life and a decent send off was always expected, no matter how much of a low life the deceased had been. After taking Daisy shopping to buy a new navy coat, mother and daughter had decided to pop in to the Roman Road shop and grab a coffee with Stevie on their way home. It was a lost leader day and the place was packed, all the tills were manned and Ivan and SJ were working nonstop to refill the shelves. When Stella and Daisy reached the rear storeroom they found Tammy and Bianca in the middle of a full blown row and the women didn't see the visitors to begin with.

"I don't give a fuck what you say; I ain't bleeding well doing it!"

"I'm sorry you feel that way Bianca but your dad said you have to."

"Oh fuck off Tammy, who died and made you god. Don't forget, one day this will all be mine and when that happens I'm going to make sure that you're the first out of the fucking door."

"There's no need to be like that Bianca, I'm only repeating what I've been told by your dad."

"Oh fuck off you stupid bitch! Do you really think my old man gives a flying fuck about you and the other low life idiots that work here?"

Stella had heard enough and marching over to her granddaughter it took all of her inner strength not to slap the girl across the face. Daisy was close behind her daughter, she loved a row and Bianca had it coming to her in droves.

"Don't ever let me hear you talk to anyone like that again Bianca Nicholson. Who the bleeding hell do you think you are? You might live in a fancy fucking house and have everything your heart desires but that don't make you better than anyone else. I take it your dad ain't here, because I know fine well he would haul you over the bleeding coals for talking to Tammy like that. Now get up them bleeding stairs and make us a cuppa and by god it had better be the best brew you've ever made my girl!"

Bianca knew better than to argue with her Nan and skulked off in the direction of the staff room. As she did she could hear Stella apologising to Tammy. How dare she make her look so small in front of the hired help, well when her dad came back she was going to tell him exactly what had happened and for once he would put her Nan in her place.

"I'm sorry you had to hear that Mrs Nicholson. I know she's family but on the weeks that she's here, it's almost unbearable. I don't want to sound as if I'm telling tales but honest to god I really don't know how much more I can take."

"No need to apologise to me my love, don't my Stevie take her in hand?"

"He does his best but when she ain't twisting him around her little finger, she's skiving off out the back. I don't want to seem like I'm a grass Mrs Nicholson but I'm at my wits end not to mention that it's causing a lot of discord and bad feeling with the other staff members." Stella shook her head slowly, as if she hadn't got enough to deal with at the moment.

"Leave it with me Tammy and I'll speak to her father." Stella linked arms with Daisy and steered her towards the door leading upstairs. They had just reached the top when Stevie came running up behind them.

"Hello there Mum, you alright Nan?"

"Not really Son, I think me and you need to have a little chat in the office about that brat of a daughter of yours. For fuck's sake where the hell does she get off behaving the way she does. You're a good man son and a wonderful husband but if you don't mind me saying, your child rearing skills leave a lot to be desired."

Stevie Nicholson grimaced as he pushed open the door but when the three entered they came face to face with Bianca who was now sitting in her father's chair behind the desk. She had at least obeyed her Nan as there were two mugs of tea perched on top of one of the storage boxes.

"Dad, thank god you're back. That Tammy is a fucking bitch and I really think you need to sack her. She talks to me like I'm the bleeding village idiot and I won't put up with it, do you hear me?"

Stella rolled her eyes upwards as she walked over and picked up the mugs. Handing one to her mother she waited to see what her son's response would be.

"Firstly Bianca I've told you before about your language. Secondly, Tammy is the best employee I have and if the two of you have a problem I would take her side every

74

time."

"But Dad...."

"No buts now get back down there and do some work for a change. If you know what's good for you, you will apologise to Tammy and remember what I said a few days ago, if you don't start pulling your weight then there won't be any wages."

Without a goodbye Bianca stormed out and feeling chuffed with himself Stevie turned to his mother for approval but he wasn't expecting to hear what she said next.

"Call that a bleeding telling off, good god son are you a man or a fucking mouse. If you don't start pulling that little madam back into line you're going to have some serious problems on your hands before too long."

"What like you have with Ray?"

His words shocked Stella to the core, they hurt, were undeserved and totally out of character. Stevie saw the offended look on his mothers face and was instantly sorry. Walking over he reached out with both hands and grabbed her shoulders.

"I'm sorry Mum that was uncalled for and I shouldn't have said it. Sometimes I really dislike my daughter. I can't for the life of me work out where she gets it from, I mean it ain't as if her mother's like it."

"I'll tell you where she gets it from son, you and her aunt Jane! As much as it goes against the grain to hear it, the three of you are picked out of your grandad's arse."

Suddenly Daisy burst out laughing and it relaxed the mood but Stella still held some concern regarding her oldest son. He never shunned her advice, in fact he usually sought it out, so for him to say those things was totally out of character and she worried that his feelings went a lot deeper than having to chastise his daughter.

75

She made a mental note to have a quiet word with him the next time they were alone. The room was silent for a few seconds but then the office door flew open and Tammy Carter came running in. Her face was red and she was out of breath as she struggled to get the words from her mouth.

"Quick Stevie, Sean Magarity is up to his usual trucks again and Ivan has sneaked off on a break so that he doesn't have to deal with him."

Stevie Nicholson ran out of the room with Tammy following closely behind. Reaching the shop floor they found the man spread eagled on the ground with Barbara Morton sitting in the middle of Sean Magarity's back. The thief's arms and legs were flailing about and Stevie could see that Barbara wouldn't be able to keep the culprit down for much longer.

"You phoned the Old Bill Tam?"

Tammy winked in her boss's direction.

"Sure did they will be here in a matter of minutes."

A small crowd had begun to gather and Sean Magarity started to panic. He was on his last warning and knew that this time it would mean at stint at Her Majesties. Turning his head sideways his eyes were pleading as he spoke to Stevie.

"Please Gov'nor don't call the Old Bill, I'll put everything back I swear.   Please, this fat cow is breaking my back!"

Stevie Nicholson wanted to smile at the spectacle sprawled out on the floor but he didn't.

"Let him up Barbara and well done, now don't try getting funny you little twat or you'll be back on that fucking floor in five seconds flat."

Sean shakily stood up and emptying his pockets handed over three packets of batteries, six cans of Lynx, a bag of brass screws, three tubes of toothpaste and a can of hairspray. As the items kept appearing Stevie shook his head and stepping towards the man grabbed the side of his coat and opened it up. Two large cloth pockets had been sewn onto the inner fabric; no wonder the light fingered little thief was able to carry so much stuff.

"I want you out of here now Magarity and you are banned from ever stepping foot through that fucking door again. Try to come in and I'll march you down the bleeding cop shop by the scruff of your fucking neck! Understood?"

Sean Magarity ran from the store and as the front door swung back and forth everyone began to laugh. The Old Bill hadn't even been contacted; it was an old East End thing, you never grassed on anyone, even if they had done wrong to you or yours. Problems were always sorted out in house and the law couldn't be trusted.

"Right ladies and gents the show is over, so let's get back to filling your baskets with all the bargains we have on offer today. Barbara you did good love and I know it must have taken some guts."

Barbara Morton was as wide as she was tall and what she lacked in muscle she more than made up with in weight. Stevie knew it had taken some balls or at least in Barbara's case some serious mental ability to tackle Sean Magarity to the ground. As he headed back up the stairs he decided a little reward would be in order come Friday. Realising that with all the commotion he hadn't seen his daughter he turned back towards the shop floor.

"Tam, where's Bianca?"

Tammy Carter shrugged her shoulders.

"I saw her sneak out of the front door when all the trouble started."

Stevie took in a deep breath, it was the final straw and

there would be hell to pay when he got back home tonight. Remembering his Mum and Nan were still upstairs he put his anger to the back of his mind as he ran up to the office. As he entered Stella and Daisy began to clap their hands. They were standing beside the close circuit television monitor and had watched the whole shenanigans from the comfort of the office. About to make a comment he was stopped when Tammy once again came into the office.

"Sorry Boss but Maggie Atkins is kicking up a stink at the tills. Says her deodorant won't squirt and is yelling at the top of her voice that we rip people off."

Stevie turned towards his mother and held out his upturned palms.

"I'd better go before we have no bleeding customers left; it's one of the many joys of retail I'm afraid Mum."

With that he turned and left the room. Stella took hold of Daisy's arm and grinned.

"Come on love let's get you home. I tell you something for nothing Mum; the next time anyone says my boy is minted and has a life of riley I'm going to bloody well set them straight about all he has to deal with!"

"Too true girl, what a fucking carry on and no mistake. Your Stevie deserves every penny he gets if he has to sort out them bleeding riff raff day in and day out. I'll tell you something Stella, the lifters of today ain't got a patch on my generation, fancy getting caught for a load of stuff that ain't worth a jot. In my day if you took the risk of shop lifting it was for a sight more than pound shop rubbish!"

Stella couldn't hold the laughter inside as she steered her mother towards the stairs.

By the time he'd closed the shop up for the night and driven back home to Essex Stevie had at last calmed down a little. He wasn't looking forward to the row he knew would definitely kick off as soon as he walked through the door but for once he was going to take his daughter in hand. Jo was in the kitchen and the food she was cooking smelled wonderful. Walking over he placed his hands onto her hips and nuzzled the back of her neck. "I hear you've had an eventful day?"

Stevie removed his hands and breathed out deeply. Jo's tone told him that she wasn't happy and that Bianca must have laid it on thick regarding her version of events from earlier. Now he not only had to deal with his daughter, but also try and convince his wife that their offspring was a lazy good-for-nothing little bitch.

"I ain't in the mood for a row, at least not with you Jo. Where is she?"

"Gone out."

"Fucking gone out! Well that really takes the biscuit."

Jo was starting to get angry, she was having a nice quiet day until Bianca had walked in and started crying. Now she was being asked to take sides and quite frankly she was sick to the back teeth with all of them.

"She was frightened by what happened today at the shop, Stevie she was in tears when she came home."

"Frightened! She really is playing you Jo. It was a shop lifter and nothing she doesn't see happen most days. The real reason she stormed out was the fact that she didn't want to do any more fucking work. Mum came in and found her having a right go at Tammy and told her off. Look babe, I'm stressed up to my eyeballs at the minute, I mean for fucks sake we might not have a business left come next week."

This was the first Jo Nicholson had thought about the shops since having tea at her mother in laws on Sunday and she instantly felt guilty that he was having to deal

79

with it all alone. Walking over to her husband who was now seated at the table she sat down beside him and took his hand.

"Is it really that bad Stevie? Could we really lose everything?"

In frustration he ran a hand through his hair and when he looked her directly in the eyes Jo could see something she'd never seen before, fear.

"Until next week we don't know who will get the shops. If its Mum or Nan then all well and good but you know as well as I do what an evil bastard Wilf could be. In all honesty, well he could have left them to anyone and to be truthful, I wouldn't put it past him to have done just that to spite everyone."

"I'm not stupid Stevie and I know that but what's the point in worrying until you know exactly what's going on?"

"Worrying!!!!"

Now he was getting angry and standing up he swiped the mugs from the table and as they smashed on the tiled floor he stormed into the hall and went upstairs. It had been a long time since Jo had seen her husband erupt like this and she knew the best way to handle him was to allow him to calm down in his own time, she just hoped Bianca stayed out until he had. That wasn't to be the case and a few seconds later when the front door slammed Jo mouthed the words 'Oh shit'. Carrying three shopping bags that just by the designer labels stamped on the side told Jo they held some expensive items; her daughter flopped down onto one of the dining chairs.

"I see the old man is home then?"

"He's your father so show a little respect B and I don't think you were being truthful when you told me what happened at the shop today was you?"

Bianca Nicholson was about to blow up into one of her tantrums but was stopped when her mother held up her hand.

"I don't want to hear it, your dad is stressed out and your behaviour today hasn't helped the situation. Now for once in your life take some advice girl, go upstairs, put that little lot away and don't come down again until I call you. When you do come down I want you to apologise to your dad and not mention what happened again. If you don't darling then I can assure you with the mood he's in, you will be the one that comes off worse."

With that Jo stood up and went over to the stove to continue preparing the meal. The next thing she heard was her daughter for once doing as she'd been asked. Hopefully, if Stevie came down in a better mood peace could once again be restored in the house, if not, then Jo would just put on her coat and leave them all to get on with it, for a few hours at least.

CHAPTER NINE

On the day of the funeral the weather was as sombre as the Nicholson's mood. Rain was sheeting down heavily and everyone was soaked by the time they arrived. The family were congregating at the flat on Roy Street and there was hardly room to swing a cat. Once again Stella had prepared a buffet so that they all had food in their belly's before they set off but this time it was covered over with a sheet to stop any temptation until she was sure that they were all here. Busying herself with making sure everyone had a drink Stella hadn't given her mother a second thought but as she walked back through to the kitchen she noticed Daisy standing on the doorstep looking out at the rain as it teemed down over the landing. Stella thought how sad she looked but knew that it wasn't anything to do with losing Wilf. It was regret for a life wasted and there wasn't anything Stella could do to change things. Her heart went out to her mother and she felt the onset of tears, almost as if she had failed the woman even though the terrible times had begun when she was still a child and unable to stand up to her father. There and then Stella Nicholson made a decision, she couldn't change the past but the future was now in her hands and she made a silent promise to herself that from now on her dear old mum would know nothing but joy and happiness for the rest of her days.

"You alright Mum?"

Daisy turned and gave her the warmest of smiles. Stella had been a wonderful daughter and she didn't know how she would have got through the past fifty plus years without her girl by her side.

"Never better love but I'll be glad when today is over and

that old bastard is gone for good."

"Sweetheart he's already gone. Your wanker of a husband and the man I had the misfortune to call my father is dead, he can't hurt you anymore sweetheart."

"Not physically, but mentally the fucker still haunts me Stella. After today when they burn the last of him, I know he will be gone for good and then I will be able to sleep easy in my bed, does that make any sense love?"

"Complete sense darling now come on inside before you catch your death. Stevie's just opened the old sod's brandy and I know he would be cursing us all to hell and back if he knew we were drinking his stash."

"I hope he does know love, come to that, I hope the fucker rots in hell."

Stella didn't know how to reply to her mother's last sentence, the woman was hurting so bad that maybe it was best if she said nothing at all but it didn't stop her thinking and silently she said to herself 'I'll drink to that'. They both saw the hearse pull into the square below along with three limousines for the family members. Stella took a deep breath and then walked in to the front room to announce that it was time to leave. Stevie and Jo headed out first followed by SJ and Bianca, who was behaving impeccably as her father was still angry and she had been warned by her mother not to put a foot wrong today. Little Wilf trailed behind, he couldn't understand why he had to be here, it wasn't as if he had even liked his great grandad and to spoil things even further it was sports day at school. Ronnie and Sam were next to leave along with their children Lee and Suzanne and between them was little Robbie. Jane and Roger linked arms and Jane held a handkerchief to her nose in a gesture that would let everyone know she was crying. Stella raised an eyebrow at her daughter's dramatics and normally she would have mentioned how ridiculous it looked but not today, today she wanted things to run as smoothly as possible. The last to leave was Raymond and as he watched them all descend the stairs he couldn't help but think what a sorry bunch of human beings they were. He wasn't trying to kid himself that he was any better, in fact he knew he was far worse but the one thing he wasn't was a hypocrite like his brother and sisters, well not Ronnie so much but the others at least. Stella and Daisy were shown into the front car along with Stella's four children. Their spouses and kids were put into the other limousines and when all the doors were firmly closed the procession slowly pulled away. Daisy's sister Lena had sent word that she would make her own way to the Crematorium, Lena always like to make a grand entrance and if nothing else, seeing a woman in her late seventies totter down the driveway in high heels that should have long been banished to the bin, would give them all a smile. Stella had hoped that Dougie would be here, she'd told him the day and time well in advance but if he'd made the choice not to attend then there wasn't much she could do about it. Studying her mother Stella noticed that not once had Daisy taken her eyes off of the coffin in front.

"You sure you're alright Mum?"

"Never better love, just making sure the old sod doesn't go anywhere before we have a chance to put him in the oven."

Stella smiled at the realisation that Daisy meant every word she had just said. Slowing down the cortege pulled left off of Hermit Road and into the East London crematorium in Plaistow. There was nothing welcoming about the place but as they all got out of the cars Stella breathed a sigh of relief when she spied Dougie and

James already waiting for them at the side of the building. Walking over she embraced her brother and when Daisy looked in their direction she could hardly believe her eyes. Now her tears fell thick and fast for the son she had lost so many years ago and who she had believed she would never see again. Dougie almost ran over and wrapping his big arms around the little woman held on for dear life never wanting to let her go.
"Oh Mum it's so good to see you darling."
Daisy tried to speak but no words emerged as she just clung to her son and sobbed. Wilf Nicholson's coffin was slid out of the hearse and there was just a single floral tribute perched on top that simply read 'From the family'.
With the hymns sung and after Daisy had been adamant that she wanted to stay and watch the coffin as it was lowered, they could all at last leave. Everyone squashed up in the limousines so that there was room to accommodate Dougie and James and then it was back to The Old George for the wake. As soon as the family entered the music began to play and the alcohol flowed. It wasn't a traditional wake where everyone toasted the dearly departed but several glasses were raised in thanks that the old man had finally gone and they could now be a real family. Stella took the best part of an hour to introduce her brother to everyone. Dougie was so polite and he made sure he gave each of them the same amount of time as he went out of his way to chat even to the younger family members. Bianca was impressed especially when she was introduced to James but it was left up to her mother to explain that the man was gay and would never be interested in her. Stevie had been on tenter hooks for the entire time and when Bernard Fuller from Milton and Gaskell solicitors arrived, he was

already pacing the floor in the back room. After introducing himself to Stella there were several seconds of awkward silence but as usual the ice was broken by the woman who hated anyone to feel uncomfortable.

"Well it's nice to finally meet you Mr Fuller, now how would you like to proceed?"

"If we could go somewhere a little quieter perhaps?"

"The back room is ready and waiting."

"Excellent, now if you would be so kind as to gather your sons and daughters and of course your mother and anyone else you may think is relevant, we can get started. This shouldn't take long and then you can all get back to your....."

Bernard Fuller didn't know how to finish his sentence as he'd never seen so many people having a good time after a funeral.

"Party Mr Fuller, it's a party. If you had really known my father then you would understand but it would take far too long to explain and I doubt very much if you're that interested."

Not giving the man time to reply Stella picked up a fork from the buffet table and tapped it on to the side of her glass as loudly as she could.

"Right you unruly lot! Listen up I need a moment of your time. Mum, Dougie, Ronnie, Jane and Ray, can you all go through to the back for a moment. The rest of you lot, well that food ain't going to eat itself so get tucked in."

As the immediate family left the room the remaining mourners besieged the table like gannets and Bernard Fuller shook his head in amazement as he followed Stella into the back. The space wasn't large but a table had been set up in the centre and several chairs had been placed in front of it. Stevie was already sitting down and when Bernard Fuller took a seat the others followed suit. "Good afternoon ladies and gentlemen, my firm Milton and Gaskell were instructed by the late Mr Wilfred Nicholson to make sure that his final wishes are carried out fully. I personally haven't been privy to anything that is contained in the Will as it was drawn up by my predecessor. Neither my firm nor I can be held responsible for its contents as they were given under strict legal instruction. Now without any further delay I shall begin. The Will reads as follows. Mrs Nicholson, Mr Nicholson bequeathed to you his pocket watch as you were never a good time keeper especially when it came to providing his meals, maybe now you won't have a problem, Mr Nicholson's words not mine I might add." Bernard Fuller handed over Wilf's half hunter watch and Daisy stood up and held out her hand. The look on her face was one of puzzlement as she stared down at the trivial item her husband had bequeathed.

"To my daughter Stella I leave ..."

Bernard Fuller began to stutter and stammer, he didn't know how to finish his sentence and it was Stella that told him no matter what her father had asked him to say, he should just continue with it.

"To my daughter I leave a packet of unopened condoms as she never knew when to keep her legs shut."

Bernard handed over the packet and the room went silent. Not because of what had been left to the woman but purely out of a deep sense of love and the embarrassment they all now felt for her but Stella could only grin.

"Come on you lot, the old fucker might think he had the last laugh but he hasn't."

Looking towards the ceiling Stella held up the packet.

"That was pathetic old man; you're a bit bleeding late with these ain't you."

"I don't know why you're looking up for girl, he ain't there."

Everyone laughed at Daisy's words and it relaxed the mood but Mr Fuller had to cough loudly to quieten them all down so that he could proceed.

"If I may continue ladies and gentlemen? Mr Nicholson further states 'If there is any cash left it will be in my trouser pocket as I've made sure I spent every penny I could. There are no savings as I've gambled, drunk and womanized for the whole of my married life and the rest of the cash I've just wasted ha ha. First one to my trousers is welcome to it, that's if you ain't been scavenging through my things already. Lastly and what all of you greedy fuckers have been waiting for, my shops. I leave the Roman Road and the Liverpool Street stores to my only son Douglas. I never gave you what you deserved in my lifetime and my only hope is that you have straightened yourself out you bent bastard.' Mr Nicholson wanted it to be noted that at his last remark he was laughing."

Again the room was silent but this time it was for totally different reasons. Dougie was too stunned to speak and Stevie had tears of disbelief in his eyes. The old bastard had well and truly screwed him over and now he had nothing, nothing to show for all the years of hard work. For a second Stevie contemplated contesting the Will but he knew his grandfather would have made sure it was watertight. His mind instantly went in to overdrive and he started to bite down hard on his finger nails. Well the house would have to go that was for sure, god how had it all come to this. When he turned to face his mother, Stella could see the sheer disbelief in his eyes and her heart went out to her eldest son. If anyone deserved those shops it was Stevie, he was the one who had toiled hard to make them what they were today. She instantly felt guilty regarding getting in contact with her brother but then she reasoned it wouldn't have made any difference either way. She could feel her boy's pain and devastation and there was nothing she could do about it, maybe Dougie would see sense and pass his inheritance over.

"And that ladies and gentlemen, concludes the reading of Mr Wilfred Nicholson's last Will and testament."

With that Bernard Fuller said his goodbyes to Stella and Daisy and then left The Old George as quickly as he could. The rest of the family headed back to the party but they were all subdued. Daisy, Stella, Ronnie and Ray all felt terrible for Stevie. Jane on the other hand was fuming that she hadn't been included; she had been counting on some kind of inheritance to bring her dream of moving out to Essex and being closer to her brother to fruition. That had now gone out of the window and she was angry, angry that some long lost member of the family that she had never even seen before today, was getting everything. Dougie stood at the bar and was in total shock, he hadn't yet commented about the inheritance to James but he knew it would only be a matter of seconds before his husband would begin a barrage of questions.

"I'd like to leave now James if you don't mind, I'll just go and say my goodbyes to the family and then we'll get off."

"Why, what's happened?"

"Not here, I'll explain later."

With that Dougie Nicholson made his way over to the family table and stopped in front of his sister and mother.

"Stella, Mum, I'm getting off now."

Stella stood up but before she had time to say anything Jane interrupted and her tone was nasty and sarcastic as she spoke.

"So now that you've got what you came for you're leaving! I really don't know how you can live with yourself. My brother has worked his socks off for years and you just walk in and pull the rug right from under him."

Stella had heard quite enough and getting to her feet she slammed her hand down onto the table.

"Shut up Jane, just shut the fuck up. I'm sorry about that Dougie we're all just a bit shocked as no doubt you are too. You get off now love and I'll contact you in a few days when the dust has settled."

Standing on tip toes she kissed her brother on the cheek and she could feel him squeeze her arm in thanks.

Bending low he kissed his mother tenderly but she didn't respond. It wasn't out of any malice, nothing could be further from her mind, it was simply down to the shock and realisation that once again her husband had been cruel to the core and that even in death he was still hell bent on making sure he got his own way. As she sat and watched her long lost son walk out of The Old George she wondered if she would ever see him again. The couple walked a short distance until they were able to hail a cab but as soon as they were inside James started his interrogation.

"So are you going to tell me what happened then? I mean I'm only your husband for god's sake!"

Dougie closed his eyes as he began to speak and knew that what he was about to say would only bring him more aggravation.

"The old man left me both of the shops."

"Oh my god, oh my god we're rich."

"Sorry James but I'm not keeping them. It isn't right and just because the old bastard left them to me doesn't mean

I can't give them back to the people that deserve them the most."

James had been elated at the news and had seen it as a fantastic wind fall. Now he couldn't for the life of him understand what the problem was, couldn't understand why Dougie's conscience was pricking him to such a degree that he wanted to hand it all back. The couple began to argue and continued to do so for the rest of the journey and even when they were once more in the flat above the bar. As usual James was gradually starting to wear Dougie down or at least he thought he was but when Dougie raised his voice, something he rarely did, James knew he had to try a different tactic. Disappearing into the bedroom he switched on his lap top and began to search for retail premises available on the open market both in Bethnal Green and those close to Liverpool Street. His eyes opened wide when he saw the prices they were commanding and he called Dougie through to take a look. Patting the duvet beside him James asked his husband to take a seat.

"You are not going to like what I'm about to say but I'll say it anyway. Now that we are married anything you inherit is legally half mine. Now I don't want to argue with you over this but there is no way that I am going to give up what could be a fortune just to keep your long lost relatives happy."

Dougie Nicholson couldn't believe what he was hearing, he had always known that James was greedy but this was a totally different kettle of fish. Standing up he removed a jacket from the wardrobe.

"And where exactly do you think you're going to?"

"I need to think and also get as far away from you as possible because right at this moment James, I really don't like what I'm seeing in you."

"Seeing in me? And just what do you mean by that little remark?"

"You are unbelievable, you greedy little bitch!"

"Fuck you!"

"Yeah, well that just about sums you up."

Dougie walked out but instead of James running after the man who had provided everything for him, he just shrugged his shoulders and glancing at his laptop typed in the words 'luxury villa's to purchase'. James had always known deep down that one day he would be rich, he just hadn't ever dreamed that it would happen so soon. When Dougie came home he would work on him again and make his husband see sense but for now he would just have to make do with fantasizing about what he was going to buy and he was in no doubt that he would be shopping until he dropped. He just hoped that it would all happen quietly, without too much fuss and more importantly, in the not too distant future.

CHAPTER TEN

Stella Nicholson had tossed and turned all night long with worry regarding her eldest son's future. Now as the bright morning sunshine began to stream through the unclosed curtains she pulled the duvet up over her head. Just for once she wished she could shut the world and all its problems out, just for once she wished someone else could deal with things instead of it always having to be her. Slowly the bedroom door opened and Daisy popped her head into the room.

"You alright girl?"

"No not really Mum but there ain't a lot I can do about it, now is there?"

Daisy pushed the door wide open, walked over and without an invite took a seat on the side of the bed.

"Now you listen here Stella, we ain't no quitters and lying in your pit never solved anything. Get yourself up and do what you do best, what you've always done"

"And what's that?"

"Pull your family back together again and put a stop to all this arguing and bad feeling."

She knew that the old woman meant well but this time Stella didn't know which way to turn. On one hand she knew her boy deserved to inherit the shops and without them he could lose everything, but on the other hand she had only just found her brother and after so many years she didn't want to lose him again.

"I'm between a rock and a hard place Mum, whatever I do it will mean turning my back on family and where Stevie is concerned, well I could never do that. I feel so guilty; I mean it was me who found Dougie again in the first place."

"You really think that things would be different if your brother wasn't back on the scene? I've never heard anything so bleeding ridiculous in all my life."

Stella pulled herself up so that her face was now level with Daisy's.

"Of course I don't think that but it doesn't stop the guilt."

"Well for the record, that old bastard wrote his last Will and testament over ten years ago so let that be an end to all of this. Whether Dougie had turned up yesterday or not, those shops had been ear marked for him a long long time ago."

It wasn't the truth, in all honesty Daisy didn't have a clue when that rat of a husband had made his wishes known and she wasn't in the habit of telling lies but she reasoned that just this once and if it brought some kind of peace to her daughter, then no harm had been done. Standing up she held her back and winced in pain, true she did have arthritis but this little show had been purely for her daughters benefit.

"Well are you getting up or do I have to make my own bloody breakfast?"

Stella laughed out loud and slowly shook her head as she hauled her legs over the side of the bed. Switching on the radio Marvin Gaye and Tammi Terrell were singing 'Ain't no mountain high enough' and Stella stopped for a moment and listened to the words. Finally she decided that she couldn't leave things as they were. Maybe it wouldn't do any good but she at least had to try and build bridges. Buttering Daisy's toast, Stella then made a quick phone call. After she was washed and changed and had checked that her mother was settled for the morning she informed Daisy that she was popping out for a couple of hours and if Daisy should want anything, then she was to call Ronnie who wasn't going to work and who would pop round to the flat if she was needed. Stella retraced her steps of a few days ago and even though she was now a bit more familiar with the area she didn't feel any easier as she walked along the streets of Soho. As before, Delphine's was closed, and tapping on the window she waited for Macy to open the doors.

"Hello there Stella love, nice to see you again so soon."

"Is he in?"

"Yeah, I'll just shout up to the flat. You're lucky, James is out so at least you two can have a bit of privacy without that lazy little sod sticking his nose into your family's business. You know something Stella, after you left last time Dougie had a grin on his face for hours, seeing you was a right tonic and no mistake but since the funeral it's been the complete opposite. I don't know what's going on and I ain't one to pry."

Waiting a couple of second in the hope that Stella would reveal all, she gave up when the woman just stared towards the front window and said nothing.

"Well like I was saying, I ain't one to pry and I just wish that whatever it is, it can be sorted out as I hate to see the boss so unhappy."

Macy Langham disappeared for a few seconds and then smiling in Stella's direction she quickly returned to her cleaning. Dougie didn't know who his visitor was but when he entered the bar and saw his sister his face lit up.

"Oh Stella, it's so good to see you. I thought that after what happened yesterday you wouldn't want anything to do with me. I really had no idea about it and ....."

She placed a finger to his lips.

"Dougie we have spent too many years apart for me to let that happen again. I've come here today to ask you and James over for Sunday lunch. There will only be six of us, me, mum, Stevie, Jo and you two. I'll move a mountain if I have to but this family will get back on track. What do you say?"

"I think it's a great idea Sis, what time do you want us?"

"Two'ish?"

"That's ideal. You'll stay for a coffee?"

"I'd love to darling but I really need to get back as I've left mum at home on her own. Ronnie is on standby but the old sod can be a real handful when she puts her mind to it."

Brother and sister embraced and a few seconds later Stella left the bar but she had no intention of returning to the flat on Roy Street. Back in Bethnal Green Stella made her way to her son's shop, though for just how much longer it would be known as that she had no idea. It wasn't so busy today and as she entered Tammy stood talking to Ivan the manager. Looking up they both smiled as she approached.

"Morning Mrs Nicholson."

"Morning Tammy, Ivan, is he in?"

Tammy nodded her head and Stella went through to the back and climbed the rear stairs to the storeroom and office. Tapping gently she turned the door handle but as she went inside she could feel her heart drop at the sight before her. Stevie was seated behind his desk and he had his head in his hands. Looking up with embarrassment he quickly wiped his eyes with his palms but it was too late, his mother could see that he was emotional and deeply troubled. Walking over she stopped in front of the desk and smiled tenderly.

"You alright Son?"

"So so, anyway what brings you here?"

"I went to see your uncle Dougie and before you start, someone had to try and sort this mess out or are you just going to hand over all you've built up without any kind of fight?"

Stevie was shocked by his mother's words but he was also secretly pleased that she was at least trying to help him but then again wasn't that what she always did where any of her kids were concerned.

"And just what did the robbing cunt say?"

"There's no need for that Son; Dougie had no idea what was going to happen so don't go blaming him. Now I've invited the pair of them to Sunday lunch and I'm now asking you and Jo. I don't want any kids there, come to that I don't want anyone other than those invited. You will show your uncle respect and we will take things slowly. Hopefully if all goes well we can come to some sort of a compromise. Tell Jo we're eating around two, now get your head out of your arse son, stop feeling bleeding sorry for yourself and get on with some work."

Stella left the shop with a positive attitude and a smile on her face; she knew it was wishful thinking but if everything went to plan they could be back on track by Monday.

Midday on Sunday and the leg of lamb was roasting nicely in the oven as Stella Nicholson sang away to the radio while she peeled potatoes. Daisy was dozing in her armchair which left her daughter free to prepare the lunch without interruption. Earlier she had hauled a heavy folding table up from the ground floor shed so that the six of them would be able to sit and eat together for a change. It would be cramped but if she placed it next to the other small table and with a little juggling she could just about fit everyone around. Lying in bed this morning she had gone over and over in her mind just how things might pan out. It had been so long since they had known each other well, that she wasn't sure if her brother had a temper or whether he was a placid man, she prayed he was the latter because if Stevie lost it like he had so many times over the years then there could be a full on fight right here in the front room. Stella had just removed the joint from the oven when the telephone rang. Glancing up at the wall clock she noticed that it was exactly one o'clock. She was still busy preparing the food and when Daisy didn't pick up Stella walked into the front room and somewhat annoyed, grabbed the phone.

"Hello?"

"Oh hello Stella its James your brother-in-law, I'm afraid we won't be coming for lunch. Sorry to let you down at such short notice."

To say she was disappointed was an understatement but she tried not to let it show in her tone.

"Can I ask why?"

"Well there really isn't any point as I'm sure you have an ulterior motive for inviting us and, well it just won't work. I have discussed things with Dougie and we are going to sell off the shops, it's a chance in a life time for us and we can't look a gift horse in the mouth so to speak. I know you are only looking out for your own and for that I applaud you but as you will appreciate, we have to do exactly the same."

"Why you little bastard, if you think......."

Stella realised that the line had gone dead and she was now talking to herself. Slamming the receiver back onto its cradle she bit down hard on her lip and hit the tip of her thumb against her chin as she wracked her brains trying to think of something to do. Her line of thought was broken when the front door suddenly opened.

"Mum, Nan, anyone here?"

It was Stevie and Jo and on hearing their voices, Stella's stomach churned over as she realised that she didn't have a clue how she was going to break the news. Well, she

98

supposed honesty was the best policy but she didn't even have to begin to explain because as soon as Stevie walked in and saw the look on his mothers face he knew.

"So the bastard ain't coming is he?"

"No son he ain't, that jumped up little wanker that calls himself Dougie's husband has just rang and cancelled."

"I knew it I just fucking knew it, well that's it then I'm fucking ruined!"

Stevie Nicholson flopped down on the tired old sofa with a gutted look on his face and taking a seat beside her son Stella could only puff out her cheeks in disbelief.

"So, did he give any reason?"

"He said they were going to sell the shops, so there wasn't any point in coming over today. Oh love I'm so sorry truly I am."

Stevie grabbed his mother's hand and squeezed it, she really was a wonderful person and the last thing he wanted was for her to feel bad. The future was going to be bleak enough without having the worry that his mother was unhappy.

"Darling you ain't got nothing to be sorry about, you tried your best and I couldn't ask for any more sweetheart."

"So what's going to happen now son? Where the bleeding hell do we go from here?"

Jo had stood silently in the doorway and knowing what her husband was about to say she retreated into the kitchen to put the kettle on.

"I suppose a liquidation sale of all my stock and then I'll have to try and find a job somewhere. The house will have to go; I just can't afford to keep it now as there's no way I will be able to make the mortgage payments every month. Oh fucking hell, I haven't even thought about my staff either."

99

"I don't understand why you can't just rent another shop."

"Oh Mum, you really don't know much about business do you. Firstly there ain't any vacant shops in this area and those that are; well they just ain't big enough for what I sell. I can't downsize because without the space to hold such a large amount of stock I couldn't cope. I make small margins on the stuff I sell, you've heard the saying 'stock them high and sell them cheap' well that's what I do. Secondly the price of the lease's, let alone the rents, well it's astronomical. I know you thought I paid grandad a good rent each month but believe you me it was nothing compared to what he could have achieved on the open market. Don't get me wrong, I've earned a good living but not so much that a bank would back me, the house is mortgaged up to the hilt and there's just no way I will be able to afford the repayments. Fuck me, those couple of poof's must have looked into market prices, I reckon they will achieve somewhere around the four million mark for each shop if they sell them, maybe even more."

"How much!"

"I know, it's crazy."

Stella stood up and began to pace the floor, this wasn't fair and she wasn't just thinking of Stevie. Those properties should have been left to Daisy and then all of them could have benefited. Removing her brother's business card from her purse she walked over to the telephone.

"What are you doing Mum?"

"I want to speak to the organ grinder not the fucking monkey. That brother of mine has some explaining to do and the cowardly bastard can tell me himself what's going on."

100

Dougie Nicholson was in the middle of serving a customer when his mobile began to ring.

After cancelling the visit to Stella's he had sent home the extra staff he had asked to work the shift. The bar was heaving as it always was on a Sunday lunch time and he was about to delete the call when he saw that it was his sister. Passing the customer his drink Dougie waved his hand and said it was on the house and then rushed out into the small rear yard to answer.

"Hello Stella love, sorry about lunch."

"Fucking sorry about lunch! I knew you were a lot of things Dougie but I didn't think gutless was one of them."

Dougie sighed heavily, he would bet that James hadn't passed the message on in the best way and now his sister was upset which was the last thing he wanted.

"What's going on Dougie?"

"I'm sorry Stella I didn't want it to come to this but I haven't got a choice. James said if I hand over my inheritance then he will leave me. He's my life Stella not to mention my husband and besides, he has legal rights. Because we're married he's actually entitled to half of what dad left me. My hands are tied love."

Without a goodbye Stella put the phone down and turning to Stevie relayed all that she had been told.

"So if that little ponce wasn't demanding half do you think he would have given the shops back Mum?"

Stella wasn't sure of anything anymore. Three weeks ago and as shitty as her life was, everything was orderly and she was able to cope but now she didn't know what was happening.

"I don't know love, I really don't know; I mean its years since I had anything to do with my brother and to be truthful people change. I now realise that I don't know

101

him at all. I think next week I might seek out some legal advice myself Stevie. I mean it ain't as if we've got anything to lose now is it? I could always challenge the will or at least try?"

Stevie didn't reply and standing up he kissed his mother on the cheek. Jo appeared in the doorway with a tray of tea but when he slowly shook he his head in her direction, she returned it to the kitchen.

"Do you mind if we get off Mum, only I seem to have lost my appetite?"

"Of course not son, mind how you go and I'll pop in the shop next week."

"Yeah but don't leave it too long or there won't be a shop to visit."

With that the couple left the flat and Stella walked through to the kitchen just as Daisy was picking off a piece of the lamb.

"Fill your boots Mum, there won't be anyone else eating it."

Daisy had heard all that had gone on and wiping her greasy hand down the front of her dress she studied her daughter for a moment.

"Why don't you go and see Micky tonight. Since all this has been going on you've hardly given him a second though. A few drinks and a good seeing to will do you the world of good."

"Mother!"

Daisy shrugged her shoulders and grabbing another piece of meat disappeared into the front room. Stella couldn't help but laugh at her mother's suggestion but come to think of it, after the day she'd had what harm would it do.

CHAPTER ELEVEN

For the past ten years Stella Nicholson had been in a relationship. His name was Micky Mackerson and he was the Landlord of the Dundee Arms on Cambridge Heath Road. The set up suited them both, it had never been serious but purely companionship and of course a little sex thrown in whenever the mood took them, which happened to be almost every time they saw each other. Micky was no Adonis but he was interesting, funny and above all else he cared for Stella deeply. From their first date they had both made it clear to each other that they weren't interested in anything deep and meaningful. Stella liked being single and Micky had already been through three wives and definitely wasn't looking for a fourth. A couple of times a week they would meet up, once to go out to lunch somewhere and the second to spend time alone in the flat above the pub. The Dundee Arms was a busy bar that screened live sports and held quizzes twice a week. Good bar staff meant that Micky could take regular time off and not be disturbed. Deciding that her mother was right, Stella freshened herself up and applied a little makeup. Daisy was asleep in the chair and not wanting to just go out without telling her Stella gently touched her mother's arm.

"Mum, I'm taking your advice and popping out for a while to see Micky."

"Good girl and if you want to spend the night you do that, I can lock up and if I need anything I can always knock at old Stan's next door. For once just relax a little love and take some bloody time for yourself."

Stella bent down and tenderly kissed her mother.

"I will and thanks."

"What for?"

"Just being you."

Putting on her coat she slipped out of the flat and began the walk to her friends. It was just after three and even though the sun was shining brightly it was chilly. Stella pulled the collar of her coat up and hoped that Micky had lit the fire in the flat, the building was old and at times it could be as cold as ice. Walking along Old Ford Road she passed the many smart terraced properties that in her childhood had been classed as rundown and unwanted housing. Now a two bedroom could command well over a half a million and Stella wondered what the world was coming to. Approaching the three storey building Stella suddenly stopped, her head was all over the place and she wasn't sure if she should really be here, it wasn't like she was very good company at the moment but then Micky usually had a knack of making her feel great about herself so pushing open the front door she entered. The Dundee Arms was very old and had a grade two listing but since being refurbished and opening up as a trendy bar and one of the best places to be in Bethnal Green, Micky had treated it like his child. Before the renovation had taken place he hadn't much bothered with the pub but as soon as it had been remodelled it was a different story. Now the place gleamed from top to bottom and he wouldn't allow any rowdy behaviour in the pub, well at least he tried not to allow it but it was a difficult task if any of the premier football matches were showing on one of the five wide screen televisions that hung around the bar. It wasn't busy yet as the match they were planning to air didn't start until eight. Julie Peters and Bobby Windsor were behind the bar and they smiled when they saw her step inside. Walking behind the bar Stella opened the door that had 'PRIVATE' emblazed on the front and then

104

entered the back hall. Empty beer crates that had earlier contained designer brands lined the entire length all the way to the back door and the evidence spoke for itself, Micky had been very busy the previous night. Climbing the stairs she stopped and peered at her reflection in the ornate mirror that hung beside Micky's front door. Happy with what she saw Stella knocked and walked in. The living quarters at the Dundee Arms were spacious and had also been remodelled. Now everything was state of the art and trendy and Micky Mackerson was extremely proud of his home. Stella's high heels began to clack away on the polished bare board floor so she slipped them off as she hung up her coat. Hearing the television blearing out she made her way through to the front room. Micky was lying on the sofa and he looked up as she entered.

"Hello there girl, ain't you a sight for sore eyes."

Stella took a seat beside him and Micky knew straight away that there was something wrong. The woman was strong and it took a lot to faze her, lord above knew that she'd had many trials over her lifetime but she seldom let anyone know she was bothered. Today was different and as he looked into her eyes Stella began to cry. The tears flowed thick and fast but Micky did nothing. He knew that she had to let it all out and when she eventually finished he took her in his arms and silently held her for a few minutes. When she was ready to talk Stella gently pulled away from him and standing up Micky went over to the cabinet to pour them both a large brandy, as he did so his tone was soft as he spoke.

"Right, you want to tell me what has got you so upset?"

Stella rubbed at her brow. She didn't really know where to start or even if sharing her problems would help but deciding to give it a try she slowly began to talk.

"I told you before that my wanker of a dad had a couple of shops. My head is all over the place of course I did, and you've been down to Stevie's Roman Road place many times. Well, when the old bastard died I naturally assumed he would leave them to my Mum or at the very least to Stevie. I mean fucking hell Micky, that kid has worked his arse off for years to build up those shops." For a moment Stella was lost in thought as she remembered back to earlier and just how crestfallen her son had been. She really was struggling to come to terms with the fact that her brothers greed could allow someone, come to that a blood relative; to lose everything they had worked so hard for.

"And?"

"Well when the Will was read after the funeral seems the old cunt had done neither and instead he left them to my brother."

"You mean the queer one, the one that you haven't seen for donkey's years?"

Micky could see by the look on her face that she hadn't liked the queer reference but she didn't say anything to him about it and he now felt bad. A lot of his customers batted for the other side and his words were just a figure of speech the same as poof, fagot or bender. It was just common banter for Micky and a lot of his regulars but he still didn't like to upset her and now he regretted his choice of words.

"Yes, I went to see him before the funeral. He lives in Soho and things seemed to be fine until his scheming husband poked his nose in."

"His what?"

Micky Mackerson was old school; he would never admit to being homophobic but all the same he couldn't stomach the thought of two men having sex and touching each other intimately. In his own words 'it gave him the creeps', it just wasn't natural.

"You heard me, seems my darling brother got married a couple of years ago but didn't bother to let any of his family know. It was my dad who threw him out but he never saw fit to contact me or my mum again. Until now I didn't let it bother me but after all this, well I don't mind admitting that it has hurt us, always did but me and mum preferred not to talk about it. I suppose if we didn't mention his name then the hurt was less but of course it wasn't and I for one always prayed that one day he would seek us out. Anyway that's getting away from the point, this James bloke won't allow Dougie to pass over his inheritance to my boy. They plan to sell both shops, which I might add and something I didn't know, are worth at least three or four million each, well according to Stevie they are."

"Probably more but fuck me girl, what a bleeding mess!"

"You're telling me!"

"So what are you going to do?"

"I ain't got the foggiest Micky I wish I did."

Micky Mackerson went over to the cabinet and refreshed their drinks, all the time his mind was trying to think of something he could say to help her. Retaking his seat he placed the glasses onto the coffee table and took hold of Stella's hands.

"How far do you want to go?"

She frowned at his question.

"I don't understand what you mean?"

"How far would you go to help your son, even if it might mean your brother getting hurt?"

Not quite grasping what he meant Stella thought for a moment. She didn't want anyone to get hurt but by doing nothing that's exactly what would happen to Stevie and his family. Dougie on the other hand, already had a successful restaurant and bar bringing in a good income and if he hadn't have been so greedy none of this would be happening now; this whole conversation wouldn't even be taking place.

"In answer to your question I will do anything I can, my kids will always come first. What do you have in mind?"

"Well not a lot but there is someone that could help but I know you won't like what I'm going to say."

"Try me."

"Tony Miller!"

Stella stood up and began to pace the floor, she hadn't heard that name in a long long time and she didn't want to hear it now. Micky was well aware of Stella's past and her association with Miller but he loved her so much that he was prepared to put aside his own feelings in the hope of helping her.

"Why him, he's nothing but a gangster and a real horrible bastard by all accounts."

"Exactly, everyone in the East End, come to that most of London, are scared of him and if anyone can get your brother to change his mind it's the Miller firm. Now you know that normally I'm against any kind of violence but this time is an exception, especially if you don't want your boy to lose everything and besides Miller owes you big time."

Stella sat back down again; this needed to be thoroughly thought out. For the last thirty seven years she had never asked Tony for a thing and he had never offered. He hadn't bothered with Stevie while he was growing up even though he was well aware of the child's existence, so why should he want to help his son now. Stella had always prided herself in the fact that she had raised all of her children alone and without help from any of their fathers. There was also the promise she'd made to her mother that Dougie wouldn't be hurt well at least not physically. If it was only his pocket that got affected then surely Daisy wouldn't mind too much.

"So what do you think?"

"I really don't know Micky; I mean from what I've been told Tony Miller is now a right evil sod, not that he was that nice back when I knew him. Even if he is willing to help me he might want something in return, change that, from memory he will definitely want something in return."

"That, you won't know until you ask, and at the end of the day you can always walk away. Now come here and give me a kiss, my little fella wants to get better acquainted with you young lady."

Stella giggled but was instantly stopped when Micky covered her mouth with his. As he ran his fingertips sensually down the length of her spine Stella could feel herself pushing against the man. Micky might not have been much to look at but between the sheets he was dynamite and right at this moment she wanted him more than anything else in the world. Standing up the couple quickly walked through to the bedroom and as Micky unzipped her dress she let it fall to the floor. There was no embarrassment even though time had taken its toll on both of their bodies. They had been together long enough that all inhibitions had disappeared years ago. Leading her over to the bed Micky gently guided her onto the mattress and then lay down beside her. He was always a tender lover who didn't like to rush things. Placing his hand between her legs Micky gently began to rub the inside of her vagina. He knew it was something Stella really liked and it didn't take long for her to vocally express her pleasure. As each wave of ecstasy powered

109

through her body she began to arch her back, her gasps were becoming more frequent and he knew she was on the verge of coming. Stopping, he moved on top of her and entered Stella with force, something else he knew she liked. As he moved in and out and his rhythm increased she began to softly groan again and with a sudden climax that tore through her entire body like an electric shock, she orgasmed. Wanting her lover to also feel fulfilled she sensually kissed and licked his lips and neck until finally his body shuddered and Stella knew that he was spent. As she smiled up at him Micky kissed her tenderly and winked in a way that always made her feel that what they had between them was very special.

"Alright girl?"

"Mmmm very alright thanks to you and your expertise Mr Mackerson."

Micky couldn't get enough of Stella Nicholson and since their relationship had begun he hadn't looked at another woman even though there had been plenty of offers and that included members of his own staff. He knew it was only because he was the Landlord but with Stella it was different, she had been there when the place was a complete shithole and he had little to offer her financially. Most of their early years together had been spent up here in the flat as neither of them had any spare cash, so now that he was earning a few bob he liked to treat her to nice things. Reaching over he removed a small box from the bedside table and handed it to her.

"What's this?"

"Open it and find out."

Micky Mackerson had long since wanted to propose to Stella but they had both made it quite clear early on that they weren't looking for a serious relationship, the only problem was, Micky's feelings had changed and he now wanted to spend the rest of his life with her. Stella lifted the lid to reveal a stunning gold bracelet with a diamond studded heart hanging from the chain. Micky removed the bracelet and carefully secured the clasp on her wrist. "Oh Micky thank you it's beautiful. You do know it's not my birthday for another month?"

"Of course I do and it's not for that, I just wanted to get you something nice. Now I'll go and get us both another brandy, are you stopping the night?"

"I won't if you don't mind, I don't like leaving mum alone for too long at least not so soon after the old man snuffed it, not that it makes any real difference to her but it makes me feel a bit better. I know deep down that she's pleased he's dead and every day since it happened she's become more and more alive, bless her."

"Well you're having a taxi home then."

"Don't be silly it's only up the road."

"Well I'll walk you then, you know how dodgy this area is after dark. Let me fetch the drinks then we can start round two."

Stella giggled like a school girl and pulling the sheet up around her neck she held out her arm and studied her gift in great detail. No one had ever given her anything so beautiful not to mention so expensive. It made her feel valued and just for a moment she was blissfully happy and nothing else mattered. For now she was just going to enjoy the moment, tomorrow would be time enough to start worrying again, after all, she knew that when the morning came and she had done what she had to do, her life would probably never be the same again. Her train of thought was interrupted when Micky walked back into the bedroom in just his socks and carrying two large glasses of brandy; the sight instantly had her in another fit of giggles much to his annoyance but she knew deep down that he was only playing with her. Micky placed the drinks onto the bedside table and hands on hips swung his body around to face her.

"Right wench! Find something funny do you?"

His words made Stella laugh even more and as he dived onto the bed their shrieks could be heard downstairs in the bar below. The staff shook their heads and the regulars smirked but didn't dare comment, Micky Mackerson was a randy old sod and his bird, though a bit over the hill, was still a looker. George Eglen, a very regular punter, eyed up the ceiling and secretly wished it was him upstairs in the flat with Stella instead of Micky.

CHAPTER TWELVE

The history of Limehouse went back many many years. In the eighteen hundreds it had gained the name due to the lime oast's that were next to the river and were operated by the large potteries that served shipping in the London docks.

Tony Miller's office was situated in a part of Limehouse that sits on the edge of a basin which runs directly into the Thames. The area boasts splendid views of Canary Wharf but its commercial use is now more for light industrial trade, however some years earlier one man had seen an opportunity for a different and more violent use entirely. Born and raised in Bethnal Green, Tony Miller was a jack the lad and by the age of eighteen he hadn't achieved anything, well nothing that was legal at least. His parents had continually told him that he was on a fast track to prison if he didn't knuckle down and work for a living like everyone else. Their advice had lasted for all of two months and after working for a fruit and veg seller at Spitalfields Market he had knocked his employer spark out over a crate of cabbages due to a short days pay in his wages. Tony then decided to follow his own path no matter where that led and no matter what the cost. Saturday nights had always been spent in the Princess Alice on Commercial Street in Whitechapel. It was a place where the latest tunes were played on the jukebox and some of the tastiest girls in the East End would gather there in the hope of getting a boyfriend. It was on one such night that Tony Miller first set eyes on Stella Nicholson. She had ignored him to begin with which had only made him want her more but after just a few dates and when she had tearfully informed him that she was expecting, Tony had packed a bag and left London as quickly as he could. For the next ten years he resided in Liverpool and then Manchester and after working for several of the notorious gangland family's, and rising in the ranks, he had returned to the capital with a considerable amount of money. Deciding that the time was now right to start up a business of his own Tony had gradually hired a crew of men that he felt he could trust to cover his back should the need ever arise. He didn't bother to contact his family, as far as he was concerned no one was aware of his return to London and in all honesty he had no wish to see them again. Notoriety travels fast and it wasn't long before people learned of Tony's reputation and knew not to bandy his name about, at least not if they knew what was good for them. Armed robbery ran alongside high end burglaries and the money soon began to roll in. The Boss, as he was known to all that worked for Tony Miller, was never satisfied and he soon decided to move into the Soho sex scene. It was seedy and hadn't gone down well with most of his men but they were all so fearful of voicing their opinions, that apart from the odd grumble nothing much was said. It wasn't that the Boss was overly tough, well at least not in stature but what he lacked in that department he more than made up for in his mental ability to put a gun to a person's head and pull the trigger without a seconds hesitation. Tony Miller ran his organised crime racket, or as he liked to call it, his business empire, out of a small lock up cabin that was situated on a piece of waste ground at Northey Street in Limehouse. Scrap metal trading was the legitimate front for the company but nothing could have been further from the truth. Cars and vans were piled up high behind a six feet tall fence and for most of the time five hefty guard dogs were running around loose. The canines were a mixture of Dobermans, Alsatians and Rottweiler's, bread specifically for the job they were expected to do and each one was attack trained. Tony kept himself and his business low profile but everyone in Limehouse still knew of the gangster and what he was capable of, so much so that most crossed the street rather than come face to face with the man or any of his henchmen. The cabin housed two rooms and a toilet. The rear office was Tony's domain and no one entered without an invite. The front reception was used as a waiting area for anyone wishing to do business or members of the Miller firm who were killing time waiting to take instruction from their Boss. Tony Miller dealt in anything and everything; at any one time he had between eight and twelve girls turning tricks for him in Soho along with a string of shops selling sexual aids that mostly catered for the gay fraternity. He was also heavily into loan into sharking not to mention armed robbery so long as it was well organised and the chance of capture was minimal. So far lady luck had shined down on the firm and it had been a long time since any of them had received a pull from the Old Bill. Most would have thought it was because the Miller firm were astute criminals and good at their trade but in reality it was down to the ten grand that Tony paid over monthly to several police inspectors. Business was booming and Tony lived the high life and was always flashing the cash when the mood took him. He had never married though he guessed he had probably fathered more kids in the East End than the ones he was already aware of. It had never worried Tony although he had often thought about the mother of his eldest child. Back in the day Stella Nicholson really had been a beauty but Tony wouldn't allow himself to be trapped by anyone and that's exactly

115

what he had believed she was trying to do. The kid was now a man and if circumstances had turned out differently he could have been part of Tony's empire. It wasn't something that the man lost sleep over but as he was getting nearer to the age of retirement than he would have liked, now and again he would quietly reflect on what might have been and the missed opportunity of having his heir take over from him someday. Situated to one side of the scrap yard was a static caravan. It wasn't used by the firm but rented out to Jumbo Smith a local car breaker. The man kept an eye on the yard during daylight hours and the business carried out at the yard was beneficial to both parties. Jumbo knew the score but was content to turn a blind eye regarding what went on daily under his own nose. Making sure Tony Miller was happy was not only paramount to keeping Jumbo's business going but also to ensure his personal health stayed intact. The Miller firm never asked him to do anything outside of the law that he didn't already do himself but if he was required to occasionally leave the keys in the ignition of the crusher he duly obliged and never asked any questions. Only once had he witnessed something that had turned his stomach but Jumbo wasn't stupid and had never mentioned what he'd seen. It had happened one Saturday lunchtime, several years ago now, Jumbo had been about to knock off work for the weekend when he was approached by big Harry Chrome. The Boss wanted the crusher to be available and Jumbo was told to leave the keys in the usual place. He thought nothing more about it until the Monday morning. It was going to be a busy day as he had four right off cars coming in but when he arrived at the yard things looked a bit different from when he had left on Saturday. A massive lump of metal, remnants of several cars that had been crushed, now stood just a few feet away from the door of his caravan. Walking over he inspected the mass and bending down he could see a large amount of what looked like dried blood. Curiosity got the better of him and leaning in to take a closer look he saw that a glove was imbedded into the metal. Reaching out he pulled on the soft leather and as he did so the glove came away revealing what appeared to be a human hand. Most of the skin and tissue had come away with the material leaving just the gnarled bones protruding. Suddenly his fried breakfast from earlier appeared all over his steel toe capped boots and Jumbo staggered backwards. It was all well and good loaning out his equipment so long as he didn't know what they were doing but this; well this was totally out of order. Entering the van and closing the door behind him Jumbo flopped down onto one of the bench seats. He began to sweat profusely as he tried to work out what to do next. He couldn't go to the police or it was a distinct possibility that he would end up as an accessory himself, he also couldn't complain to Mr Miller because if he did, the same fate as the victim would probably befall him. Jumbo Smith realised that if he wanted to keep on breathing then he just had to suck it up and keep silent. From that day on he decided to keep a handwritten diary and even though he was aware that if Tony Miller ever found out he would be a dead man, Jumbo also knew that he had to have some kind of leverage if the Old Bill ever came down heavy. Each day he would jot down and date, anything that happened out of the ordinary and also who called at the yard and at what time. The black book was stored in an empty compartment under one of the caravan's bench seats and Jumbo would constantly check to make sure that it was still there.

117

After saying goodnight to Micky Mackerson Stella had closed the door to the flat and out of nowhere she had begun to cry. The rest of the night was no better and she had paced the bedroom floor for hours. Finally deciding that she couldn't take anymore she made her way into the kitchen and was surprised to see Daisy in the middle of making a drink.

"You're up early Mum?"

"And is it any wonder, you kept me awake most of the night stomping about like a bleeding elephant."

"Sorry love I've just got a lot on my mind."

Daisy passed her daughter a mug of steaming hot tea.

"Now why don't we have a chat about it all? I know what's on your mind but I can't for the life of me understand why you just won't let it go?"

Stella wanted to talk, god she was desperate to talk and there was no one she trusted more than her mother but there was just one problem, if she revealed what she was planning to do and what the outcome might result in, well she just didn't know what Daisy's reaction would be.

"I'd like that Mum but I can't."

"And why not might I ask? You've never kept anything from me before; well not as far as I know."

"It's different this time."

"Why is it?"

If Daisy Nicholson was anything it was persistent and Stella knew that like a dog with a bone her mother wouldn't let go until she found out what was going on.

"Alright, alright but you're not going to like it. I tried to talk to Dougie but he wouldn't budge, said he and that James bloke are going to sell the shops and Stevie will be out on his ear. The poor little sod will have to sell everything and that includes the house. I was planning on paying his dad a visit to ask for his help."

118

"Tony Miller!"

"That's right but you know as well as I do that if he agrees to help me, not only will there be a price to pay and probably a heavy one at that, but things could also get nasty."

The room was silent as Daisy thought for a moment. When it boiled down to it there was a choice to be made, Stella had to choose her son or her brother whom she had been estranged from for years. This really was a dilemma because it also concerned her own son. Taking her daughters hands Daisy stared into Stella's eyes as she spoke.

"Believe me, I know the love a mother has for her son and I don't want any harm to come to my Dougie. You have to make that clear to Miller, promise me Stella because I really don't think my heart could take it if anything happened to him."

"I promise Mum."

"Then do what you have to love, ask that toe rag to help you if you must. I mean it isn't as if he doesn't owe you big time after what he did."

Kissing her mother tenderly on the cheek Stella then got dressed and set out to find the only person who could offer any chance of rescuing her sons business. It took over an hour to learn where Tony's firm was situated. Calling in at Hal's mini cabs on the corner of Globe Road she asked Sheila the radio controller if any of the drivers had ever mentioned Tony. The woman shifted about in her seat and shrugging her shoulders simply shook her head, Stella could tell that Sheila was nervous and wasn't about to offer any information. Continuing along Roman Road Stella soon bumped into one of her old school friends. Jersey, real name Norman Royal, was a small time villain and well known by most people living in

119

Bethnal Green.

"Hello babe how you doing?"

"Not so bad thanks Jersey and you?"

"Things could always be better sweetheart but then I suppose it's the same for most of us. I was sorry to hear about your old man's passing."

"Well you must be the only person on the manor that is! Jersey can I ask you a favour?"

"Fire away love."

"I'm trying to find Tony Miller and I wondered if you could....."

Jersey didn't let her finish her sentence and had already begun to walk in the opposite direction while shaking his head.

"Sorry love but I don't know anything. Take care Stella and if you know what's good for you you'll stay well away from the likes of Miller."

Whatever was wrong with everyone, was there no one who was even prepared to discuss the man. About to give up she suddenly had an idea, it was a long shot but there just might be one person able to help her. Crossing Cambridge Heath Road Stella walked into the Dundee Arms. After telling Micky about the difficulty she was having he made a telephone call and seconds later handed her a piece of paper with an address written on it. Micky Mackerson was worried, it might have been his idea in the first place but now in the cold light of day it didn't feel like one of his best. As Stella turned to leave he grabbed her hand.

"Be careful love."

"I'll be fine Micky, it isn't as if I don't know the man, you forget we have a child together."

"That might be true darling but it's been years since you've seen him and I very much doubt that he's the

same Tony Miller as he was all those years ago."
Stella smiled and winked at her friend and then
disappeared out of the front door. At Bethnal Green
underground station Stella boarded the central line and
after changing at Liverpool Street she soon arrived at
Limehouse station. It wasn't an area she was familiar
with but after asking a friendly looking member of the
transport police she was soon heading in the right
direction. Passing the newly built apartments that cost
thousands of pounds to rent each month Stella wondered
if Tony lived in one of these places. People were coming
and going but no one smiled or gave you the time of day,
now back in Bethnal Green it was a different story and
Stella imagined that for all the wealth that these people
had it must still be a very cold and lonely place to live.
Along Narrow Street she crossed over the waterway that
lead into the Basin and turning left she quickly arrived at
her destination. The scrap yard was less than a half a
mile from the station so it hadn't taken her long and as
Stella approached the high fence two of the dogs came
charging over bearing their teeth and she suddenly
wondered if she was doing the right thing. Jumbo Smith
stood watching from the doorway of his caravan and
when he saw the stranger try and open one of the front
gates he quickly ran across the yard. It had rained
heavily the night before and he had to dodge the large
puddles that had formed on parts of the sunken ground.
To Stella the sight was quite comical as Jumbo was a
large man, well actually if she was being brutally honest
he was downright fat and as he darted in and out his huge
stomach wobbled up and down. By the time he reached
the fence Jumbo Smith was panting heavily.
"No no no! Don't come in here Mrs; they ain't the
friendliest of beasts as you can see."

As Jumbo stood on the other side of the fence, he studied Stella and could instantly tell that she was decent and not like the usual brasses that regularly paid a visit in order to hand over their so called rent.

"Who you looking for love?"

"Tony Miller, have I got the right place?"

"You have doll but are you sure it's Mr Miller you want?"

Stella smiled at the scruffy looking man that she would normally have gone out of her way to avoid and who was now being so polite to her that she felt guilty for being so judgemental.

"I'm sure thanks, is he in?"

"Not yet. Why don't you call back later?"

"Could I not wait for him inside?"

Jumbo shook his head.

"Afraid not love, Mr Miller would have my guts for bleeding garters if I let anyone in here no matter how nice they seemed. Even the Queen herself wouldn't get passed these gates without Mr Millers say so."

Stella thanked the man as she turned and walked away. Taking a leisurely stroll back she stopped to gaze over the Thames. The sun was shining brightly but Stella could feel a dark cloud looming over her head and she was worried. With time to kill she decided to go and see Dougie and try one last time to get him to change his mind. Stella headed towards the station and prayed that if things went well, she wouldn't ever have to return here again.

CHAPTER THIRTEEN

Lunchtime at Delphine's was always hectic. A few months earlier the food had been highly rated in a couple of the glossy magazines and since, and much to their happiness, Dougie and James had been rushed off their feet. As the main cook Dougie Nicholson was pleased as punch that his food was going down a storm but in reality and unbeknown to him, James had paid for the advertisement via several sex sessions with the magazine editors. It had taken him a while to seek them out but after that it had been easy and his child like good looks had seen the older men eating out of the palm of his hand amongst other things! The menu was mostly gastro fare but it suited the many office workers and actors that worked in the area. The novelty of actually having to pull his weight had soon worn off and now James was dreaming of the day when he could put his feet up around a swimming pool in some hot exotic country. It had only been a few days since he'd found out about the inheritance but that hadn't stopped him filling the coffee table with brochures and magazines. Along with her cleaning duties Macy was also helping out waiting tables but only when it was absolutely necessary as James didn't think she was sophisticated enough for Delphine's. Yesterday and during a heated argument regarding the tipping system James had blurted out how she just wasn't what they wanted for the place and his revelation had hurt her deeply. Usually she would have gone straight to her boss but this wasn't just a silly argument, Macy Langham was heartbroken and too upset to talk to anyone. Lying in bed she'd contemplated handing in her notice but in the cold light of day she had known that it wasn't even an

123

option. Money was tight and she was only just managing to cover the rent and bills as it was and if it hadn't have been for Dougie feeding her while she was on shift she would have ended up destitute. For now she had no choice but to stay and take every nasty insult that James felt like dishing out.

As Stella slowly walked towards the restaurant she racked her brains as she tried desperately to think of a solution, any alternative to the one thing she didn't want to do and that was go back to Tony Millers yard but nothing was coming to mind. Finally she pushed open the front door and was surprised to see the place so busy. Almost every table was taken and people also stood at the bar drinking. From the way they were dressed she could only assume they were city types, a breed she had very little experience of. Suddenly Macy noticed the woman out of the corner of her eye and she instantly rushed over.

"Hello Stella love, do you want me to get Dougie?"

"Thanks but not just yet love. Are there any tables free Macy only I ain't half come over peckish."

No more needed to be said and within seconds Stella had been guided to a small table just opposite the kitchen. Macy slid out one of the chairs and trying to be as professional as she could, removed the tea towel that was tucked in the front of her apron and then proceeded to flick the nonexistent dust from the chair pad.

"You take a seat while I grab a menu; want something to wet your whistle?"

"I don't mind if I do? Can I have a brandy and coke please?"

Macy turned and walked briskly over to the bar where James was serving. When she gave the order and asked for the drink to be put on the bill for table number two James looked over in Stella's direction. It was obvious from the expression on his face that he wasn't pleased to see her there but that wasn't going to put Stella off one little bit. When she smiled he returned the gesture but it was plain to see that it was grudged. James placed the drink onto a tray and informed Macy that he would take it over himself. As he approached her table Stella inwardly groaned.

"Well what a surprise to see you here?"

Stella smiled but the sarcastic undertone to his words hadn't gone unnoticed.

"I'm sorry to say it but I very much doubt you'll get to see Dougie today. As you can see we're rushed off of our feet and he's on chef duties so I would imagine you won't be staying for lunch?"

"I most certainly will! I'm quite happy to wait James; I'm not in any hurry as it happens."

Now the sarcastic tone was in Stella's voice and he couldn't help but slightly pout his lips and twitch his body in a bitchy manner. It had all been a waste of time because Macy had taken it upon herself to go into the kitchen and inform Dougie that his sister was in the restaurant. While James was still writing down Stella's order Dougie appeared. His chef's whites were heavily stained, beads of sweat stood out on his brow but his flushed face was beaming when he saw her.

"Hello darling, I'm so pleased you're here, I couldn't bare it if we fell out."

"Me neither sweetheart."

Stella got to her feet and embraced him but James was quick to intervene and roughly grabbing his husbands arm he spoke loudly.

"We really don't have time for this today Dougie we are just too busy. Now I think it's best if you return to the kitchen don't you?"

125

Dougie didn't reply and taking a seat and completely out of character, he totally ignored his partner. He knew that he would be made to pay for his actions later but for now he was going to enjoy his sisters company.

"I said...."

"I heard what you said James but Macy has stepped in and even though you might not think she's sophisticated enough to serve out front; by god that woman can cook. Now run over to the counter and get me a drink would you, there's a dear."

James quickly minced off in the direction of the bar and Stella could no longer suppress the giggle that she had been trying so desperately to hold inside. Instead of her brother looking annoyed he suddenly joined in with her. A few moments later his drink was slammed onto the table but James didn't loiter around, he was so angry that he knew to remain would only end up with him tipping the drink over his husbands head and it wouldn't have been the first time.

"So honey what brings you here?"

Stella took a large gulp of her drink; she'd been dreading this moment. Placing her glass back down, she took in a deep lungful of air.

"We really need to talk about the shops Dougie. I know that you and James want to keep them but I just thought that if I explained what would happen if you do, well you might see things a little differently. Stevie has put everything into those shops but he's also mortgaged up to the hilt and will lose not only his business but his home. Isn't there anyway we can come to a compromise? I mean couldn't you join forces or something or couldn't he rent them from you like he used to do from the old man?"

By the time she had finished speaking Stella had tears in

her eyes and it upset Dougie to see her in such a state. Reaching out he grabbed Stella's hand and gently squeezed it.

"I never wanted it to come to this Sis. Let me have a word with James tonight, it's best to leave it until after we've closed when he's had a chance to wind down and relax. Tell Stevie to come and see me in the morning and we'll see if we can work something out sweetheart. Exactly what I don't know but I promise I'll try to sort this mess out."

In a second Stella was out of her seat and wrapping her arms around her brother's neck. James was monitoring things from behind the bar and when he saw the woman's show of affection he threw the glass he was holding into the sink. As it loudly smashed everyone in the bar looked round including Stella and Dougie. Knowing it was time for her to leave Stella cancelled her meal order and after kissing her brother and thanking him again she left Delphine's with a smile on her face as wide as the Thames. For the rest of the day James had given his husband the cold shoulder and by the time they locked up and made their way up to the flat you could cut the atmosphere between the couple with a knife. Dougie had planned on going straight to bed but he hadn't bargained on what would happen next. James stormed into the kitchen and began throwing plates and cups onto the floor. The sound of breaking crockery brought Dougie running in.

"What the fuck are you doing, have you gone completely mad?"

James spun round and his words came out like venom.

"What am I doing? You've fucking ignored me all day and don't think I didn't see you conniving with that bitch of a sister of yours. I'm not putting up with it Dougie so

127

you'd better tell me what's going on!"

Dougie walked over and taking his husband in his arms, tried to calm the man down. Tenderly kissing James's neck, which usually did the trick, he was shocked when his husband roughly pushed him away.

"That won't work! I'm so angry with you that right at this moment I don't even know if we have a future together. You treat me like a second class citizen, like a rent boy you've picked up off the street and I'm not going to put up with it, do you hear me?"

His words were like a stab to Dougie's heart. He absolutely adored the man and there was no way he could live without James. Holding his hands up Dougie accepted defeat.

"Ok ok, come into the lounge and I'll explain everything."

James stood exactly where he was, his arms were crossed and he wore a look of defiance.

"Please baby, just listen to what I have to say."

Reluctantly James did as he was asked and when they were seated and after James had promised to remain calm, Dougie repeated everything that Stella had told him. For a moment James didn't comment, he was trying to keep his cool but he also knew that now was not a time to back down, now he had to be firm and lay it on the line once and for all.

"I'm sorry to hear about your nephew but as far as I'm concerned that doesn't change a thing. Now I'm not making silly idle threats here Dougie but this is what will happen if you go ahead and hand over those shops. I will fight you in court to get my half and that will cost us both thousands."

"I'm not on about giving Stevie the shops, perhaps we could go into business with him?"

"You've got to be kidding me? I want out, I want luxury and selling those premises is the only way that's going to happen. If you persist with this then I have no alternative, I will divorce you."

"You don't mean that James."

"Try me, actually I'll move out tomorrow if you want. Gene has always said that if I needed a place to crash I could stay at his."

"I bet he did! That horny old queen has always been desperate to get his hands on you."

"The choice is yours; you have until the morning to give me your answer."

With that James stood up and marched towards the bedroom but not before he looked back over his shoulder and bluntly informed his husband, that the sofa was the only place Dougie Nicholson would be sleeping that night.

Stevie had woken early and was on tenter hooks waiting for an acceptable time to call at his uncle's bar. Yesterday when his mother had visited the shop and revealed the conversation she'd had with her brother he had jumped for joy. There now seemed to be a light at the end of the tunnel and even though it would still be a struggle as he didn't know what the compromise would be, there was just the slightest chance that they could keep the house and some sort of business. Jo cooked him a light breakfast and then joined him at the table. The kids were still asleep and today she was happy for once not to have them all downstairs.

"You ok love?"

"To be honest girl I feel sick to the stomach but things still look a bit brighter than they did a few days ago. If it goes well with Uncle Dougie, we're going out tonight for a slap up meal and no arguments."

129

Jo studied her husband's face and noticed a few new lines that hadn't been there a couple of days ago. Lying in bed last night she had mulled over everything in her mind and as far as she was concerned it wasn't as bad as it could have been. They were all together and healthy and if they had to start from scratch then so be it, Jo desperately wished Stevie could see it like that but she knew he never would. Her husband was all show and without his status symbols he felt a failure, Bianca was just the same and Jo was sometimes scared for her daughter's future.

"And if not, I'll cook us both a nice steak."

She regretted the words as soon as they had left her mouth and as her husband glared at her she prayed for the ground to open up and swallow her whole.

"Don't even say that! If we lose everything, well I don't think I could handle it Jo. I'm approaching forty fucking years old and in all that time I've only ever worked for myself. Can you really see me going into rented accommodation and working some shitty eight till five job? I would be a laughing stock down the golf club, no change that, because I wouldn't fucking be able to afford the membership fee would I?"

Stevie Nicholson snatched up his car keys and left the house, if he wanted to find out his fate then now was as good a time as any. Driving over to Soho took just over an hour and Stevie was seething with anger for the whole of the journey. He had a bad feeling regarding his future and he was totally pissed off with his wife's lack of faith. Parking up in Lexington he then began the walk to find Delphine's bar. Unlike his mothers first trip a few days earlier Stevie was able to locate the place within a few minutes. It was just after eleven and thankfully the bar had only been open for a short while and was yet to get busy. Pushing on the front door he walked inside.

Only two or three tables had occupants and making his way up to the counter he stood and waited for his uncle to turn around. When he did, Dougie took a step backwards. Since giving James his decision this morning he had been dreading seeing his nephew. Several times he had got out his mobile to call Stella and cancel but when it came down to it he just couldn't do it. He was going back on his word and the least he could do was front up and be a man about it.

"Hello Stevie, can I get you a drink?"

"No thanks Uncle Dougie I'm driving and besides I'd like to get this over with as my bleeding nerves are in a right old state."

Just then James appeared from the kitchen but when he saw who the visitor was he disappeared back inside just as quickly. It was all well and good laying down the law to his husband but when it came to arguing with a well built heterosexual man, he would avoid it at all costs.

"I'm sorry Stevie really I am. After your mum left yesterday I thought long and hard but it isn't just down to me, and James won't budge an inch on the matter. Surely you can see it from my point of view, I mean in all honesty would you hand over the shops if the boot was on the other foot? I had hoped we could reach a compromise but once again James won't hear of it, if I go against him it will end in divorce and I am just not prepared to let that happen. I have an appointment booked with our solicitor in a couple of days to finalise everything, now I'm not an unreasonable man and you are family so of course I we will give you notice so that you have time to clear the shops. I really am very sorry Stevie but that's the best I can do under the circumstance. I wish with all my heart that I hadn't inherited the shops in the first place but I did so there's no going back.

In one way or another, that old bastard has screwed us all over."

"Have you told my mum?"

Dougie didn't reply he didn't need to; the look on his face was enough. Stevie Nicholson didn't say another word as he left the bar. His head was spinning and he couldn't think straight. He was finished and he didn't have the first idea what he was going to do. Back inside the car he gripped the steering wheel and rested his forehead on the backs of his hands. To begin with there was only silence but soon he started to sob, it wasn't a state he would ever allow anyone to see him in but right at this moment he needed to release all the pent up hurt and frustration he was feeling. When he at last felt cried out, he started up the engine and drove back to Bethnal Green and the Dundee Arms. Drowning his sorrows wouldn't achieve anything but it would make him feel a whole lot better, even if it was only for a few hours.

CHAPTER FOURTEEN

It was a quiet day for Micky Mackerson as he stood leaning over the bar reading the newspaper. He glanced up when the door opened and was surprised to see Stevie Nicholson walk in. Micky hadn't heard from Stella and wasn't sure if she had done anything regarding the family's predicament yet. Deciding not to mention it just in case she hadn't, he smiled broadly at his first customer of the day.

"Hello Stevie! What can I get you?"

Stevie nodded his head and taking a seat at the bar asked Micky for a large scotch.

"Not like you to be drinking shorts mate, having a bad day?"

Stevie didn't reply and after necking the drink in one mouthful, he asked for another. By the time he'd finished his sixth Micky was more than a little concerned.

"Whatever it is that's wrong mate, the answer doesn't lie in the bottom of bottle believe you me!"

Again Stevie necked down the drink and held out his glass.

"Stop with the fucking lecture Micky and just give me another will you, oh what the hell, make it a double."

Micky Mackerson filled the glass and after replacing the bottle turned back to face Stevie.

"You don't look too good son, why don't you let me get you a cab home."

"Nah you're alright and besides I've got the motor outside."

Micky saw the man's car keys laying on the top of the bar and pretending to wipe the woodwork he discreetly covered them with a bar towel and drew them down onto the shelf below. Excusing himself with the ruse of having to change a barrel he walked into the back hall and removed his mobile. Not one to usually meddle in things that didn't concern him, Micky knew that there was always an exception to the rule. Dialling Stella's number he impatiently rapped his fingertips on the doorframe as he waited for her to answer.

"Hello?"

"Stella girl is that you? Thank fuck for that!"

"Yes it is and hello to you as well Micky Mackerson!"

"Sorry love but I ain't got time for pleasantries. Your Stevie's in the bar and he's fast getting off his face. I offered to call a cab but he reckons he's going to drive. I don't know what's occurred but he's in a bad way girl."

"For fuck's sake! Whatever you do don't let the daft sod go anywhere until I get there."

"He can't sweetheart; I've hidden his keys but for god's sake get a move on love before he falls off the bleeding stool."

Micky hung up and then quickly returned to the bar. Stevie was still in the same spot but his glass was now full to the top with whisky so it was obvious he had helped himself. The door opened and a couple of regulars came in but apart from giving Micky a look that said 'what's going on here then', they collected their pints and took a seat at the far end of the pub. Stella must have run all the way because a short time later the front door to the pub flew open. As she reached the bar she was panting heavily and Stevie just smirked when he saw his mother.

"Hello there mum! What can I get you?"

"Nothing son and by the looks of you I'd say you've already had a bleeding skin full. Micky, order us a cab will you?"

134

Micky again disappeared and when he returned he mouthed the words 'five minutes'. Stella wasn't looking forward to going back to the flat and trying to get her son up the stairs but she would just have to manage as there was no way Micky could help her, not with punters now in the bar. By the time the taxi pulled into Roy Street Stevie Nicholson was sound asleep and trying to get him out of the vehicle wasn't easy but somehow with the help of the driver together they managed it. Placing her sons arm around her neck, Stella almost dragged him up the stairwell and by the time they reached the flat she was totally exhausted. Pushing open the door and guiding him into the front room she gave a small shove and he landed flat out on the old sofa. He probably wouldn't come back to normality until the morning, so covering him with a blanket, she then phoned her daughter in law so that the woman didn't worry.

"Jo, its Mum. Stevie's had a skin full and I expect he will be kipping on my sofa for the night. I don't know what was said between him and Dougie but I can only guess it wasn't what he wanted to hear."

"So is he alright Stella?"

"He's fine love; though I wouldn't want his head come tomorrow morning. Now don't you worry darling, he'll be as right as rain the next time you see him."

After hanging up Stella quietly slipped out of the flat and headed back to the Dundee Arms to try and find out what had happened. Micky smiled when she entered but when she started to fire question after question he could only hold up his palm for her to stop.

"Stella love there's nothing I can tell you except he turned up here with a face like a smacked arse. He wouldn't talk but something's bothering him that's for sure and I can only assume it's what you told me about."

Walking outside into the bright fresh air Stella dialled her brother's number. He picked up after a couple of rings but when he saw the number appear on the screen he didn't let her speak.

"If you're calling to have a go at me you can save your breath, I already feel bad enough about all of this as it is. I told Stevie that there was nothing I can do so let that be an end to it."

"I didn't know what you had told him Dougie that's why I'm bloody ringing. I've just had to go and collect my boy from the local boozer as he's paralytic but from what you've just said, I now realise that you've gone back on your word."

"I didn't promise anything Stella, well only that I'd have a think and see if we could reach a compromise but that's not going to happen. I'm sorry if this is going to cause a rift between us but my loyalties have to lie with James, after all he's the only one that's been there for me in the past."

Stella couldn't believe what she was hearing and now knew there was no way back. As much as it broke her heart she would have to go cap in hand and ask for Tony Millers help, she also knew that things wouldn't end nicely.

"Well, you've made up your mind Dougie and as much as you feel you have to stay loyal to your husband, my loyalties lay with my son. I love you Dougie, I always have but now we know where we stand, I just hope you will be happy with the outcome."

"I am, so that's an end to it."

"I don't think so Dougie. As far as I'm concerned it's only the beginning of something that I think we will both come to regret."

"Are you threatening me Stella? Stella? Stella?"

With her phone already tucked away in her handbag Stella Nicholson once again set off for Limehouse.

After her visit the previous day, Tony Miller hadn't returned to the yard as Jumbo had anticipated. Instead he had enjoyed an afternoon at one of the West End casinos and after losing heavily had returned to his home. Arriving at work the next morning he wasn't in a good mood and when Jumbo had come running over to tell him about the visitor he could only grimace at the state of the man not to mention his disgusting body odour.

"Not now Jumbo I ain't in the best of moods today."

"But Mr Miller you had a visitor yesterday."

When Jumbo had explained that the woman was a bit of a sort and nothing like the usual brasses that frequented the yard, Tony suddenly became intrigued. Inviting Jumbo into the cabin Tony walked through to the office and immediately opened up the windows.

"Don't bother getting comfortable just tell me what she said and for fuck's sake Jumbo, get yourself some deodorant man."

"Yes Mr Miller."

"Do you think that she was Old Bill?"

"Nah I don't think so Mr Miller, there was just something about the way she said your name, like she already knew you."

"Description?"

Jumbo rubbed at his chin as he tried to remember the visit. His memory had always been dreadful and to him twenty four hours might just as well have been a month. "She was average height I suppose. At a guess I would say mid fifties and she had a bleeding good chassis for her age. I wouldn't say she was a stunner but there was definitely something about her. Let's put it like this, I

137

wouldn't say no if you know what I mean."

Tony waved the man away and as he sat perched on the corner of his desk, wracked his brains trying to think who it might be. A few minutes later and when no one came to mind Tony shrugged his shoulders and took a seat behind the desk ready to start planning a job that was in the offering. Whoever it was would come back if they really wanted to see him. Two hours later and as Jumbo was about to pick up a clapped out old Skoda with the grabber he noticed the dogs tear off in the direction of the gates. Straining his neck he could just make out that it was the woman from yesterday. Climbing down from the cab he ran over to the cabin and informed big Harry Chrome that the Boss had a visitor. Jumbo had a set routine whenever anyone called, he was to gather up the leads and make sure each of the dogs was secure and not able to bite anyone, unless of course it was Old Bill. It took several minutes as the mutts loved to give him the run around but finally he managed it and motioned to Stella that it was now safe to enter. Sliding the large bolt across and after stepping into the compound she closed the gate behind her and secured the premises. Big Harry was walking towards her and suddenly Stella felt intimidated. She was sure the man wasn't Tony but then again it had been years since she'd last seen him, if it was then he'd certainly put on some timber. As Harry got closer Stella realised that it wasn't Tony Miller and for some strange reason, she didn't know why, but she breathed a sigh of relief.

"Can I help you darling?"

"I'd like to see Mr Miller if I may."

"What's your name love?"

"Stella, Stella Nicholson."

"Well you wait here Stella and I'll go and see if he's in."

She wanted to laugh at the absurdity of it all but instead she thanked the giant of a man and did as she'd been told. Glancing around the yard she noticed the scruffy man from yesterday. He was standing inside a clapped out old caravan and she could clearly see through its open door that he was scribbling furiously into some kind of book. Jumbo looked up and when he saw the strange woman watching him he kicked the van door shut with his boot. Stella didn't know what he was up to, but whatever it was he obviously didn't want anyone else to see. Seconds later and the big man was once again by her side.

"The boss will see you now."

Entering the timber building she was surprised at how clean and neat the place was. Smart furniture lined the walls and various plants filled each corner of the room. The big man gestured with his hand for her to enter the office at the far end. Tony studied her for only a second and then making his way over he grabbed her hand.

"Bless my soul, it really is you. When Harry said your name I thought I was fucking dreaming. How are you girl, keeping well I hope?"

"Thanks Tony and yes I am, I'm doing fine actually."

"You look it, mind you, you always was easy on the eye girl."

He didn't comment further but he knew she couldn't be doing that well or she wouldn't be here now. He was struggling to take his eyes off her, true she had aged but then hadn't they all. Stella still had the looks and figure that had first attracted him to her and now all these years later she was back on the scene.

"Take a seat and tell me why you're here. I mean I take it this ain't a social visit now is it?"

The office was plush and she followed him over to two expensive looking leather sofas. Tony poured out a

139

couple of glasses of brandy and handed her one before respectfully taking a seat on the opposite sofa. Stella took a swig of the golden liquid in an attempt to calm her nerves. Regardless of the horror stories she'd heard Stella wasn't scared of Tony Miller, the one and only thing she was scared of, was him refusing to help her.

"The old man passed away a couple of weeks ago."

"Bet that fucking upset you!"

She knew he was being sarcastic but she couldn't blame him, Wilf had chased Tony away from her many times when they were younger.

"I don't know if you're aware but he had a couple of shops, one on Roman Road and the other close to Liverpool Street station.

"No I didn't know that, so the old cunt was a man of property?"

"Anyway, for years Stevie has rented the places and run them as pound shops. Stevie's your son just in case you are interested. He's worked so hard and now has a house out in Brentwood. His wife and three kids, your grandchildren, are great and life was going good for him."

Her words had shaken Tony to the core. It wasn't the fact that the boy had made something of himself, Tony didn't expect anything less, and after all, he was from Miller stock. No, what had shocked him was the revelation that he was a grandfather something he'd never even thought about.

"So what's changed?"

"The old man only went and left the shops to my brother Dougie."

"You mean the funny little kid with the freckles?"

"Not so little now! Anyway, a few months after you disappeared he came out and shouted from the bleeding

140

roof tops that he was gay. As you can imagine Wilf went ape shit and disowned him there and then. For years we didn't hear a thing and then I tracked him down when the old man snuffed it. He now lives in Soho with his husband. When he came to the funeral I thought we were beginning to build bridges but that all changed after the Will was read. Seems that husband of his is a greedy bastard and wants it all for himself. In a nut shell my boy....."

"Our boy!"

Stella didn't want to argue as she needed Tony's help like never before but it still stuck in her craw that after years of having no contact with his son he now wanted to refer to Stevie as his.

"Our boy, is about to lose everything including his home. I've tried to get a compromise but they won't have a bar of it and to tell the truth Tony, I'm at my wits end, that's why I'm here now."

For a minute or two Tony Miller didn't say anything as he took in all that she had said. Of course he would help her that went without saying, but still, he didn't want to come across as a push over.

"So what are you asking me to do about it?"

"I don't know, I don't know anything anymore, in all honesty I'm sick to the back teeth with it all but what can I do, I can't turn my back on my boy when he needs me." She was striking a low blow with what she had just said but Tony let it go. Stella began to cry and the tears weren't crocodile, for the first time the enormity of it all was really starting to sink in and the woman, who was normally such a great leader that sorted out all of her family's problems, now felt totally and utterly lost. Tony made his way over and taking a seat beside Stella he tenderly held her hand.

141

"I had to promise my old mum that whatever happens, Dougie wouldn't be hurt, at least not physically. Is there anything you can do to help me Tony?"

"I'll need to give it some thought. Let me sleep on it and I'll get back to you tomorrow, what's your number?" Stella removed a pen and a piece of paper from her handbag and scribbled down her mobile, she didn't want him calling the flat in case anyone else answered. Standing up she thanked the man that had at one time been the love of her life and then she slowly but with as much dignity as she could muster, walked out of the cabin. Tony Miller was lost for words; he couldn't believe how she still made him feel after all these years. Usually he had at least one young bird hanging on his arm but none of them, unlike Stella, had ever meant a thing to him. Stella Nicholson was a different matter altogether, she stirred something up in Tony that he didn't even know existed and it was a feeling he liked. Deciding that he would give her time enough to get home and then he would call her, he sat back on the sofa and smiled to himself. Stella made her way back home but her heart didn't feel any better as nothing had been sorted out yet. She would remain uptight and wouldn't be able to rest until her boy got what he deserved. Placing her key in the lock she glanced at the screen of her mobile when it began to ring. Not recognising the number she was about to dismiss the call when she thought better of it.

"Hello?"

"Hi Stella its Tony. I will need a few more details and I wondered if we could talk about things over dinner tomorrow night?"

Stella knew that she couldn't decline and at the same time she hoped she hadn't given Tony Miller the wrong impression; still, even if she had she didn't have much choice now and would have to play along for Stevie's sake.

"That would be lovely Tony thank you."

Hanging up she had a terrible feeling of foreboding, if Micky ever found out it would be the end of their relationship and he was far too dear to her to risk letting that happen.

CHAPTER FIFTEEN
(Six months earlier)

Anna Hillman worked behind the front kiosk of 'Take A Look'; the place was one of the many peep show venues on Dean Street. Anna had lived in the area for quite some time and at twenty four years of age thought she knew all there was to know about the seedy world of Soho. True she had been witness to some awful things in her short life, many personally suffered at the hands of her stepfather but unbeknown to her she still had a long way to go when it came down to Soho's sex industry and the evil that went on there. Running away from home just after her sixteenth birthday, Anna was soon all alone in the world but that didn't last for long and it turned out that she would be one of the lucky ones. Making her way to the capital as a lot of homeless young people do she was soon befriended by a group of six teenage girls who were all roughly about the same age as her and who were all running away from home for very similar reasons. The gang mostly consisted of girls from up north who were street wise and desperate for a better life after years of abuse. The leader, a girl that went by the name of Betsy Turner, was the off spring of a prostitute and she hated anything to do with the sex trade. A pact was made that they would do anything to survive, anything except to sell themselves. Things worked out fine for two or three years and they all ate well and had ample warm clothing in the winter but when Betsy was arrested for shoplifting, her fifth offence in as many months, she was sent to Holloway prison and the rest of her little gang seemed to fall apart over night. Now Anna was alone and scared but luck shone down on her for a second time when she was befriended by Nicky Naylor a woman from

a similar background but several years older. The pair
had hit it off immediately while they were queuing up at
the local burger van that pitched up daily behind a club
on Great Windmill Street. Nicky offered Anna a place to
stay and swore on her life that there would be no funny
business. She was true to her word and Anna would
contribute to the weekly household bills with no strings
attached. Everything was fine until Nicky found out how
her lodger earned a living, shoplifting and picking
pockets wasn't acceptable and Anna was told to stop or
get out. After a few days of worry and fearful that she
would be kicked out of the only real home she had ever
known, the position at 'Take A Look' became available.
Five years down the line and life was good, Anna
Hillman covered her bills and when Nicky moved on to
pastures new Anna took over the flat and found herself a
lodger. Macy Langham was ancient and not the kind of
flat mate that Anna would have chosen but when push
came to shove Anna needed to pay the rent so she had
relented and offered the older woman a room. It was the
same sad story over and over again. Macy Langham had
been the victim of abuse but where Anna had been used
by her father, Macy had been sold by both her parents to
satisfy their alcohol addiction. The young woman had
arrived in the capital much the same as Anna but Macy
hadn't been so lucky. A pimp had been on the lookout at
Kings cross station and had homed in on her as soon as
she stepped from the train. There began many years of
life as a prostitute. The only reprieve she had was when
she reached the age of forty and was no longer of any use
to her pimp. Macy had struggled on alone but punters
were thin on the ground and when Anna had entered her
life Macy said a silent prayer. It didn't take long for the
two to become inseparable, Anna because she looked on

145

the older woman as a mother figure and Macy because to begin with she was just grateful for somewhere to lay her head but over time she also came to look on Anna as family. Anna Hillman had never sold her body, well at least not as far as she saw it. A quick blowjob in the early hours after 'Take A Look' had closed didn't count as far as she was concerned and the few minutes she was forced to spend pleasuring a man allowed her a few of life's luxuries. That had suddenly all come to an end the night she met Tony Miller. The man had arrived at her place of work to see her boss Alan Mendham and when he smiled at her she could feel the hairs on the back of her neck instantly stand on end. Anna lowered her gaze and to Tony she seemed to have an innocent quality, though how that was possible in Soho he really didn't know. Making his way up the stairs he knocked and walked into the office to carry out his business but the girl was still on his mind.

"Hello Tony! Blinding to see you again, how's tricks?"

"Brilliant thanks Alan. Before we get started, who's the little blonde tart downstairs in the front booth?"

"That's Anna, why do you fancy a little bit do you?"

Tony Miller just smirked but he was surprised at his old friend's next sentence.

"Well you'll need to get in line mate there's already a long queue. I wouldn't hold out much hope though, as far as I know and as strange as it may seem working in a place like this, she's a good girl just trying to make a living. Been with me over five years and not one spot of trouble from her, fuck me mate she doesn't even swear."

Unknowingly Alan Mendham had thrown down the gauntlet and Tony loved nothing better than a challenge.

"Is that so, what do you say to a little wager then?"

"Ok Tony how much are we talking?"

"A ton if I get to take her out, and to make things a bit more interesting, a grand when I bed her."

Alan burst out laughing; Tony Miller was so cocky it was comical.

"You mean if?"

"I know what I mean."

"You're on but let's make it a little more interesting shall we. I reckon if you're going to lay her you will have done so in, let's say two weeks."

"Two fucking weeks! If she's as pure as the driven like you say she is, then it ain't giving me a lot of time."

"You can't have it all fucking ways Tony; you set the figure so I'm setting the time limit. Fuck me, two weeks for a stud like you, that's a fucking lifetime."

The old friends shook hands both sure that they would come out victorious. As Tony left the office he turned to Alan.

"And no bad mouthing me to the girl you old cunt, or the bet is off!"

"Now would I?"

As he walked past the front booth he winked in Anna's direction and this time she gave the slightest hint of a smile. The following afternoon when she arrived for her shift at 'Take A Look' there were a large bouquet of red roses waiting for her. The card only had the picture of a winking eye but she still knew who they were from. The following day was exactly the same and by Friday Macy had started to complain that there were more flowers in the flat than in a chapel of rest.

"So who's your secret admirer?"

"I'm not really sure I should say."

"Oh go on you know I can keep a secret."

Anna was desperate to share her news and deep down she did kind of trust Macy, well sort of.

147

"His name is Tony Miller."

Macy just stared open mouthed. Of all the people for Anna to get mixed up with, Tony Miller definitely shouldn't be among them. Now she was in a quandary, tell Anna all that she knew about the man from her days working on the streets and risk falling out with her, or keep her mouth shut? The only problem was, Macy was well aware of what he was capable of, she'd seen too many women's lives ruined over the years and all at the hands of Tony Miller.

"You don't know him then?"

"I know him or know of him very well and if I could give you one piece of advice it would be to stay well clear. Not only is he a gangster, one of the worst in fact, but he is also a very cruel human being Anna and he will break your bleeding heart without a moment's hesitation. Now you know I have never tried to interfere in your life but this time I have to have my say."

Anna Hillman was angry, in all the years she'd lived in Soho she had avoided getting into a relationship at all costs, now when she finally felt she had found a nice man her flat mate was slagging him off.

"I hear what you're saying Macy and thanks for your concern but it's my life and I will live it how I please." The girls tone said in no uncertain terms that the conversation was well and truly over and as much as Macy didn't want Anna to see Tony, she knew she had to back off. If the shit hit the fan then hopefully she would be here to pick up the pieces and if he hadn't done too much damage, be here to wipe away Anna's tears.

The next day the flowers arrived again only this time the card had a message written on it. Tony was inviting her out to dinner and if she was comfortable going out with him, he had already cleared it with Alan for her to have the night off. She had been on the early shift today and at five o'clock she collected her coat and bag and made her way home to the flat. A leisurely bath would be followed by a pamper session as she wanted to look her best for him. At seven she walked the short distance back to 'Take A Look' and waited outside to be collected. When the glistening Jaguar pulled up complete with chauffer Anna was overwhelmed. Tony Miller was already inside and as she climbed in he passed her a glass of champagne. When the car pulled away they began to chat, Tony had booked two restaurants, one very upmarket and the other not so posh that Anna would feel out of her depth if she hadn't ever experienced the high life. As he hadn't yet spoken to the girl before he'd invited her out, Tony didn't know how common she was and one thing he hated with a vengeance was being shown up in public. He needn't have worried and as they talked away he told the driver to make his way over to the Ivy restaurant on the Kings Road. Walking inside Anna couldn't remember in the whole of her life going to anywhere so beautiful but smiling sweetly there was no way she would ever let that be known. The couple enjoyed a sumptuous meal and the conversation flowed freely which somewhat surprised Tony but he had quickly realised that she was confident and perfectly at ease with the surroundings. Playing the gentleman he had the car drop her off at home and all he did was lean over and give Anna a kiss on the cheek. Climbing out she was on cloud nine and silently prayed that he would want to see her again. The flat was empty as Macy was still on her shift at Delphine's but Anna had no intention of going to bed, she was far too excited. Pouring a glass of wine she relived every second of the evening over and again in her mind, never wanting it to end. Anna

149

Hillman's prayers were answered and several more dates followed in quick succession. Tony took her to the theatre, casinos, private clubs, and finally he invited her to his home. Sleeping together hadn't been mentioned yet but she knew the time was fast approaching and in all honesty she was actually looking forward to it. Oh Tony hadn't said he loved her, well not in so many words but she knew he did and it would only be a matter of time before he said it. On the night in question, almost two weeks to the day they had met, he had sent a car over to collect her and as she entered the foyer of his apartment block she was greeted by the concierge and taken straight up to the penthouse. When the lift doors opened she had to stifle a gasp, the place was stunning and not what she was expecting at all. Sumptuous earth tone fabrics had been used for the soft furnishings and when she stepped onto the carpet the pile was so deep that she could feel her shoes sink right in. Tony Miller emerged from the kitchen wearing an apron and he had a light dusting of flour on his nose which made her giggle. It was so sweet that he had wanted to cook a meal for her personally. Of course it was all just an act, Tony had sent his driver to collect the food from his favourite restaurant an hour earlier and all he had to do was reheat it. The apron and flour had been his own idea and when she tenderly wiped the white dust away and planted a lingering kiss on his lips, Tony knew that he would be receiving his payout from Alan Mendham the very next day. The couple enjoyed a light dinner which was intentional on Tony's part as he never liked to feel full if he was going to have sex. When a bottle of wine had been consumed he took hold of Anna's hand and led her through to the bedroom. Tony Miller was experienced and knew how to please a woman and as he began to seductively undress Anna she

150

didn't resist. He started to slowly open the buttons on the front of her blouse and as he did so he kissed her luscious plump red lips teasingly and nibbling them. Expertly unclipping her black lace bra Anna's pert ivory breasts came into view and at the same time Tony could feel his penis harden. Now the kissing became passionate and Anna's bra fell to the floor. Her breasts were firm and perfectly formed and as Tony noticed her nipples were erect and inviting, he took one into his mouth and sucked hard. Anna groaned with pleasure and then Tony dropped to his knees and kissed her stomach over and over again as he slowly moved his way to her skirt. By now Anna Hillman felt as if her body was on fire and not willing to wait any longer she unzipped the garment herself. Her matching lace panties came into view and as she stood before him he couldn't take his eyes from her. Black stockings, suspenders and high heels were a mega turn on and as he glanced upwards she flicked her mane of golden hair from side to side. Anna slowly opened her legs and Tony didn't need an invitation. Placing his hand up and inside her delicate panties, his fingers slipped inside with ease as she was already so wet and again Anna groaned with pleasure. Grabbing Tony's head, she pulled him tightly to her body and at the same time he placed another finger inside of Anna and began to vigorously stimulate her. When he at long last kissed her on the mouth she playfully bit his lip as she thrust her hips towards him.

"Harder harder, I like it hard!"

Tony was amazed at the girl who he had wrongly thought was shy when she grabbed at his wrist and started her own rhythm, pulling him harder and forcing his fingers further inside of her at an even greater speed.

"Be rough with me, I like it that way!"

Tony placed his hand around her throat and pushing her down onto the bed he knelt at her feet. Ripping off her panties he quickly unzipped his trousers releasing his hard penis. Anna pulled at his shirt ripping it from his body like a woman possessed and as she did so she clawed at his naked back with her nails.

"Arghhh! You fucking bitch!"

Taking Tony's erect penis into her mouth Anna clawed at his buttocks. It was pleasure and pain both at the same time and apart from wincing slightly, Tony Miller loved every moment of it. Anna greedily worked on Tony for several minutes but just as he was about to climax he pulled her head away. She was reluctant to release him and tried to hold on but he was to strong and when he roughly pulled her legs apart and rammed his hard penis into her she screamed out in pleasure. Anna was tight and wet and Tony didn't last long but as they climaxed together they were both clawing each other and were actually drawing blood as they did so. Panting heavily Tony then rolled off of her but Anna wasn't finished just yet. Taking his now limp member into her mouth it wasn't long before Tony was hard again. As he lay on his back she climbed on and rode him while pleasuring herself at the same time. It took a further three orgasms before she was finally satisfied but at long last she had a wide smile on her young pretty face. Stepping from the bed she walked towards the bathroom as Tony pulled the sheet over his body, it was about all he could manage and closing his eyes he was exhausted and partly relieved. Back on the bed she had reached out to him but there was no response. With the sex over and even though they had both enjoyed the experience, Anna now felt used. It wasn't anything he'd said but his attitude afterwards had felt almost dismissive. Totally out of character and she

152

didn't really know why, but lying alone in the bed Anna started to cry. Tony stepped out of the sheet and got dressed and it was clear that he didn't want her to stay the night so once more getting out of bed and after making her way into the en suite, she slowly pulled on her clothes. When she lifted her bra strap over her shoulder Anna winced in pain and looking into the mirror she could see the claw marks which were now very sore. She sighed deeply, maybe this was how it was supposed to be, maybe this was the way a man showed a woman that he loved her and she belonged to him. Entering the lounge he smiled when he saw her and as Tony walked over and kissed her, his attitude seemed totally different from a few minutes ago and all of Anna's doubts instantly disappeared.

"Fancy going to a club tomorrow night?"

"I would love to thanks."

After that night a strange relationship began between a man who was only using a young woman for self gratification and a girl who thought she was so desperately in love. Six months later and Anna Hillman was still regularly seeing Tony Miller. On the day that Stella Nicholson arrived back on the scene things had come crashing to the ground, Tony was now happy to discard Anna without a second thought. People's feelings weren't his concern but then again, he wasn't yet aware that none of their lives were ever going to be the same again.

CHAPTER SIXTEEN

To say Stella was nervous was an understatement. She still had just under an hour before Tony was due to collect her but as hard as she tried she just couldn't find anything to wear or at least nothing she was happy with. Daisy sat on the edge of her daughter's bed watching Stella remove dress after dress from the wardrobe. When there was only a dressing gown left hanging she finally spoke.

"Stella, can I ask you a question?"

Stella only nodded her head as she continued to rummage through a chest of drawers.

"Are you planning on sleeping with that fucking villain?"

"Mother!"

"Don't mother me, no one takes so long to get ready if they ain't trying to make an impression and besides, them lacy knickers you've laid out are new and don't try telling me any different. You're making a huge bleeding mistake love, I mean just look at what happened last time."

"In case it's slipped your mind Mum, I happen to be in my mid fifties! My child bearing days are well and truly over."

"Many a cow has shit their heels before now!"

"Whatever are you on about Mum?"

Daisy was losing her patience and standing up she headed towards the door. Touching the handle she turned in her daughter's direction.

"All I'm saying is don't be so sure, in this life anything can happen. He might not be able to get you pregnant but he's certainly capable of breaking your bleeding heart again. And I remember only too well what he did to you last time and the months it took for you just to feel normal again, so just think on when you make any decisions tonight ok?"

Stella ignored her mother's advice and picking up the navy dress that she'd already discarded twice, decided that it would have to do.

Anna Hillman was already getting ready for her date when the telephone rang. She had been looking forward to tonight and when she picked up her mobile and saw who was calling she smiled. Macy had a night off and was curled up in the chair watching some history programme that she didn't really understand and Anna didn't want the woman poking her nose in. Leaving the front room she made her way into the bedroom and closed the door before answering.

"Hi Tony babe!"

She listened intently to what was being said on the other end of the phone and her expression visibly changed as she looked into the mirror. After saying goodnight she sighed heavily as she ended the call. Anna walked back into the front room and Macy studied her flatmate out of the corner of her eye, the look of disappointment was clearly visible.

"Stood you up has he? I knew it wouldn't last five minutes, I warned you but would you listen, oh no, you still went ahead and let that bastard have his way with you."

"Oh don't start, if you must know he's inundated with work and can't make it that's all."

"And if you believe that you're a bigger fucking idiot than I thought. Mark my words Anna Hillman, your so called relationship with Tony Miller is coming to an end and best you start getting used to that fact."

Anna stormed out of the room, she didn't want to hear

anymore and pulling on her coat decided to go for a walk. She had always loved the streets of Soho at night; they were so vibrant and alive that it never failed to lift her spirits when she was down and she decided that she might even stop off somewhere for a bite to eat, anything other than having to listen to Macy going on and on. It was still relatively early and there wasn't much happening yet so she continued to stroll along not really bothering where her feet took her. When she did take notice of just where she was she had already arrived in Covent Garden which was a favourite place as she loved a bit of celebrity spotting. At around the same time as Anna's call Stella Nicholson had also received one but it wasn't Tony Miller on the other end.

"Hello there girl, how are you doing?"

His voice instantly made her feel guilty even though she hadn't done anything wrong, at least not yet. Stella knew that she would have to lie and it was something she hated doing but at least it would save causing any hurt to the one man who had always been good to her.

"Hi Micky. I'm fine thanks."

"Did you go and see that Tony Miller?"

"Yes I did and he said he would think about helping me so I'll just have to wait and see what happens."

"You fancy coming round later, I've got the night off?"

Stella inwardly groaned as she tried to think up an excuse.

"I can't tonight Micky, Mums not too well and I'd rather stay here and get an early night if you don't mind?"

"Mind? Why ever should I mind? Give the old girl my love and maybe I'll see you next week?"

Stella had already hung up and Micky wasn't sure that all was well, something in her voice had told him she wasn't being entirely honest but there was little he could do

156

about that. Pulling himself a pint he made his way
upstairs to watch the DVD he'd purchased over two
weeks ago but as yet hadn't had the time to view. Stella
continued to get ready but her heart was heavy and she
didn't like the feeling. The same old draw from over
thirty years ago was pulling her towards a man that she
knew would only cause her heartache but just like before;
Stella also knew there was no point in fighting it as she
couldn't win. At seven thirty she pulled on her coat,
picked up her handbag and then popped her head around
the front room door.

"I'm off now Mum."

There was no reply, Daisy had the right nark and when
her mother was put out Stella knew there was no way
anyone could win her around. Closing the front door she
just hoped that the old woman would be in a better mood
in the morning. The Jaguar was already parked up in the
square below and as Stella approached she smoothed
down her raincoat and hoped that she looked alright.
Tony Miller beamed as she climbed into the car, Stella
may have been from the East End but she sure scrubbed
up like a girl from the west of the city.

"So where do you fancy going?"

"Surprise me."

Tony knew exactly where to take her. Tonight wasn't
about making an impression like he had done with Anna,
tonight was about being with a woman that he had known
for years, had fathered a child with and if all truth was
told, someone who had never been far from his thoughts
though Tony would have been loath to admit it. There
was no chauffeur on this date and pulling the car out onto
Roy Street he headed in the direction of Soho. Little Italy
was situated on Firth Street and right opposite Ronnie
Scott's jazz club. It was well known for its traditional

157

Italian food as well as having a very intimate setting. As usual Tony stopped right outside the restaurant, the local Bobbies and traffic wardens had been informed to stay clear of the car and Tony Miller never had a problem parking. Walking around to the passenger side door he held it open while Stella climbed out. The maitre d' made his way over as soon as he saw the couple enter and then showed them to the best table in the house. Stella was well aware that Tony's name put fear into people wherever he went and it wasn't something she liked or agreed with but then this was his world and she had no right to voice her opinion. Being treated like royalty was new to her and she couldn't deny that she liked the feeling. The food was outstanding and Tony had laughed at the amount she was able to put away. He remembered back to the days when all they could afford was a couple of bags of chips and even then she would eat hers in record time and be pestering for some of his. Anna Hillman walked down Old Compton Street on her way back from Covent Garden. The streets were getting busy with the many tourists that filled the place nightly in the hope of seeing something or someone out of the ordinary. Of course that wasn't always the case, oh there was still a heavy sex industry and some of it wasn't very savoury but at least it was discreet and the Old Bill left the workers alone, well most of the time. Deciding to go down Firth in case there was anyone famous entering or leaving Ronnie Scott's, Anna stopped dead in her tracks when she saw Tony's car. Her heart began to race, was he cheating, but he couldn't be they were still sleeping together. Maybe he was just having a business meeting and anyway, the place looked a little shabby and nothing like the upmarket restaurants he usually took her to. All the same she decided to wait and watch to see who he came out with. Situated next door to Little Italy was the stage door entrance to the London casino. It was set back just enough so that Anna was hidden from view to anyone exiting the restaurant. Leaning against the wall she was in for a long wait as the conversation and jokes flowed between Stella Nicholson and Tony Miller. The years seemed to fall away and it felt just like it had when they were teenagers. It was freezing outside and glancing at her watch and seeing that it was just past ten Anna finally decided to go home. About to step out from the shadows she immediately retreated when the restaurant door opened and Stella walked out followed by Tony. Anna felt a lump in her throat, she was heartbroken and couldn't for the life of her work out why he would cheat with someone so old. The couple climbed into the car and when they had driven off and Anna was confident that she wouldn't be seen she began the walk home. Macy Langham was still seated in front of the television but switched it off the instant she saw her flat mates tear stained face.

"I knew no bleeding good would come of it, I told you but would you listen?"

Anna dropped down onto the sofa and began to sob which immediately made Macy regret opening her mouth. Taking a seat beside her friend she took Anna into her arms and held the young woman tight until the tears at last started to subside.

"Why Macy, why would he do that. I mean I ain't ugly am I?"

"Oh darling of course you ain't, you're beautiful but some men, well most in my experience, like to put it about. You can never change men like Miller love and there ain't any point in trying."

"But Macy you should have seen her, she was old enough

159

to be my mum."

"Fanny's fanny love and some men don't care how old it is or in what condition. Look, you have to see it as you've had a lucky escape."

"I don't feel lucky!"

"Believe you me honey it could have been a whole lot worse. I mean imagine if you'd been seeing him for a couple of years or lord forbid you'd gotten pregnant! No Anna, you definitely had a lucky escape.

"But I love him Macy I really do love him."

"Babe there's no point in loving a man like Tony because he will never be able to return that feeling. Men like Miller only ever love one person and that person is themselves."

Anna's tears began all over again only this time they quickly turned into wracking sobs that would last long into the night.

Pulling up in the underground parking space Tony turned in his seat to face his date. Stella braced herself for what she knew he was about to say but in all honesty they were both far too old to be pussy footing around with each other.

"Would you like to come up for a coffee?"

Stella burst out laughing at the absurdity of his words.

"What?"

"Well I suppose it's better than offering to show me your etchings. Look Tony, we ain't twenty anymore so what you actually mean is do I want to stay the night and the answer is yes."

A broad grin spread across his face and they both climbed out of the car and made their way inside. Unlike Anna, the apartment didn't make Stella's jaw drop, oh she liked nice things but a person's personality and heart was far more important to her.

"Drink?"

"Please."

Grabbing a bottle of champagne from the fridge and two glasses from the cupboard Tony then led the way through to the bedroom. As he unzipped her dress she said a silent prayer of thanks that she'd purchased the new underwear and wasn't wearing her usual Big Bertha's, a name that she had always called her oversized but very comfy knickers. Tony was gentle and laying her down on the bed he began to explore every inch of her body. There was no giggling like there normally was with Micky, this was intense and sensual. Stella wasn't embarrassed about the few stretch marks that were on her stomach, she had long since given up on them but when Tony slowly ran his finger over each one, and then gently kissed them he made her feel like a goddess. He took his time but when he at last entered her she let out a cry of ecstasy. He couldn't believe how good it felt, how intimate, how beautiful, unlike the young girls that he had surrounded himself with for the last god knew how many years. When their lovemaking had finished they shared the champagne and it wasn't long, much to Stella's pleasure, that he was ready to go again. They would become one several times that night and when both were exhausted they fell asleep in each other's arms. For the first time in years Tony wanted a woman in his bed all night long but then Stella Nicholson wasn't just any woman, she was the only female to have ever really touched his heart.

When the morning sunlight shone through the open blinds of the window Stella could feel the warmth on her face. Screwing up her eyes it took a few seconds to focus and to remember where she was. Like a bolt of lightning the guilt hit her from all sides and holding her brow with

161

her hand she couldn't believe what she had let happen. Tony was still sleeping beside her and as quietly as she could Stella slipped from the bed grabbed her clothes and went into the bathroom. After dressing she looked at her reflection in the mirror. Last night's carefully applied makeup was now smudged under her eyes and she looked exactly how she felt, like a whore. There was nothing else to explain why she had allowed this to happen, other than she had sold her body in the hope of helping her son but it still didn't make things right. Rubbing at her face with some wet tissue she removed the smears of mascara and then walking through to the hall she pressed the button and waited impatiently for the lift to arrive. Outside on the street she was soon able to hail a cab and within a short time she was once more climbing the steps to her home and the dreary bleak flats that she knew so well. Making her way along the landing Stella prayed that Daisy would still be asleep, but her prayers weren't answered. As soon as she placed her key into the lock and pushed open the front door she came face to face with her mother and it was plain to see that Daisy Nicholson wasn't happy.

"And just where the bloody hell have you been?"

"You know fine well where I've been Mum and before you start bleeding ranting and raving, I'm a middle aged woman and I do not answer to you or anyone else."

"So you keep telling me but from where I'm standing it looks like you'll be answering to that tosser pretty soon, you're one soppy cow Stella and before you know it he'll be pulling your strings good and proper."

"I don't want to talk about it mum, now I'm going to have a bath."

With that Stella walked into the kitchen, lifted off the lid to the tub and turned the taps on. She ached all over and

162

the thought of what had caused her discomfort brought a smile to her face. The moment was soon lost as she turned around and saw Daisy leaning up against the door frame watching her.

"What?"

"Micky Mackerson is what! That poor sod thinks the sun shines out of your arse and this is how you treat him? Tony Miller might well be able to help you but he's a fucking gangster Stella as well you know."

Daisy turned and stormed off in the direction of the front room leaving Stella standing open mouthed. Her mother never did mince her words and this time she had given it to her daughter with both barrels but as much as it pained Stella to admit it, when it came down to the cold hard facts, every word that had came out of Daisy's mouth had been the truth. Wearily Stella locked the front door and after pulling the kitchen blind, climbed into the bath. Her mind was racing, she knew Tony would want to see her again and as much as she didn't like admitting it, she wanted to see him too. The only problem was she didn't want to hurt Micky, poor honest reliable Micky Mackerson who had never once hurt her or asked anything of her. Stella realised she had a lot of thinking to do but that would all have to wait until this mess with the shops was sorted out. Lying back in the bubbles she closed her eyes and at the same time she began to cry.

CHAPTER SEVENTEEN

Tony had woken up feeling great but as he moved his hand over the sheets to touch her he suddenly sat bolt upright when he realised that the rest of the bed was empty. He called out her name but when there was no answer he realised that Stella had gone. He had presumed she would at least have stayed for breakfast and in preparation he had bought everything to cook a full English or if she was into healthy eating, fresh salmon. Strawberries, croissants, in fact everything you could think of to make a sumptuous spread. Normally Tony ate out so his fridge was usually bare but he had been so desperate to impress her, not that he would admit to that in a million years, he had spent over an hour in Harrods buying the best of everything. Tony Miller was used to getting his own way and the feeling of disappointment was new to him and one he didn't much like. By the time he arrived at the yard his mood was dark and when Tony was in a bad mood you stayed well clear if at all possible. Harry was making a cuppa when he heard the cabin door open, one look at his boss's face and as big as he was, he instantly ducked back into the kitchen area. Pete and Gazza were lounging on the reception sofas and didn't have time to sit up before the boss entered.

"What the fuck do you think this is a bastard hotel? I don't fucking pay you two tosser's to lie about all day. Now get some fucking work done or sling your fucking hooks."

Walking into his inner sanctum Tony slammed the door shut. The sound echoed throughout the cabin and no one would now dare to go into the office until they were called.

In just a couple of days Stella had got right under his skin and the feeling of wanting and needing someone so much was alien to him, not to mention the fact that anyone being able to do that to him was pissing him off big time. The only trouble was, Tony Miller liked it, liked the feeling that he was no longer alone and as much as she had wound him up this morning by disappearing, he really wanted to speak to her. Tony didn't want to come across as being pushy but as she hadn't explained all that he needed to know regarding her father's Will, he picked up the telephone. Just the thought of her made him tingle inside and he could feel the butterflies in the pit of his stomach. He longed just to hear her voice and as he dialled her mobile he anxiously awaited like a teenager for her to answer. Still in the bath, she reached over the side and slipped the phone out of her handbag as it began to ring.

"Hello?"

"Well hello there beautiful, you snuck out early?"

"I'm sorry Tony but I needed to get back to mum, anyway you was still snoring your head off when I left. I really must have worn you out last night?"

"I do not snore and for your information I could have gone on all night!"

They both laughed and Tony realised that he wanted to see her right now.

"What are you doing?"

"I'm in the bath."

"That sounds nice, fancy a bit of company?"

"Firstly I don't think mum would approve and I don't know if you remember what these flats are like Tony but right at this moment I'm laying flat out in the kitchen tub."

165

Again he laughed and when he asked if he could see her that night, there was silence on the other end of the line and he didn't have a very good feeling.

"I'd love too but..."

Tony's heart started racing with fear, was she about to dump him after just one date?

"You know how it is with family Tony; I come with a lot of baggage not to mention a whole load of bleeding trouble at the moment."

"I know sweetheart and there was just one question I wanted to ask, have the solicitors started changing over the ownership yet?"

"Not as far as I know but then it isn't anything to do with us now. I know Stevie hasn't had notice to quit or anything but I suppose it all takes time. Oh Tony, what a bloody mess and just when I thought things were starting to turn around for my family!"

"Well hopefully I can soon sort things out for you, as it happens I've got a couple of my blokes looking into it today so I'll give you a call tomorrow and let you know how it goes. I really enjoyed last night Stella and I don't just mean the sex, although I have to say for an old girl you've still got it."

"Cheeky sod! So I'll wait to hear from you and thanks Tony."

"No worries love, I'll sort it"

Stella Nicholson laughed as she hung up, Tony always was a charmer who could make a girl laugh herself out of her own knickers and she was no different, it was probably the reason she had ended up pregnant in the first place but if he helped her sort things out then all that would be forgiven. In all honesty she would forgive him anything so long as he helped to save their sons livelihood. Lying back in the bath she was now relaxed and finally felt able to enjoy the warm water as it caressed her body.

An hour later and now in a better mood, Tony Miller was still sitting behind his desk mulling over how he was going to handle the situation. Under normal circumstances he would have gone in all guns blazing but this wasn't normal, well not if he wanted to keep in Stella's good books. The only trouble was, queers could be hard to deal with at the best of times and when there was a large amount of money involved, Tony knew that this little problem probably wasn't going to be so easy. That said, he hadn't built his reputation on being soft and if it turned out that violence was the only option then he was the master when it came down to administering it. Calling through he told Harry Chrome to come into the office.

"What's up Gov?"

"I want you to go over to Soho. Ever heard of Delphine's?"

"Walked passed it a few times, looks a bit poncy if you ask me."

"I didn't. A friend of mine is having a bit of trouble with a pair of queers. They have inherited a couple of shops that don't rightfully belong to them and my friend wants them back. I want you to put the fucking frighteners on them but don't go over the top Harry, remember this is only a warning at the moment."

"So how far do you want me to go Boss?"

"You know what poof's are like, pretty things everywhere no doubt. Smash a few plates and make a nuisance of yourself and it scares the shit out of them. A few slaps here and there should be enough for now."

"Ok Gov, shall I take Gazza along?"

Tony thought for a moment, maybe just the sight of his

men would be enough; it was worth a try at least.
He wasn't worried about things getting nasty but he
needed to use the soft approach to begin with. If that
didn't work then the intensity and violence on the second
visit would have far more of an impact.
"Yeah, he's a big cunt and his size alone might be all
that's needed to scare the queer bastards without having
to use any muscle."
Tony gave his right hand man the details of who they
needed to see and then instructed Harry in exactly what
he wanted him to do. Jumbo was outside in the grabber
when Harry and Gazza came out of the cabin and he
stopped what he was doing to watch the men. When he
saw Harry carry a couple of pick axe handles over to the
car and when the big man placed them into the boot
Jumbo picked up a diesel receipt, the only piece of paper
to hand, and scribbled down the time of departure, the
men's names and what they had put into the car. He
wasn't sure that anything was going to take place but it
was always best to be prepared and over the years Jumbo
Smith had seen so many things that he wasn't about to
take any chances As far as he knew they could have just
been popping to the cafe but Jumbo knew that if he didn't
write it down he might miss something big happening.
Just recently he had seen a change at the yard and he
didn't think it was for the good. Tony Miller was getting
far too big for his boots as far as Jumbo Smith was
concerned and he suspected that it wouldn't be long
before the big man had his collar felt. Jumbo had seen it
happen many times in the past and he wanted to make
sure that when the shit hit the fan his own back was well
and truly covered.
It was just before eleven when the men pulled up outside
Delphine's. Macy had finished her cleaning duties and

168

was tired so had gone home for a couple of hours rest before the lunchtime rush began, leaving James and Dougie alone on the premises. James was busy prepping the salads out back in the kitchen; he preferred food prep to what his husband was doing, on his hands and knees bottling up behind the bar. Dougie didn't hear the door open and once inside Gazza slid the latch so that they wouldn't be disturbed. The two men walked up to the bar with the pick axe handles hanging loosely by their sides and Harry stepped behind the counter. Picking up a glass he proceeded to smash it onto the floor before approaching Dougie from behind. At the sound of the noise Dougie suddenly looked up from the shelves and to say he was startled was an understatement. The men's stature and attire spoke volumes and Dougie had been in Soho long enough to know the type and that when they called at your premises it was never for a social visit. As he spoke his voice came out in a slight stammer. He didn't mention the smashed glass deciding that politeness was the best policy although he somehow doubted that it would do him any good.

"Can I I I I help you gentlemen?"

"Dougie Nicholson?"

Dougie quickly stood up and wiping his hands on his apron, tried desperately to appear calm and in charge of the situation.

"Sorry but I would really appreciate it if you went around to the other side of the bar, back here is only for staff."

"Just answer the question cunt! Are you Douglas Nicholson?"

Dougie could feel himself begin to shake with fear and glancing down at his trembling hands he swiftly placed them behind his back. He was tall and thick set but when it came down to anything nasty he was a pussy cat and

169

even back on Roy Street when he was a teenager he had always been a push over for the bullies.

"Well I would really like to know who is asking before I reply to your question."

Gary Wilson, known to his associates as Gazza, stepped forward and after crushing the shards of glass under foot he slammed the pick axe handle down hard onto the bar and with one massive hand he quickly grabbed Dougie's cheeks and squeezed with a vice like grip. As he thrust his victim backwards, the shelves containing all the freshly stocked soft drinks began to wobble causing a few of the bottles to crash to the floor and smash. Using his other hand Gazza grabbed Dougie's genitals and as he again squeezed Dougie screamed out in pain. The man then moved his face to within an inch of Dougie's as he began to speak but remembering that Tony had given strict instructions not to go in heavy as this was only a warning, he lessened his grip just a tad.

"Now you listen to me cunt and listen good! My Boss has asked me to come and have a quiet word with you, if it had been down to me there wouldn't be anything quiet about it but I always do as I'm told just like you are going to do. Now you have something that really isn't yours and if you don't give it back and fucking pronto, you and your family jewels will soon part company. Understand?"

Harry began to laugh at the scene. They had been sent to do many jobs for Tony but dealing with a poofter had to be the easiest and most comical. Harry Chrome had little feeling for anyone; his whole life had been shit right from childhood. As far as he was concerned he didn't care who got hurt as long as there was a nice wedge to pick up at the end of the week. He didn't have a woman; they were all more trouble than they were worth, again a view

170

that stemmed from his childhood, and picking up a brass once a week was enough to satisfy his needs. If the woman in question just happened to be one of Tony's girls, then all the better as he received a discount but a permanent woman on his arm was a definite no no. Seeing the man writhe in agony made Harry feel good, to him there was nothing more satisfying than seeing someone suffer. Through the pain and with tears streaming down his face Dougie vigorously nodded his head. His screams from a few seconds earlier coupled with the sound of the smashing bottles had alerted James and when he ran through from the kitchen and saw what was happening he started to shake uncontrollably. "You've got one week to sort it all out faggot, if not we'll be back and if that happens I really wouldn't want to be in your shoes sunshine. Now I'm sure I don't have to remind you that calling the Old Bill ain't an option?" Again Dougie nodded his head and was still doing so as the men picked up their axe handles and walked from the restaurant. Gazza's nails had dug in deep and as Dougie wiped away a droplet of blood from his cheek he could only stare open mouthed. James, being the coward that he was, didn't try to help in any way. When Gazza and Harry had passed him on their way out he had pushed himself as far back onto the wall as he could and when Harry had ruffled his immaculate hair and then laughed, James thought he was about to piss his pants. Seeing the front door slam shut and only when he was sure they weren't coming back did he run over to his husband. "Oh my god Dougie, who were those men and what did they want?"
Dougie Nicholson staggered over to one of the chairs and almost fell as he went to take a seat. He had never been so scared in the whole of his life and he was well aware

171

that men like those didn't make idle threats.

"I don't know but they must be connected to Stella because they were talking about the shops or at least I think they were. They want me to hand them over James; whatever are we going to do?"

"Well you can just phone that bitch up and tell her to fuck off, those properties are ours and...."

Dougie slowly held up his hand and for once the gesture stopped James from continuing. Whatever was going on, he wasn't about to rush into making any rash decisions.

"I need time to think James so I'd be grateful if you could leave me alone for a while."

"But I..."

"I said!!!! I need time to think!!!!"

James minced off into the kitchen, he didn't like his husbands tone but just this once he would make allowances. Dougie had better make sure that he did the right thing or without a shadow of a doubt James would walk out. Dougie Nicholson sat with his head in his hands; he really didn't know what to do. If he gave into the men's demands then he would be left alone but if he just ignored the threat, well he was scared to even consider where that might leave him. Picking up his mobile Dougie dialled his sister's number. Stella was in the middle of making Daisy's lunch and without looking at the screen she picked up her phone to answer.

"Hello?"

"Stella it's me. I've just had a couple of gorillas in the bar threatening me. Why have you got other people involved Sis, this is family business."

Stella couldn't believe the nerve of her brother but whatever had happened must have scared him or he wouldn't be phoning her now. She decided to make a stand and not feel sorry for him; after all he hadn't shown

172

Stevie any sympathy.

"Oh so its family business now is it? Pity you didn't see things that way when I asked for your help. I'm sorry Dougie but it's out of my hands, I asked Stevie's dad for help and that's who you will have to deal with from now on."

"Not Tony Miller! Oh Stella how could you, the man's an animal and my life could be on the line."

"You should have thought about that in the first place. Goodbye Dougie."

Dougie Nicholson was left with the phone glued to his ear even though he knew there was no one on the other end. He couldn't believe his sister could do such a thing; well there was nothing left for it he would have to hand over the shops. Making his way to the kitchen he was dreading what James's reaction would be and pushing on the swing door he took a deep breath as he walked inside. "So?"

"We hand them over or rather we don't accept them when the solicitor gets in contact."

"But that's our future you're throwing away Doug and I ...."

"For fucks sake are you thick or something? If I don't do what they want I won't have a fucking future and neither will you or do you really think that they will just let you keep hold of the shops and no more will be said?"

James began to cry and walking over Dougie took his husband in his arms.

"We already have a good business babe so nothing's going to change, we just won't be millionaires but we do have each other."

Still in the embrace James stared over his husbands shoulder and rolled his eyes upwards. He hadn't envisaged spending that much longer with Dougie, after

173

all, he had only married the man for a better lifestyle and now it would be years before he could squirrel away enough money to move abroad on his own.

CHAPTER EIGHTEEN

The following morning Stella was putting the finishing
touches to the Sunday joint before placing it into the oven
when her phone rang. Daisy was peeling the potatoes
and trying hard to listen to every word her daughter was
saying. When the words 'thank you' were used several
times she knew it must be good news but she was
annoyed when Stella ended the call but didn't utter a
word to her. Finally when Daisy's patience had got the
better of her she slammed the knife down onto the
draining board.
"Well?"
"Well what?"
"Don't play silly buggers Stella; are you going to tell me
what's going on?"
Stella Nicholson had only been toying with her mother
and had wanted to see how long it would take to get this
response and laughing she shook her head. She was
happy to explain but there was a nagging doubt in the
back of her mind that it had all been just a little too easy.
Dismissing the thought she turned in Daisy's direction
and smiled.
"Seems Tony has managed to change my brothers mind
and don't worry, not a hair on his pretty head was
damaged in the negotiations. I can't wait to let Stevie
know, the poor sod has really been through the ringer in
the last few days, well mentally at least."
About to pick up her telephone Stella was stopped when
the front door slowly opened and her daughter Jane
tentatively stepped inside. Looking up at the same time
both Stella and Daisy gasped simultaneously. Jane's face
was so swollen it was hardly recognisable. Both eyes

were black and one of them was completely closed shut. Her top lip was also cut and as she made her way into the kitchen she was limping slightly.

"Oh my god! Whatever's happened?"

Stella ran over to her daughter but as she hugged her Jane winced in pain. Daisy instantly put the kettle on and Stella led her daughter into the front room and down onto the settee. Gently holding her daughters chin she slowly turned Jane's face from side to side as she examined the damage. For a long time Stella had been having a niggling thought that maybe her son-in-law wasn't all that he was cracked up to be and on a couple of occasion she'd seen him grab Jane's wrist in a none to friendly way. Years back just after they had married he'd hit her but he had promised his wife that it was a one off so nothing had been said since. In her naivety and the need for her family to be happy Stella had believed that the couple were now alright but she should have known better, a leopard never changed its spots. Her son in law was a sneaky one that was for sure and for a second the thought crossed her mind that she should tread carefully where her daughter's marriage was concerned but then in all honesty after this little episode there wasn't much of a marriage left, or at least she hoped there wasn't. She kept her tone low and calm as she spoke, even though inside Stella felt like screaming.

"I swear to you Jane, if I get my hands on that bastard I'll fucking swing for him."

"Oh please don't mum, he's a good man really."

Stella couldn't contain herself any longer and instantly her calmness was replaced by rage and a rise of several octaves in her voice.

"A fucking good man! What planet are you living on Jane? No man has a right to lay his hands on a woman;

176

he's a cunt and a coward!"

At her mother's words Jane slowly nodded her head and at the same time she began to cry.

"I thought after the last time he would never lay another finger on me and in all honesty Mum he hasn't for nearly five years. I know he's still been going to his anger management course because I drop him off there every Friday night but something must have just tipped him over the edge."

Her daughter's choice of words made Stella again blow her top, whatever was wrong with the soppy mare.

"Tipped him over the fucking edge! Get a grip Jane, he might try and come over all high and mighty but he's nothing but a bleeding bully. Nothing! Nothing do you hear me, gives a man any excuse to hit a woman. Now this time you must leave him and never go back, fuck me girl, the next time he could end up killing you!"

Daisy came in with the tea and taking a seat in her chair she listened intently to what was being said but she didn't yet offer an opinion. Stella was waiting for her daughter to promise she wouldn't go back but no words escaped Jane's mouth.

"Well, I'm waiting?"

"Look Mum, most of the time I couldn't wish for a better husband. Anyway this is all granddads' fault. None of it would have happened if he'd left his affairs in order, well that's what Roger reckons anyway."

"He did leave his affairs in order just not to Rogers liking, so how the fuck is Wilf to blame for any of this? I know the old man was a bastard but even he ain't capable of causing trouble from the grave, isn't that right Mum?"

Stella glared at her mother willing for Daisy to back her up or at least offer some advice but still the old woman said nothing. What with everything else that had been happening recently this was all getting too much and right at this moment Stella wanted to get out of the flat and as far away from Bethnal Green as she could. There was just one problem; she knew she couldn't now leave her daughter alone.

"I need to get back mum, he'll be home soon and if he finds out I've been outside I...."

Stella couldn't believe what she was hearing.

"Get back? What the fuck are you talking about Jane! You are going nowhere Mrs, do you hear me?"

Stella grabbed hold of her daughters hand and Jane screamed out in pain. Looking down Stella could immediately see that her face wasn't the only thing he'd hurt. Jane's fingers were cut and badly swollen like someone had stamped on her hand.

"Is it broken?"

"I don't think so but I'll give it a day or so and then pop down the hospital if it ain't any better."

"And you're talking about going back to that wanker!"

"But you don't know what he's like mum."

"Oh don't I? Every time I look at your poor battered face I know what that pig is like so don't you try telling me I don't! For once you are going to do as I say young lady!"

Making her way into the kitchen Stella picked up her phone and dialled Veronica's number. Her eldest girl was level headed and as much as the sisters didn't always see eye to eye, Stella knew that Ronnie would be here in a heartbeat when she found out what had happened. It was an age before Ronnie answered and for a minute Stella feared her daughter might not be at home but finally the phone was picked up.

"Ronnie?"

"Hello Mum, everything alright love?"

178

"No it bleeding well isn't. That scumbag Roger has beaten our Jane to a pulp. I'm trying to make her see sense but she keeps on about going back home. Oh Ronnie you should see her face love; its pitiful and her hand, her poor hand looks like he stamped on it or something."

Stella started to sob and as she desperately tried to hold it inside it only made things worse. The noise Ronnie could hear on the other end of the telephone broke her heart.

"Oh mum please don't cry."

Stella sniffed loudly and at the same time wiped her nose with the back of her hand.

"I'm sorry Ronnie."

"Sorry? You ain't got anything to be sorry about, just don't let her leave the flat Mum and I'll be around as soon as Sam gets back from the pub. My sister can be a right stupid cow at times but over my dead body will she go back to that spiteful cunt! I've kept my mouth shut for years but I always knew there was something dodgy about that bastard!"

"Me too, please hurry and get here Ronnie."

With that Stella ended the call and wearily made her way back into the front room. Once more taking a seat beside her daughter and holding Jane's one good hand in hers she stared directly into the young woman's eyes.

"Right, from the beginning tell me exactly what happened and don't leave anything out."

Jane swallowed hard, she was a very private person who usually didn't confide in anyone, least of all her family and this was going to be difficult to talk about.

"I don't know if I can and it won't change anything will it?"

"It will make me feel better if I know exactly what that

179

arsehole did, and don't try and sugar coat things."

"Well when Roger came home from his course on Friday night he seemed agitated and didn't want to talk. I know when he gets like that its best to leave him alone and he usually comes around after a few hours. We went to bed but on Saturday he was still in a foul mood. We were supposed to be going out to dinner last night with friends but past experience has taught me that it isn't a good idea when he's feeling down."

"Feeling fucking down!"

"Please don't Mum. Roger was hoping to get something out of the Will, he knows what those shops are worth and when we weren't even mentioned, well to be honest he was devastated."

"Look sweetheart, if your grandad had left you anything then it would have been exactly that, yours! It had nothing to do with that toe rag Roger. Where the fuck does he get off thinking he's entitled to a penny of the old man's money?"

Before anything else could be said the front door flew open and Ronnie came running in. Seeing her sisters battered and bruised face she immediately took Jane into her arms.

"Oh darling whatever has he done!"

Her sister's words made Jane start to cry again and it took several minutes to calm her down. Finally winking in her mother's direction was Veronica's signal to Stella that she would now take over. Stella didn't need telling twice and grabbing her coat and without a word to anyone, she quietly stepped from the flat. Walking past the Dundee Arms she contemplated going to see Micky but as lovely as he was, the only person on Stella's mind was Tony and his apartment was where she was heading. Hailing a cab she asked to be taken over to Kensington and sitting back in the seat she wondered if she was doing the right thing, after all he might not even be home or worse still he could be entertaining another woman. Never one to give in easily Stella knew that she wouldn't find out if she didn't at least pay him a visit but then deep down she couldn't really understand why she was here, it wasn't as if she wanted him to get involved any deeper in her family business than he already was. Maybe she was falling for him again and Stella Nicholson knew that if that was the case, then it would only end up causing her more pain in the long run.

Tony Miller was taking a nap on the couch when the concierge telephoned the penthouse and informed him that he had a visitor. As soon as her name was mentioned he immediately asked for her to be shown up. This was an unexpected pleasure and heading into the hallway he checked out his reflection in a large Venetian mirror. Happy that all was as it should be he wore the biggest smile as the door slid open.

"Well this is a nice surprise I must say!"

Stella started to cry which was totally out of character and Tony took her in his arms.

"Hey hey, whatever's the matter?"

Stella revealed all that had gone on and she could see his face becoming angry.

"Do you want me to sort the cunt out because believe you me nothing would give me greater pleasure."

Stella dried her eyes and followed him into the lounge where he poured them both a large scotch.

"Thanks but no, this is one problem my girl has to deal with herself. I never liked the slimy bastard, he always thought he was better than any of us and Jane has been acting like that herself for the last few years. Maybe getting away from that arsehole will bring her back into

181

the fold. Sorry to put all this on you, I feel as if I've done nothing but bitch about my problems since we hooked up again but I just wanted someone to talk to."

"Don't be silly, you can have a right old moan to me anytime you like. Now about the other business, your brother and his partner have a week but I ain't a hundred percent sure he will come through. I know what I said earlier but I just want you to be prepared if things don't go to plan. I've dealt with queers in the past and they can be tricky little fuckers. I've given it some though and if things do get a bit heavy its best if you ain't around."

"Well that's easier said than done and just where do you think I'm going to go?"

Tony Miller lent in and kissed her tenderly on the lips.

"I have a villa in Marbella and I want you, your mum and daughters, come to that take Stevie as well then no blame can be laid at your door. Go for a week's holiday, it will do you all the world of good."

Standing up, Tony disappeared into the bedroom and a minute or two later returned holding an envelope. His smile was warm and tender as he handed it to Stella.

"What's this?"

"There's five grand in there, plenty to get you and your family some flights with a bit left over for spends."

"But I can't accept this Tony."

"Yes you can, it ain't as if I don't owe you big time for raising my son, a son I didn't contribute a penny towards. Now go and book the flights for as soon as possible and when everything is sorted out I'll let you know."

Tony stood up and Stella knew that it was probably her cue to leave. Placing a kiss onto his cheek she thanked him several times before leaving the apartment but as she left Stella wondered if she would see him again when this was all over. Maybe he did feel that he owed her and when he had sorted out her mess he wouldn't want to see her again but something deep inside told her that wouldn't be the case. Again Stella hailed a taxi and this time asked to be taken to the Dundee Arms. Guilt was playing heavily on her mind and she had to at least try and explain to Micky why she had been so aloof over the last few days.

As she walked into the pub Micky Mackerson took one look at her and instantly knew. He didn't know how he knew, he just did and when she smiled in his direction he felt as though his heart would break. Motioning for her to join him out back he walked through the door into the rear hallway and waited for her to join him.

"Hello love, I was hoping you'd pop in."

"Were you Micky and why is that?"

"I know this is going to sound so cruel after everything you've gone through lately but I can't string you along and we were never exclusive anyway. I've met someone else and I want to give it a shot as I think it could become serious. I hope you understand, I mean it wasn't planned or anything. I'm sorry if this upsets you Stella really I am."

Micky was making every word up, there was no one else, never would be not after Stella but he knew the score and he was a proud man. Stella felt nothing but relief, she liked Micky, probably loved him deep down but he didn't excite her in the way that Tony did. Daisy would tell her she was a fool and that all she would ever get from the likes of Miller would be heartache but on the wrong side of fifty Stella didn't want to lose her last chance at happiness.

"That's fine Micky, we had some fun and now it's over. I wish you and your new lady all the luck in the world." With that Stella turned and walked out of the pub. As he

183

watched her close the front door he made a quick exit out to the back so that none of his staff saw him wipe away the tears that had escaped from his eyes. If things turned sour then maybe they could try again but for now he loved her too much not to let her go.

Stepping over the threshold of the Roy Street flat Stella was full of purpose. Ronnie was still seated beside Jane and Daisy was in her chair watching and listening as the pair of them talked. They all looked up when Stella entered and they couldn't be off noticing the strength and determination in her manner.

"Have you managed to talk any sense into the silly mare?"

"If by silly mare you mean me mother, then yes my sister and I have talked and no I will not be going back to Roger. Happy now?"

Sometimes Stella felt like slapping her daughter but today was definitely not one of those times.

"I wouldn't call it happy Jane more like relief."

Ronnie waited for her mother and sister to pause and was then about to try and lighten the mood but was beaten to it by her grandmother.

"You look like the cat that's got the fucking cream and no mistake!"

"Mother you always have such a nice way with words."

"Sarky!"

"Jane, Ronnie, I want you both to take a week off work and no arguments."

"But why?"

"Because dear daughters we're off on holiday and it ain't going to cost anyone a penny. I'm going to call Stevie and tell him to get packed. You know something? This is the first time I will have ever been on holiday with my kids. Well not all of them, I mean I can't ask Raymond,

184

and I doubt he's even got a passport."

Daisy knew exactly where the money had come from for this so called holiday and she was damned if she would accept a penny from that toe rag Miller.

"Well I hope you ain't including me in any of this? I ain't going on no plane at my age and besides it would stick in my craw taking money off of that wanker."

"You can please yourself Mum but I ain't looking a gift horse in the mouth and besides I need to get away."

For once Stella was putting herself first and she was sure that Stevie's wife Jo would take care of Daisy so there really wasn't anything to worry about. Daisy studied her daughters face but didn't make any further comment. Ronnie did and as she looked quizzically at her mother she spoke.

"Who's paying for all of this Mum, and why do you need to get away?"

Stella's patience was fast running out but taking in a deep breath she tried to remain calm as the last thing she wanted was another argument. Just lately it seemed that all her family did was fall out with each other and she'd had a gutful.

"It's none of your business who has paid and as for getting away, don't you think that after all this family have been through in the last few days we deserve a treat, I know I do or do you think I was just put on this earth to bleeding fetch and carry for you lot. I'm going down the travel agents in the morning and booking four flights to Spain, if you decide to come then great, if not then that's your loss."

With that Stella walked out of the room and her daughters could only stare at each other in silence. Even Daisy, who would have normally chased after her daughter with a few choice words, remained tight lipped. Alone in her bedroom Stella telephoned her son and explained all that had happened.

"Is Jane alright mum?"

"In all honesty? No but with her family around her she will be in time."

Stella proceeded to tell her son about the holiday and expecting the same response as she'd received from the others; she was surprised at Stevie's words.

"That sounds great Mum, just let me know when and what time."

"I will love but you don't think Jo will mind?"

"You know my Jo; she will be fine sweetheart, although what that stroppy mare Bianca will have to say is another matter."

Mother and son laughed out loud and when Stella hung up she felt on cloud nine. Walking across the bedroom she began to trawl through the wardrobe to find suitable clothes to take away with her. Deep down she knew she was trying to busy herself rather than face the real reason Tony wanted her out of the country. She was positive she had made it crystal clear that she didn't want her brother harmed and she just prayed that Tony would honour her request.

CHAPTER NINETEEN

The atmosphere in the bar the day after Dougie had received the threatening visitors had been very sombre and realising that something had happened Macy Langham had kept her head down and not asked any questions. Usually she could tell if the couple had been arguing, a pastime the two men seemed to be doing more and more of late. Their antics at Delphine's had started to get noticed by the customers and she had planned to have a word with Dougie and warn him but a gut feeling told her that for once this was probably a matter she shouldn't interfere in. By Monday morning her curiosity was getting the better of her and she was desperate to find out what had occurred. A bit of gossip would liven things up as it felt like all she'd been doing for the last few days was playing wet nurse to Anna and it was starting to get Macy down. The girl was sweet but a person could only hear 'but I love him' so many times before it started to wear thin. Macy was really beginning to worry about Anna's state of mind as she hadn't been to work since seeing that moron Miller out with his new bit of skirt. The girl wasn't bothering to get dressed, wasn't eating properly and just sat around the flat moping until the small hours with a vacant look in her eyes. Anna's boss Alan Mendham, was known in Soho for being a fair man to work for but even he wouldn't put up with it for long. The rent on the flat was due at the end of the week and if Anna didn't stump up her share then Macy didn't know what would happen. Maybe if she pulled Dougie to one side she could squeeze a couple of extra shifts out of him, after all he had always been good to her in the past. Deciding to bide her time and wait until she was sure that James wasn't about she began to do her daily cleaning. Suddenly from the flat above she heard screaming and shouting and plates being smashed. Those two were always at it like cats and dogs but never as bad as this, and where usually it was James doing the shouting, this time Dougie was taking the lead and standing up for himself. Macy couldn't think of a time when things had ever been this bad and she hoped that whatever it was, it would all soon blow over. The door from the upstairs flat suddenly flew open and James Nicholson came running into the bar. His face was tearstained and when he saw Macy he sneered back his lips.

"What are you fucking staring at, get back to work." James disappeared into the kitchen and Macy bowed her head as she scrubbed vigorously at some invisible stain on the wood plank floor. A few minutes later and Dougie appeared carrying a brief case, his facial expression was like thunder but when she looked up at him he was still able to manage a weak smile.

"Hi Dougie, everything ok love?"
He wasn't stupid and knew fine well that the woman had heard all the commotion of a few minutes ago, so walking towards the front door he ignored Macy's question.

"Can I have a quick word about my hours Dougie?"
"Sorry Macy but I've got a very important appointment to go to and I'm late as it is, you'll just have to ask James I'm sure he will sort it out."
With that her boss disappeared outside. Macy didn't want to ask James anything, the only trouble was she didn't have any choice so laying down her mop she headed for the kitchen and prayed that he was in a better mood. Her prayers weren't answered and as she pushed

188

open the swing doors James Nicholson was violently slashing at a lettuce. For a second he looked up and then once again brought the knife down onto the vegetable that was being so badly mutilated it would never actually end up on any of their diner's dinner plates.

"What?"

"Sorry to bother you James but Dougie said to have a word as he's a bit busy today."

"Of course he's busy; the bastard is about to sign away our future but as far as he's concerned it's nothing to do with me. Oh no, Dougie always has to have the last word, Dougie always knows best."

As Jamie's rant continued his assault on the lettuce speeded up and pieces began to fly all over the kitchen floor. Macy Langham was now having serious doubts about the man's sanity and decided at this point she wouldn't ask for extra hours. She turned to leave the kitchen but she wasn't getting off that lightly and stopped dead in her tracks when James shouted out.

"And just where do you think you're going to? I haven't finished talking yet!"

Macy rolled her eyes upwards and then turning around she uttered the sentence that would see her world fall apart.

"I didn't think you were in the best mood to be granting favours so maybe I'll leave it until later."

James slammed down the knife and stared coldly into Macy's eyes. She had always thought of the man as weak and a bit girly but right at this moment he was actually frightening her and Macy didn't usually scare that easily.

"And just who the fuck are you, to decide what kind of mood I'm in? You're nothing but an old slag who sold her body for money, well at least you did until you got so old and ugly that no one wanted you. If it hadn't have been for my Dougie you would be walking the fucking streets begging you old hag. I tell you what Macy Langham, instead of me doing you a favour I'm going to do myself one, you're sacked!"

Macy couldn't believe what she had just heard and for the few seconds that it took to register what he had said her mouth hung open in surprise.

"You what?"

"You heard me you old slag!"

"Please James I need this job, I won't be able to manage if I'm not working. My rent is due at the end of the week and........"

"Oh stop whining!"

"Please James I really need this....."

"Just fuck off out of here and don't bother trying to grovel your way around my husband because if he has to decide between me and you there won't be any contest."

Macy ran from the kitchen in a flood of tears and grabbing her bag and coat she fled the place that up until a minute ago had held such wonderful memories. Soho was beginning to get busy as all the businesses were starting to open up for the day but no one took any notice of the crying woman. No one stopped her to ask if she was alright but then Macy Langham didn't expect anything else. Soho was alive, vibrant and exciting; it was also at times the loneliest place in the world. Continuing to run as fast as her legs would carry her it didn't take long to reach the flat and closing the front door she went straight into her bedroom and slammed the door. Anna Hillman was lying on the sofa covered in a faux fur throw and feeling totally sorry for herself. She was expecting her flatmate to appear so that she could cry on her shoulder just like she had done every day since

190

she'd seen Tony with his other woman. After waiting a few minutes and when Macy still hadn't appeared Anna hauled herself from the sofa and went to find her friend. Knocking on Macy's bedroom door she waited to be invited in but when there was no answer she turned the handle and went inside anyway. Macy sat on the edge of the bed with her head in her hands and Anna could clearly see that the older woman was sobbing her heart out. Running over she dropped to her knees and took Macy in her arms.

"Whatever's the matter darling?"

"I've been sacked and I ain't got the foggiest idea how I'm going to pay the rent."

"Sacked but why? You love that job and you're bloody good at it. I thought the boss was a friend of yours?"

"He is but his husband hates me and it was James that fired me."

"Didn't your boss stick up for you?"

"He wasn't there."

"Well you'll just have to go back when he is, I'm sure he'll reinstate you."

Macy stared at Anna and at the same time she slowly shook her head.

"You are so bleeding naive Anna, there's no way Dougie will go against his partner no matter how much he disagrees with him. My job at Delphine's is history."

"Oh honey, don't cry we'll work something out."

Macy pushed Anna away and her eyes were cold and hard. Sniffing loudly, her tone was one of anger as she spoke.

"I sometimes fucking think you live in cloud cuckoo land Anna. The rent is due next week and I'm skint. You ain't been to work in ages and you're fucking lucky you still have a job though for how much longer I ain't sure.

Between us we ain't got a bleeding pot to piss in so don't insult me by saying 'we'll sort something out'. You know what Azam is like and he won't wait for his money, fuck me we could be out on the streets in a few days."

Her friend's words were like a wakeup call and for the first time in days Anna Hillman could see things more clearly. Standing up she began to pace up and down on the bedroom carpet and Macy didn't like the crazed look in the young woman's eyes.

"I'm not having this, do you hear me I'm not fucking having it!"

"Calm down Anna, it's me that's got the sack. I'm just worried that I won't be able to get another job; I mean who's going to take on a bleeding old pro like me. I've always given them two faggots all I could and at times I've worked my fucking fingers to the bone for no thanks. They think just because they paid me and not a lot I might add, they think a thank you is never needed."

Anna was still pacing and Macy wondered if the girl had heard a word she'd just said. Standing up she grabbed hold of Anna's arm and swung her around so that they were face to face.

"Anna!!!!"

"I'm alright Macy honest I am but I do think some payback is on the cards. I never told you what I did when my step father raped me did I?"

Macy Langham stared wide eyed but she didn't ask what Anna meant, in fact she really didn't want to know. Her lack of questioning went straight over Anna's head as the girl began to ramble on to herself.

"I was desperate for revenge but I was also patient and waited for the right opportunity. One night when I was confident that the bastard was as drunk as a skunk, I slipped into my mum's room where the pig laid snoring

192

his fucking head off. Mum was asleep on the couch downstairs on account of me putting four of her sleeping pills into her hot chocolate. He hadn't tried to wake her, just left here there, that was what he was like, the cunt! Anyway, as I went into the bedroom I was armed with a hammer and bread knife. I smacked him hard on the head twice and that alone should have killed him but just to make sure I unzipped his flies, pulled out his tackle and fucking cut it off. God there was so much blood and then the dirty fucker suddenly woke up and began screaming. That's when I ran away, I thought they would lock me up but then I heard that the old cunt had lived so finding me wasn't such a high priority. Shame really, I would have loved to have known I'd put the cunt six feet under. I left the house straight away but before I went I phoned the police, well I didn't want my mum to get the blame. No, don't you worry yourself Macy, those bastards will pay for what they've done to you and so will fucking Tony Miller for what he did to me. Now I'm going to my room to think and make plans."

Anna kissed her friend on the cheek and then disappeared through the door. Macy had never seen the girl act like this and the look in Anna's eyes was scary. Macy Langham started to panic but there was nothing she could do. She knew it would be impossible to talk Anna around, when the girl got something into her head there was no reasoning with her. Of course Macy could warn them but then there really was no reason why she would want too, not after what they'd done to her. Going to the police was definitely out of the question so for now all she could do was to sit back and wait to see what Anna had planned and she just prayed that the girl wouldn't take things too far. Hopefully she would calm down and by the morning after she'd had time to reflect she would realise that it was all getting out of hand.

It was raining heavily when Dougie Nicholson arrived at his solicitors in Great Russell Street ten minutes after his scheduled appointment. Ever since opening Delphine's he had used the firm and had always found them to be very professional and today of all days he needed the best help he could get. Walking into the reception area he placed his umbrella in the stand and hung up his coat. He was also full of apologies but it wasn't necessary as Thomas Hughes, his personal solicitor, was a long standing friend not to mention ex lover and he was still very fond of Dougie even if the feeling wasn't returned. Taking a seat on the opposite side of the desk to Thomas he bit down on his bottom lip and waited for his friend to begin. Dougie's nerves were in tatters and he just wanted everything done and dusted so that he could tell those bullies when they returned that he had carried out their instructions. He was still having trouble believing that his sister could resort to such measures but then in all honesty she was probably more like their father than anyone and Wilf had been the biggest bastard that ever walked this earth.

"Good morning my old friend it's a pleasure to see you." Dougie thought back to the first time the two had met. Thomas was fresh out of law school and even fresher to Soho's gay scene. The pair instantly hit it off and had soon become a couple but back then Dougie was promiscuous and he couldn't stay faithful to one man much to his lovers dislike and it had broke poor Thomas's heart. Things had fizzled out six months later and Dougie had moved on to pastures new, in fact over the years he'd had many new pastures or at least he had until he met James. Thomas Hughes on the other hand had never formed a relationship with anyone else, oh he

194

had a regular sex life and often hired the services of a rent boy but no one had ever touched his heart like Dougie Nicholson.

"So Doug, what brings you here today?"

"Oh Thomas darling, I'm in a right fucking pickle and no mistake. You know I haven't had anything to do with my family for years?"

Thomas nodded his head, he was well aware of Dougie's background and it had been a sad affair all round.

"The old man passed away a couple of weeks ago and he left me a couple of shops, shops that are worth a considerable amount of money I might add. Anyway, it didn't go down so well with my sister and her kids and now I've got some gangster on my back threatening all sorts if I don't hand everything back to Stella."

"My dear friend, I really don't think it's me you should be talking to, you should go to the police. People can't just get away with making threats in this day and age you know."

Dougie frantically ran his hand through his hair.

"You don't understand! These men are above the law, men you really wouldn't wish to have any dealings with."

Thomas sat back in his chair and studied his old friend.

"If I didn't know you better I'd say you were scared!"

"Scared? That's an understatement, now can I sign things over, is it possible?"

Thomas Hughes sighed and nodded his head.

"Everything is possible but you do understand that once it's done then there's no going back? I mean you can't stroll in here in a couple of month's time and say you've made a mistake."

"I might be a lot of things Thomas but stupid isn't one of them. All I want is for these people to leave me alone and the only way that is going to happen is if I agree to their terms. What do I have to do?"

"Not a lot really. I will prepare a letter for you to sign and once I have your sister's details it could all be arranged relatively quickly. If you would like to make an appointment for next week we should have things sorted by then."

Dougie Nicholson stared wide eyed and panic was evident in his voice as he spoke.

"I can't wait until next week Thomas! I need this done within a couple of days. Oh please you've got to help me; I really really have no time to waste!"

Dougie's solicitor couldn't believe the fear he was witness to. Whoever was threatening his friend had done a splendid job. Thomas also knew that if they could put the fear of god into Dougie Nicholson then they were more than capable of paying his firm a visit and that was the last thing he wanted.

"Calm down Dougie! Leave all the paperwork with me and I'll get the ball rolling today. Now who has the title deeds and whose name are they in?"

"Mine I think or at least they are in the process of being changed by the firm of solicitors that drew up the Will."

"Pop back tomorrow afternoon and I should have everything ready for you to sign. In the mean time if I need anything else I will call you."

Dougie sat back in his chair and sighed with relief though he wouldn't be completely content until it was all over. Thanking his friend he left the building and deciding that he really couldn't face James and another row, he walked the streets of Soho for over an hour. It always calmed him down and being known by many of the traders he stopped to chat to several on the way. The sun was now shining and as he walked he put things into perspective. He was in the same place as he'd been two weeks ago

196

and if his life was good enough for him then it was certainly good enough now. Sometimes money had a way of spoiling things and he realised that maybe he'd had a lucky escape. Stopping to buy a bunch of red roses he then set off for Delphine's and the serious amount of grovelling that he knew it would take to get James back on side. Maybe he would book a meal for two in a fancy restaurant, anything so long as his husband was happy again. Removing his phone from his pocket he dialled Macy's number in the hope that she would do an extra shift tonight so that the couple could go out. When she saw who was calling Macy breathed out a sigh of relief.

"I knew you'd phone Dougie, I knew you wouldn't agree with him."

"What are you talking about Macy?"

"James sacked me, said you wouldn't take me back and that if it came to me or him it would always be him." Dougie couldn't believe what he was hearing; things seemed to be going from bad to worse.

"It's the first I've heard about any of this love, leave it with me and I'll have a word with him and get back to you."

With that Dougie Nicholson hung up. He liked Macy, liked her a lot in fact but he sensed that this time he would have to go along with James and let her go. How things were at the moment it must have seemed to James that Dougie was undermining him at every opportunity so this time he couldn't go against James. The thought pained Dougie but at the end of the day his marriage was more important to him than anything in the world.

CHAPTER TWENTY

D day had finally arrived and Dougie Nicholson was a bundle of nerves. Tony Miller's heavies had said they would come back and he was in no doubt that they would, he was also more frightened than he'd ever been in his entire life. He tried to busy himself with the cleaning that was now an added daily chore since James had dismissed Macy but it wasn't helping to calm him. The atmosphere between James and Dougie was still frosty and he knew that when the heavies arrived his husband would disappear in an instant. At exactly eleven am the front door to Delphine's swung open and Harry Chrome and his side kick Gazza entered. They strolled up to the bar without a care in the world and the sight angered Dougie though he didn't dare utter a word. This time he was actually taken in by the enormity of their size and just what level of damage they could possibly do.

"Morning sunshine, get that little bit of business sorted out did you?"

Dougie slammed the paperwork down onto the bar and for a second but only that, tried to stare Harry out but when the man wasn't fazed in the least he lowered his eyes.

"That's a good lad; my boss will be over the moon. See, when you do as you're fucking told there's no need for anyone to get nasty. How about something to eat before we go?"

Dougie couldn't believe the cheek of the man, they had fleeced him out of a fortune and now they wanted feeding as well! This time Dougie found the courage to stand up to Harry but as he spoke he could feel himself tremble.

"We're closed!"

198

Harry Chrome and Gary Wilson burst out laughing and Dougie's face instantly turned crimson with embarrassment and anger. How dare they treat him with such disrespect, how dare they just storm in here and take away all that was rightfully his.

"I hope you and your so called Boss can sleep at night but then I don't suppose Tony Miller has ever lost sleep over anything in his entire life has he?"

Harry suddenly stopped laughing and studied the man closely. Not once had he mentioned Tony's name and he wondered how the queer knew who was behind the threat. Harry took a menacing step forward and as he did so Dougie took a step backwards.

"I hope for your fucking sake that you ain't been in contact with the Old Bill or you are going to have trouble like you wouldn't believe sunshine. Come on Gazza let's get out of here! We wouldn't want to indulge anyway; you never know what diseases are around, not when faggots are preparing the fucking food!"

The anger on Dougie's face was still evident but his lips remained tightly shut. When he was once again alone he breathed out a sigh of relief but when he glanced down at his hands he could see that they were shaking uncontrollably. Turning around he poured a very large measure of brandy and downed it in one just as James made an appearance.

"Decided to finally show your face did you?"

"I really don't think it's a good idea for you to be drinking before those bullies even get here Dougie?"

"They've already been and gone so you can stop nagging me alright."

Without even looking at his partner Dougie poured himself another drink and James just shook his head. If this was how things were going to be from now on then

199

he would really have to do some serious thinking regarding his relationship. Dougie was alright to be around when he was dishing out the cash and falling over backwards to please James but this nasty rude side of him was unacceptable and James wasn't going to stand for it.

When Tony's men arrived back at the yard Jumbo Smith was drinking a cup of tea while looking out of his caravan window. It had been a busy morning and he was making the most of a well earned ten minute rest but he instantly removed his ledger when he saw the car pull up. Removing a pencil that conveniently sat behind his ear he began to jot down notes of who was in the car and strangely, his own inner feelings regarding what he could only imagine the men had been up to. There was no telling what that manic Harry had been doing but he still noted all of the men's comings and goings, times and dates, in fact anything that he thought could possibly curry favour with the law if it was needed. Yesterday he had seen and logged them bringing in three shotguns and a hack saw which they placed inside the old dilapidated steel building at the rear of the cabin. All afternoon he could hear them cutting and grinding and Jumbo knew that little snippet of information would make for very interesting reading should the need ever arise. Harry made his way straight to the office but didn't go in; instead he knocked and waited for an invite. Tony was a stickler for his men obeying orders and Harry could remember a time when one of the younger firm members had forgotten his position and walked straight into the office. The lad's name was Pete and after Tony had beaten him almost senseless he had never made the same mistake again.

"Enter!"

Harry walked over and laying an official looking letter

onto Tony's desk, stood there grinning like a Cheshire cat.

"All present and correct Boss."

"What's this, where's the deeds?"

"It's a letter from the queers brief saying that all the relevant paperwork has been filed. The creepy cunt said that it takes time but that this was an assurance that it had all been done and I might add, without any bleeding bother which makes a change. Shame really as I was looking forward to slapping that pair of poof's, they really give me the creeps with all that arse shagging, it's not fucking normal Boss."

Tony laughed, it was good to have his men alert and up for a spot of bother.

"I'm sure something will happen soon and you'll be required to flex your muscles but for now keep your powder dry. Oh and Harry, by the way, a fucking good job done mate."

"There was just one thing Boss, the poofter knew your name and I definitely didn't mention you personally. Do you think he's contacted the law?"

Tony wasn't worried, Dougie might be queer but at the end of the day he was still an East Ender and knew the score. No, it was just a case of Stella explaining things that was all.

"No Harry it's all good and thanks again for a job well done."

Harry left the office with a spring in his step. He adored his boss and loved to keep him happy. Tony on the other hand couldn't stand the man but Harry was good muscle to have around and until he found a replacement he would keep the man close to him. The trouble with Tony Miller was the fact that he was always looking for something bigger and better and that included his staff.

Picking up the telephone he dialled the villa and was impatient when his call wasn't answered straight away. He paid a fortune each year to keep the place staffed with a cook, cleaner, pool man and security and he was now wondering if a visit was in order to let them know just who they worked for if they didn't start pulling their weight.

"Hello?"

"About fucking time Carla, it's Mr Miller. I want to speak to Stella."

"Miss Stella not here, gone to market."

"Well make sure you ask her to ring me when she gets back. Oh and Carla, don't make me fucking wait so long next time I call!"

With that the line went dead and Tony was far from pleased. The peasants that he hired seemed like they were taking the piss and no one took the piss out of Tony Miller. Within the hour Stella had called back. She sounded relaxed and full of life and he wished that he could have been there with her.

"Hi babe how's it going?"

"Oh Tony it's fabulous. Never in my wildest dreams did I think you would have a place like this. My kids love it."

"Glad to hear it. Now everything went to plan and by the time you get back the shops will be yours."

"Mine?"

"It had to be that way, what you choose to do with them is up to you. Enjoy the rest of your stay and you owe me big time lady. I think I might take my payment in kind. See you soon."

Stella began to laugh but when she realised the line was now silent she placed the telephone back into its cradle and went outside to tell her son the good news.

202

Stevie, Jane and Ronnie were lying by the infinity pool and they all looked up as Stella coughed loudly.

"Right you lot, as nice as it's been it's now time to go back home to reality."

"I haven't got a home to go to."

Stella turned to face her daughter and her heart went out to Jane.

"You will always have a home with me; or come to that, with any of us. We are family Jane and don't you ever forget that darling. Son, can I have a quiet word please love?"

Stevie walked over to his mother and she lovingly placed her hand onto his shoulder.

"I can't go into any great detail at the moment as I'm not a hundred percent sure exactly what has gone on, what I can tell you is that the shops will be remaining in our little family and your businesses are safe. We'll talk more when we get home. Come on you two or are both your arses glued to those seats?"

When her daughters slowly got up from the sun loungers and solemnly walked towards the villa Stella laughed out loud. She had enjoyed the last few days like never before but now it was time to get back to their lives and in all honesty Stella had missed Daisy and the rest of her brood and if she was totally honest she had also missed London. Micky Mackerson kept invading her mind and as much as she tried she couldn't dismiss him from her thoughts. He would have loved this place and deep down she would have loved being here with him. Stella didn't understand what was happening to her, on one hand she had got back with the supposed love of her life who just happened to have a shed load of money not to mention a fabulous apartment and this place, but something deep inside was telling her it was all wrong. Tony had abandoned her when she needed him most whereas Micky had been there through thick and thin. He had never cared what she did or didn't have or even how she had looked, Micky had loved her for her. When she got home to London Stella knew that she had some serious thinking to do.

Anna Hillman had called her employer and told him she would be back at work for the evening shift that night. She apologised for being under the weather and luckily for her Alan Mendham was a forgiving sort and welcomed the young woman back with open arms. Hearing through the grapevine all that had happened between Anna and Tony, Alan couldn't help but feel somewhat responsible and he deeply regretted the wager he'd had with Tony. The girl was sweet and Tony was well out of order for giving her the run around. Alan also knew that to say anything to Tony Miller would result in the end of a long and very lucrative friendship, not to mention the possibility of a visit from big Harry Chrome. The Miller firm were excellent businessmen and while things were going well they made good friends but Alan had been witness to Tony's wrath on several occasions and he didn't want to ever be on the receiving end of it himself.

Like she had never been away, Anna took her seat behind the booth and served each punter in a professional and friendly manner but when she wasn't busy she was mentally planning her next move. She wasn't worried about dealing with the gays but when it came down to Tony it was a different matter. Everything had to be done with military precision if she was never to be suspected. Anna wanted the man to suffer but she wasn't stupid and knew that if he found out she was responsible, then her life would be on the line and at the very best she would never feel safe again and would constantly be looking over her shoulder. At one am and when the streets had at last started to quieten down Alan appeared at the front of the booth.

"I'm off now love. Give it a half hour and if there's not much doing you can close up. I think the clubs are starting to fill up so no one is interested in having a look at the girls now. Bernie will stay with you until then." Alan slid the keys to the roller shutter under the glass partition.

"Pop them through the letterbox before you go. Night love!"

"Goodnight Mr Mendham."

Alan smiled at her words but he could see the sadness in Anna's eyes and it was a crying shame as she was such a nice girl, still there was nothing he could do to fix things and he only hoped that in time she would be back to her old self and view it all as a lesson learnt. Things were working out perfectly and as soon as her boss disappeared out of sight Anna put the closed sign up on the glass. Bernie Samuel was a large man of Caribbean descent who wasn't much interested in doing any work but his sheer size made sure that there wasn't any trouble and in all honesty that was the only reason Alan Mendham allowed the man to continue in his employ. Anna let herself out of the booth and making her way out back told the two girls who were inside the glass box's that they could go home early. They were both on their way in seconds and Anna then went to the small staff toilet where she collected her handbag and Jacket. Bending down she picked up the two litre bottle of drain cleaner. Due to its industrial strength this particular product was now banned in the UK but was regularly purchased on the black market to clear the drains

whenever they got a blockage which was often the case at
'Take A Look'. Reading the label she smiled when she
saw the words 'ninety nine percent Sulphuric acid'.
Laying her jacket over her arm to disguise the bottle
Anna switched off all the lights and made her way
outside. Handing Bernie the keys she asked him to lock
up and he didn't argue as it meant he could get home a bit
earlier for once. The area was still noisy with punters and
club goers who were standing outside the bars drinking
and chatting. Anna was oblivious to the many whistles
and chat up lines that were called out as she passed and
she continued to walk the short distance home with a
broad grin on her face. The first part of her plan had been
achieved and now all she had to do was decide when and
where to take action and make the guilty culprits pay.
Letting herself into the flat Anna crept about as she didn't
want to wake up Macy. The last thing she needed was
for her lodger to see any evidence and start asking
questions. To all that met her, Anna Hillman came across
as sweet and gentle but nothing was further from the
truth. She was sly and cunning and had a cruel streak
that could rival that of her former lover. Once inside her
bedroom she hid the acid in the bottom of her wardrobe
and at the same time retrieved the wash bag that sat on
the bottom shelf and contained all of her old medication.
Rummaging about inside, she pulled out two containers
of sleeping tablets. One was Temazepam and the other
Diazepam and both were at least two years old. Anna
had experienced insomnia for a short while after
accepting the job with Alan as the shifts were all over the
place so she had sought out some cheap tablets to help
her relax. Few people that lived in Soho ever purchased
their medication from a chemists as most items could be
bought on the black market for a lot less money than the

cost of a prescription. After two nights and suffering a couple of nasty side effects Anna had given up on the tablets and decided to let nature take its course. It had only taken a few days before she was back into her old ways by learning to sleep the natural way and allowing her body clock to adjust on its own. Now Anna was so glad that she hadn't disposed of the pills as they would be perfect for her needs. Popping into the kitchen she pulled a clear plastic food bag from the roll and looked around for something to crush the pills with. Picking up an empty wine bottle she made her way back towards the bedroom but Macy's light came on just as Anna was about to close her door. Stuffing the items under her covers she started to undress as Macy tapped and walked in. Her flat mate was wearing an old fashioned winceyette nightdress and when she yawned loudly Anna could also see that she wasn't wearing her dentures.

"You alright Anna love? How did it go?"

"Fine thanks, I'm just a bit tired that's all. How are you feeling now Macy?"

"Still just as gutted but it's nothing for you to worry about, now get your head down darling and I'll see you on the morning. Goodnight love."

"Night Macy."

Waiting to hear the toilet flush and when she was sure that Macy was back in her room Anna continued with her task. Emptying both containers of pills into the plastic bag she took a seat on the floor and began to move the wine bottle back and forth. It didn't take long for all the tablets to turn to powder and when she was happy that there were no lumps Anna placed the bag back into the bottom of her wardrobe. It was a job well done but now she would have to wait until the morning before she could make her move. Checking her list she saw that it would be a very full day, she was due at work by twelve so her first assault would have to take place in the morning. Macy had told her that the queers started getting ready for opening at around ten o'clock so the timing couldn't have been better. Laying in the dark her imagination ran wild, the anger was still as strong and she told herself that revenge would be sweet. As Anna Hillman drifted off to sleep there was just the slightest glimpse of a smile upon her lips.

CHAPTER TWENTY ONE

It was the final few hours in Marbella for the Nicholson clan and boy was Stella making the most of things. The day they arrived had been a real eye opener regarding how the other half lived and Stevie couldn't believe that his old man actually owned a property of this magnitude and splendour. A limousine had been sent to collect them from the airport and when it pulled up outside the palatial villa there had been gasps all round from the occupants inside the car. The first thing they saw was the grounds which were magnificent and when Ronnie noticed the uninterrupted sea view she squealed with delight. The main house was vast with a grand balcony that ran along the whole width of the property. When they entered through a set of highly polished double doors they were greeted by three staff members who were there to wait hand and foot on the family. The housekeeper introduced herself as Carla, next was Jose the gardener and pool cleaner and finally Maria the cook. Stevie thought he lived the high life but it was nothing compared to this and for a second he wished Jo could have been here with him. "Fuck me Mum, have a look at this little lot!"
Ronnie and Jane were already poking their noses into the first doorway leading off from the large imposing hallway and as they gasped at the splendour Stella couldn't help but laugh. After they were shown to their rooms to freshen up they met at the pool side where an array of cocktails had been prepared for them to sample. The housekeeper, Carla Santiago, had been given strict instructions by Tony to treat his guests like royalty and when they were invited into the dining room and served a feast of lobster and steak Stella knew that she could

easily get used to a lifestyle like this. The days were spent sunbathing and just resting up and in all honesty they had no inclination to leave the villa or the grounds it stood in. On their arrival Stella had banned any conversation regarding Wilf's Will, this holiday was for rest and enjoyment only. Now all too soon it was coming to an end and as Stella packed her case she was a little down hearted. By eleven Spanish time and one hour ahead of British summer time the Nicholson's were once again at the airport waiting for their return flight home. Stella studied her daughter and noticed how well Jane's bruises had healed over the last week, time eventually healed most things and for that Stella was grateful. Sitting at the departure gate she noticed that the jovial chatter of their arrival was now gone and it was just a quiet sombre time for them all to reflect and think about what life would hold for them once they were back in London. Stella was deep in thought weighing up the pro's and con's between Tony and Micky, and Stevie still couldn't stop worrying about the shops even after his mother had reassured him. Then there was poor Jane who didn't have a clue where she was going to live, the only one who seemed to be happy at the thought of heading home was Ronnie; as unlike the others she was more than happy with her lot.

In London Anna Hillman had been up with the larks and couldn't wait to get started. The first thing she did was pop down to Lemon's butchers on the corner of Romilly Street to get a pound of best braising steak. Anna asked for the meat to be cubed and then returning to the flat she placed the meat into the bag of powdered sleeping pills and gave it a good shake. Glancing at the bedside clock she saw that it was a quarter to ten and it was now time to make a move. Going to her bag she removed rubber gloves, a pair of safety glasses and a bottle of washing up liquid that she'd purchased the previous night at the local Spar shop. Putting on the gloves and glasses Anna then went into the bathroom where she proceeded to empty the contents of the washing up bottle down the sink and then carefully refilled it with the acid. Anna wiped away any overspill and for a second she worried that the bottle might melt but when it didn't she breathed a sigh of relief. Stashing the excess sulphuric acid in the bottom of her wardrobe she then set about packing her shoulder bag in readiness. Macy wasn't about which pleased Anna but at the same time she just hoped the woman wasn't anywhere near Delphine's when she carried out her revenge. Leaving the flat Anna reached Brewer Street in good time and as she strolled along she looked as if she didn't have a care in the world, the sun was shining and even though what she was about to do was sickening, Anna was excited at the thought that justice would soon be done. She had never been into Delphine's but she did know where it was and reaching the posh fronted facade she hesitated for a second before taking a deep breath and finally pushing open the front door. Anna wasn't bothered about anyone seeing her, she'd lived in Soho long enough to know that people kept themselves to themselves and didn't get involved in anyone else's business. The bar area appeared to be empty as she made her way up to the counter. Dougie and James had been rowing nonstop since yesterday and now the couple were trying as hard as they could to stay out of each other's way. James was in the kitchen prepping for lunch and Dougie as usual was kneeling behind the bar restocking the shelves. To begin with Anna thought that the place was deserted but when she heard a slight clink of bottles she peered over the

counter top just as Dougie Nicholson looked up. Anna
proceeded to remove the gloves and glasses from her bag
and all the while Dougie just stared up in a bemused way
at the strange woman.
"Can I help you love, what's going on?"
Anna ignored him and grabbing the squeezy bottle,
moved in close as she took aim. The liquid shot out from
the container in a powerful jet and Dougie leant back as
he tried to protect his face with his hands but it was to no
avail and the acid hit its intended target directly in the
face and splashing down onto his shoulders. As soon as
the liquid touched his skin the screams began and Anna
quickly removed the safety glasses and gloves then
turned on her heels and ran from Delphine's. Once
outside she composed herself so as not to attract any
unwanted attention. Hearing the noise James pushed on
the kitchen door and peeked into the restaurant, he was a
complete coward and after the earlier visit from the
gangsters he wasn't about to take any chances. Dougie
was still screaming and James, after checking that the
coast was clear, ran behind the bar. His hand flew up to
his mouth and his face grimaced in horror at the sight that
greeted him. Dougie's skin appeared to be melting in
front of James's eyes, his hair on the right side had
disappeared and the stench was horrendous. For a few
seconds James was mesmerised but when Dougie reached
out a hand in a gesture that was begging for help, James
moved closer to his husband and led him over to the
small sink they used to wash the glasses. Dougie
couldn't see and just stood there screaming, panic had set
in and he was going into shock. James quickly turned on
the cold tap and began to splash as much water as he
could in the direction of his husbands face, the relief was
instant but short lived as the damage had already been

done. As gently as he could James steered Dougie's head down closer towards the basin so that the running water could continue to do its job. Pulling his mobile from his trouser pocket he then called for an ambulance. His words were babbled for a few seconds making no sense at all but the operator was well trained and managed to calm him. When asked what had happened, James said he didn't know but that the skin on his husbands face was peeling away and that he'd poured water onto the wounds but it didn't seem to be helping much. The tap was still running but as Dougie was still screaming James was struggling to hear what was being asked. The nonstop questions were pointless anyway as he really didn't know what or who had caused this horrific act. The operator informed James that he had done the right thing and to continue with the water until the ambulance arrived. Ten minutes later and when he didn't think he could take anymore of Dougie's screaming, the front door flew open and two paramedics rushed in. They knew instantly that is was a chemical injury and surmised that it was probably acid of some kind. Dougie's face had been under the cold running water for over ten minutes and as gently as they could they guided him away and down onto the floor where he was then heavily sedated. After asking for a larger volume of water, one of the paramedics followed James through to the kitchen where they both filled up giant steel mixing bowls and carried them back into the bar. The process of rinsing off the acid began again and after James had run back and forth several times with more and more water the highly polished restaurant floor resembled a lake. When he at last stopped and stared down at his husband James was repulsed, even more of Dougie's hair and skin had disappeared and when he heard one of the say that the ear

213

cartilage had been destroyed, James ran into the toilets to vomit. He eventually returned just as they were about to put Dougie into the ambulance and locking the restaurants front door James climbed inside the vehicle. He didn't want to go but he had to be seen to be standing by his husband, at least for the moment. Inside the accident and emergency department it was all hands on deck and James was led into the relative's room. He didn't have a clue what was going on and it fleetingly crossed his mind that Dougie might even die. The thought didn't break his heart and for a moment he imagined selling the restaurant and moving abroad. When the door eventually opened two hours later he was instantly on his feet as the doctor entered.

"Mr Nicholson?"

"Yes?"

"Your partner is..."

"My husband!"

"I am sorry to have to tell you that your husband has suffered some serious facial injuries. He will survive, but the injuries will be life changing both physically and emotionally."

"What do you mean life changing?"

Doctor Phillips gently led James over to a small leather sofa that had long since seen better days and after they had both taken a seat the doctor slowly began to speak. "Unfortunately whatever was thrown into Mr Nicholson's face was extremely strong. We suspect that it was sulphuric acid but can't be sure. The cartilage to his right ear was all but destroyed along with the right eyelid. His sight in both eyes has been severely affected but to what degree we won't know for several days. His scalp and part of his left cheek were burnt away and he will need many skin grafts over several months, now I know......"

John Phillips stopped talking when James burst into tears. Not wanting to be accused of being blunt and unfeeling, Doctor Phillips gave a weak smile and walked towards the door.

"I'll leave you in peace to take in all that I've said; when your husband is more comfortable I'll send a nurse to fetch you."

When the plane touched down at Gatwick Airport the mood of the Nicholson family was still very sombre. Not one of them, and that now included Ronnie, was happy to be home and the drizzling rain did little to lift their spirits. As the taxi pulled out into the lunchtime traffic they stared out of the windows and barely a word was spoken until they reached the flats on Roy Street and Stella had paid the fair.

"Well here we are again you happy campers, time to get back to reality. Are you lot coming up for a cuppa?"

"Thanks mum but I need to get home to Jo and the kids."

"What about you Ronnie?"

"I think I'll get off as well. You staying here Jane, or are you coming back to mine?"

Stella had a puzzled look on her face as she stared at both her daughters in turn. Ronnie knew when her mum was getting the nark so she decided to just spit out what the two sisters had discussed while they had been in Spain.

"Look mum, we were talking and to be honest you've got enough on your plate with Nan and..."

"I'll say when I've got enough going on thank you very much Veronica. Jane needs to stay strong and stay away from that wanker Roger and if she's here with me I can make sure of that."

"I know she does but being with me, Sam and the kids, well let's face it mum, sometimes it's like gods waiting room up in that flat. Jane needs noise and life around her,

215

not two old women going on and on about what a complete tosser the old man was."

"Well thanks a fucking bunch and for your information Veronica, I ain't drawing my bleeding pension yet! Stella had heard enough and picking up her suitcase marched towards the stairwell. It wasn't that she wanted Jane living with her, lord above knew that there wasn't enough room to swing a cat in the flat as it was. What had really hurt was being called old, she didn't feel old and realising that her kids saw her as that was like a slap in the face. Her daughters knew their mother well enough to know that apologising now would do no good at all and it would be best to just let her mull it over for a couple of days. By the time Stella reached her front door she was worn out, the travelling had taken its toll and as much as it stuck in her craw to admit it, she was beginning to wonder if Ronnie was right after all. Stepping inside she called out.

"I'm home! Mum?"

Stopping in her tracks she listened and when she heard muffled sobs Stella let go of her case and it fell to the floor as she ran into the front room. Dropping to her knees in front of Daisy she tenderly took the older woman's hands in hers as she stared into her mother's eyes.

"Oh mum, whatever's the matter darling?"

Daisy didn't reply and when she felt the warmth of her daughter's hands she began to sob even harder. Stella didn't push things and waited patiently for her mother's tears to subside. A couple of minutes later Daisy sniffed loudly and wiped her eyes with the back of her hand. Taking in a deep breath she stared hard in Stella's direction as she spoke.

"It's Dougie! Oh Stella, James phoned a little while ago

216

and someone has hurt my boy, hurt him real bad."

"Who hurt him mum?"

"I don't know but James was crying when he called and I couldn't get a lot of sense out of him."

Stella didn't wait to hear more and pulling out her mobile she ordered a mini cab from the local firm down the road. Within ten minutes the two women were on their way to the University College Hospital, thankfully Daisy had remembered to ask where they had taken her son and for that Stella was grateful. After telephoning Daisy, James had mooched about and when he was escorted to the treatment room to see Dougie he felt scared at what he was going to find. His fears were founded as his husband resembled something out of a horror film. Still sedated, Dougie didn't know that he was being gazed upon with disgust. As James stared down he instantly came to a decision, there was no way he could ever care for this man, no way he could even bear to look at Dougie let alone anything else. Making a decision on the spot James left the hospital and hailing a taxi made his way back to Delphine's. Stuffing as many of his clothes as possible into a suitcase, he opened the safe and took out his passport and the entire weeks takings. Seeing the credit cards he hesitated for a moment and then grabbed all four and placed them into his back pocket as he reasoned it would be a while before anyone knew they were gone and there was enough credit available to set himself up somewhere nice. As he closed the front door to Delphine's he felt nothing but relief and hailing a cab for the second time that day, asked to be taken to Heathrow airport. After all the aggravation of the last couple of weeks, James Nicholson was now looking forward to the future and any thoughts regarding his husband and all the pain and suffering that Dougie was going through, had

217

already been pushed to the back of his mind.

CHAPTER TWENTY TWO

Within half an hour of Stella arriving home from Spain, she and Daisy were being dropped off outside the accident and emergency department of University College hospital. The building was vast and in the mid afternoon sun the massive glass panels that covered most of the outside had a green hue that was strangely comforting. Entering through the electronic doors they made their way to the reception and as soon as Stella explained who they had come to see the two women were escorted along a corridor and then into a small side room. Dougie lay motionless in bed and seeing the state of her son instantly made Daisy burst into tears. Stella gripped her mother's shoulder with one hand while wiping away her own tears with the other.

"For god's sake Mum, whatever's been going on?" Daisy could only shake her head in despair.

"Mum you stay here and I'll go and find a doctor. Hold his hand love; they say people can hear you even when they're asleep so talk to him and tell him we all love him."

Through sobs Daisy Nicholson nodded her head and as Stella walked out of the door she could hear her mother muttering comforting words into her brother's ear.

"It's alright my boy, your old mum is here now and she's going to take right good care of you darling."

Making her way back out into the corridor Stella stopped the first nurse that passed by and asked if she could speak to a doctor. Right at that moment finding out what happened to her brother was more important than anything; although she had a feeling she already knew who was responsible. Doctor Phillips soon approached and after steering Stella into the relative's room, relayed for the second time that day how serious Dougie's injuries were. Listening intently, Stella bit down on her bottom lip as she tried to take it all in.

"He's had acid thrown over him! Oh my god! how could someone do such a thing?"

It was a rhetorical question and the doctor could only stand there like a spare part waiting for the woman to speak again.

"Did his partner come in with him?"

"If you mean Mr Nicholson's husband, then yes he did but I saw him leave the hospital a short while ago."

"That's just typical!"

Stella thanked the doctor for all that he was doing to help her brother and then made her way outside to the rear open space where the ambulances parked. It wasn't cold, but she still pulled the collar of her coat up as she took a seat on one of the benches. Fishing in her pocket she removed her telephone and after staring at the screen for several seconds, she finally dialled James's number. It was answered after a couple of rings but she was instantly on her guard when she heard the man's snappy tone.

"Yes?"

"James its Stella, where are you?"

"Not that it's got anything to do with you but I'm on my way to Mexico. I've left the restaurant keys with Billy who runs the newsagents over the road."

"I beg your Pardon?"

"You heard me. If you thought for one second that I was going to stay around to be a wet nurse to that ugly disfigured man I have the misfortune to call my husband, you can think again. I was looking for a way out and as sorry as I am that Dougie got hurt, I can't hang around to be with someone that I would end up hating. I suppose in

220

a way it's been a blessing, well for me at least. You shouldn't have interfered Stella, if we had received Dougie's inheritance then none of this would have happened. When it comes down to it Stella, this is all your fault and it's your duty to pick up the pieces not mine. See how well you manage caring for him!"
Stella couldn't believe what she was hearing and suddenly a thought crossed her mind.
"It wasn't you was it?"
"Wasn't me what?"
"You didn't do this to my brother did you; you didn't throw acid at him?"
Stella heard him gasp on the other end and wondered if he would now hang up on her but thankfully he didn't.
"I can't believe you could even think that I would be capable of such a thing, I might be a lot of things Stella but I'm definitely not sadistic. I think you need to look a little closer to home as it was most likely one of your gangster friends. I mean they've already threatened us but you already know about that don't you?"
Stella didn't respond to the accusation, she was feeling guilty enough already with the thought that it might have been Tony. Now as James firmly laid the blame at her door it made her feel totally responsible for all of this pain and heartbreak. Deciding to change tactics she continued with another question.
"What about the restaurant?"
"Do what you like with it; I doubt very much it will be busy from now on, not with Dougie looking like an extra from a hammer house of horror movie. I mean, it's enough to put anyone off of their food."
"Why you nasty little bastard, I never did like......"
Stella stopped speaking when she realised that he had hung up. Her poor Dougie would be heart broken when
221

he found out he'd been dumped and as usual it would be down to Stella to relay the bad news when he woke up. Sighing heavily she dialled Tony's number not really knowing what she was going to say but at the same time feeling the rage that was beginning to build up inside. Whatever it took she would get to the bottom of this, she had to if she ever wanted to feel any peace again.

"Hi Tony, it's me."

"Hello sexy, did you have a good holiday?"

"Fucking good holiday! In answer to your question no I fucking did not."

"Why, didn't my staff take care of you all? Just wait until I speak to fucking Carla again, I'm really sorry about that Stella, I wanted you all to have a good rest."

"You're an evil cunt Tony Miller!"

For a second there was only silence as he couldn't quite believe what he'd just heard.

"What did you just call me?"

"You heard me! I knew you were capable of a lot of things Tony but hurting someone in such a barbaric way wasn't one of them, especially when that person just happens to be my brother. I asked you not to lay a hand on Dougie but I suppose that's the only way thugs like you know how to deal with a problem."

"Hurt your bother? Stella I haven't got the foggiest idea what you're on about girl but I don't appreciate being called a cunt by anyone and that includes you! Come round to the office and we can talk about it."

"Fuck off Tony; I never want to lay eyes on you again you bastard!"

With that Stella switched off her telephone and made her way back inside. She was still shaking with anger when she saw Daisy sitting alone in the corridor. Instantly she went into panic mode and began to run the rest of the way. It was only a short distance but she hadn't run for years and when she reached her mother she was panting heavily.

"What's wrong, what's happened? Oh Mum, please tell me that he isn't....."

"Of course he bloody ain't! He's just woken up that's all, but oh Stella he's in so much pain. I've never heard a human being scream in such a way, it sent bleeding chills right through me I can tell you. The doctor is in with him now; I think they're giving him some strong pain killers or at least I hope they are because the poor sod can't carry on like that."

A few minutes later they were both escorted back into the room by a nurse. Dougie was now under sedation and it would be a further five hours before he woke again. Stella had wanted to take her mother home but Daisy wouldn't hear of it, she did relent somewhat and allowed her daughter to take her for a long stroll and then to the cafe for a coffee. Several hours later when they returned, Dougie was propped up in bed, his eyes were bandaged and his head, neck and shoulders were covered in some sort of thick greasy looking lotion. Hearing the door open he turned his face in their direction but didn't know who was there. Stella walked over and gently took hold of his hand.

"Hello my darling, whatever has been going on?"

It was obvious that it was a struggle for him to speak but even with all the pain he was in Dougie was only concerned about his family and in almost a whisper he managed a few words.

"We'll talk about it later Stella, is mum ok?"

Daisy ran over to the bed and grabbed his other hand.

"I'm here son; your old mum is here. Now I don't want you to worry about a thing, from now on we'll take care of you. When the shit hits the fan Dougie, family are the only ones you can rely on."

Her words did nothing to alleviate his fears and he began to move his head from side to side in an agitated manner. "Where's James? I want James."

Stella looked in her mother's direction and gently shook her head. She didn't know how to break the news and she could feel the tears begin to well up in her own eyes. Holding her brother's hand a bit tighter she took in a deep breath and then slowly began to speak.

"I've just spoken to him and...."

"Is he coming to see me Sis, will James be here soon?"

Stella looked up at the ceiling, this was the hardest thing she had ever had to do and god knew poor Dougie didn't deserve it. His life had been difficult enough and now he was going to have to live the rest of it disfigured and most probably alone.

"I'm afraid not love. James has gone sweetheart."

"Gone, gone where? Please don't mess about Stella it's not fair."

"Believe me darling, the last thing I'm doing is messing about. He said he was going to Mexico. I'm so sorry sweetheart but there isn't any point in trying to sugar coat things. Apparently he came to the hospital with you but when he found out how badly you were injured, well he says he can't live with it or the thought of having to be your carer."

The room was silent and for a second Stella didn't know if her brother had understood what she'd just explained but when she noticed a tear trickle down his cheek from a gap under the bandages she knew nothing more needed to be said. Daisy gently nudged her daughter away from the bed and taking her sons hand in hers she lent in close.

"The main thing is that you're still alive Dougie.

You need to concentrate on that fact and get yourself well. When you're fit enough to leave you're coming home with me and Stella so that we can take proper care of you."

"But what about the restaurant?"

Stella hadn't given the place a second thought and for a moment she was stumped for what to say.

"For now it will remain closed, there's plenty of time to think about that place later but for now you need to rest. Come on Mum, let's get you home and leave Dougie to get some sleep."

They both kissed his hand as there was nowhere on his face that hadn't been affected. Dougie didn't utter another word; he was already drifting off to sleep as a third set of sedatives began to take effect. By nightfall every member of the Nicholson clan had been informed regarding what had happened and Stella knew that the following day they would all congregate at the flat. For now she just wanted to sleep and after making sure that Daisy was tucked up in bed, she turned in for the night.

Over in Soho Anna Hillman had been pacing the floor waiting for dark to fall. Macy had come home at tea time and was all smiles as she informed Anna that she had a couple of shifts down at the Admiral Duncan pub on Old Compton Street, so they might be able to afford this month's rent after all. When Macy left at around seven Anna had breathed a sigh of relief. Dressing in black trousers, a dark coloured top, anorak and trainers she collected the meat from her wardrobe, placed it into a rucksack along with a small set of bolt croppers, jemmy bar and a torch and at ten o'clock she slipped out of the flat. Hailing a cab was out of the question, Tony knew so many people that someone would be bound to grass on her she was sure of it, so instead she headed for Leicester

Square underground and boarded a tube for Limehouse. Pulling up her hood she kept her head down as she walked along the almost empty road. The area was dimly lit and with her dark clothes Anna blended into the night. Thankfully as it was mostly a commercial district there were only a handful of cars about. Reaching the front gates to Tony's compound she stared into the darkness and coughed loudly knowing that the dogs would hear her and be growling and baring their teeth within a few seconds. Right on cue Tyson came roaring up to the gates but stopped dead in his tracks when he smelled the juicy aromas of the beef. Anna pushed three or four large chunks of meat through the wire mesh and watched as the dog greedily gobbled them down. The others dogs were soon beside him and she continued to push the contaminated beef through the fence. Aware that it would take a while for the sedatives to take effect, Anna watched intently for any change in the dog's behaviour. After about twenty minutes she noticed Tyson begin to sway on his feet and the realisation that things would soon get moving made her smile. Leaving it a few minutes longer until she saw the others start to waver, Anna then began to climb the fence. Making her way towards Tony's office she removed a balaclava from her rucksack as she was well aware that the place was being monitored by close circuit television. The bolt croppers and torch that she'd had the good sense to pack came in handy and after cutting the padlock and then forcing the Yale lock with the jemmy she was soon inside. She had only been here on one occasion but it was enough for her to remember the layout. The torch allowed her not to have to switch the lights on and entering the inner sanctum she took a seat in her ex lovers chair for a moment. Mentally going over the hurt he had caused her made Anna ball her hands into fists, he was going to pay for what he'd done even if it killed her. Methodically she opened each drawer in turn but there was nothing damning in any of them. Removing the picture from the wall she saw the safe but it would be futile trying to open it so re-hanging the picture she moved back into the reception area. Now more than a bit disheartened she was starting to wonder if it had all been a waste of time. Deciding to have a nose about outside she smiled when she stepped from the cabin and her eyes fell on Jumbo's old caravan. Anna didn't know why but she had a strange feeling in her gut that she was going to find what she was looking for inside. The door was easy to break which she was glad of, time was moving on fast and she didn't want to be here any longer than was necessary in case the dogs started to wake. The dilapidated old van stunk of sweat and god only knew what else but it didn't stop her going through everything and opening up all of the wall cupboards. A few minutes later and when she'd found absolutely nothing she sat down on one of the benches. Anna's shoe accidently kicked into the wood below her seat and there was a hollow rattling sound. Quickly getting to her feet she bent over the bench to take a closer look and sliding the ply front sideways revealed a hidden compartment. Placing her hand inside Anna felt about and soon pulled out what felt like a book. Once more taking a seat she shone her torch downwards onto the pages and after scanning only the first few she just couldn't contain herself.

"Fucking jackpot!"

Grinning like a Cheshire cat Anna knew the little she had seen would be more than enough to get her revenge. Stuffing the book into her bag she once more scaled the fence and dropping to the ground, pulled off the balaclava and was soon on her way. She loved it when a plan came together and she couldn't wait to get back to the flat and tell Macy all that she had achieved.

Over in Kensington it was a different story entirely. Tony Miller had spent a restless evening pacing the floor of his apartment. He couldn't work out what was going on with Stella and as much as he hated to admit it, the situation was really starting to get to him. In just a couple of weeks this woman had turned his world upside down and he wasn't about to lose her for a second time. He decided that first thing in the morning he would call at the Roy Street flat and find out what the hell was going on.

CHAPTER TWENTY THREE

The Following morning at six am and just a few hours after Stella had blown her top at him; Tony Miller was tossing and turning in the bed desperate to get some sleep. The woman had consumed his thoughts for most of the night and now as the sun shone brightly into the bedroom window of his apartment he finally accepted that he wasn't going to be able to rest so he might as well get up. After making some fresh coffee he telephoned Harry and instructed the man to collect him at nine sharp, it would be too early to pay Stella a visit so his intention was to go into the office for a while. When the car reached the compound Tony instantly knew that something was very wrong. The gates were still locked but the dogs were nowhere to be seen. Slowing down Harry turned in his seat to face his boss.

"You want me to keep driving Tony?"

Reaching inside his coat Tony Miller removed a handgun and with it he motioned for Harry to get out and open the gates, if this was a set up he would at least be ready. As the car pulled up outside the cabin he heard Harry say 'what the fuck?' as they both saw the dogs lying spark out asleep on the dirt. Slowly they stepped from the car and Tony's eyes darted in every direction but there was nothing. Harry Chrome walked over and bending down to Tyson he rubbed the dogs head roughly. There was no response and the dog just continued to softly snore.

"They've been fucking drugged boss."

Harry's voice sounded emotional, he hated humans but when it came down to animals it was another matter. He loved these dogs like children and his blood was boiling with the thought that anyone had dared to harm them.

"Chain them up in case they wake while the gates are open. Phone Gazza and tell him to get his arse here now!"

With that Tony walked up to the cabin door. It was slightly ajar where Anna had forced the lock and as he pushed it open there was a creaking sound. Tony released the safety catch on his gun and then cautiously stepped inside. He really didn't think that there would still be anyone around but all the same he wasn't about to take any chances. The reception area looked untouched and with his gun still firmly held in his hand, Tony made his way through to the office. That too looked just as he had left it yesterday but when he opened up the desk drawers he knew that someone had gone through all of his paperwork. Tony knew exactly how things were laid out in the drawers and he would know if the slightest item had been moved.

"Harry! Get your fucking arse in here now."

A few seconds later big Harry Chrome ran through the doorway.

"What's up boss?"

"The cunts have been through my papers."

"We got anything to worry about Boss?"

Tony wouldn't even dignify the question with an answer; it was exactly that kind of thinking that made him the boss and Harry just a lackey.

"Come with me!"

Marching over to Jumbo's caravan, Tony roughly pushed on the door with his foot and the two men entered. Harry screwed up his face at the stink but by the look of anger on his boss's face he knew better than to say anything. They started to search the van and Tony was the first to find something. Under the bench seat the plywood sliding door was wide open and it was evident to Tony that it had held something important, something that whoever had broken into his premises wanted badly and had got. Bending down Tony placed his hand inside and felt around.

"What the fuck is this? I didn't even know it was there."

"Nor did I boss!"

"Go and check the container and then get Joe and Terry over here pronto! I've got a little job for them. Whoever has had the audacity to try and fucking mug me off are going to regret it dearly."

Harry knew that when Joe McKinney was called then there was some serious violence in store, Harry was well known for how vicious he could be but Joe was on another level entirely. Back in the sanctity of his office Tony took a seat behind the desk and rapped his fingers on the woodwork as he tried to think if he'd left anything incriminating in the drawers but he couldn't recall a single thing. Whatever they had wanted must have been in that stinking caravan but he didn't have the foggiest idea what it could be. He didn't want to think that Stella had anything to do with this but after the phone call yesterday he now wouldn't put anything past her, especially if she believed he had hurt her brother. Switching on the close circuit monitor he began to study the screen. For several minutes it was just the night image of the yard but then suddenly he pressed pause and leaned in closer. Whoever it was that had the audacity to break into his yard had made sure that they were well covered. It was impossible to recognise the culprit and the only thing Tony had to go on was the fact that they were of slight build. Within the hour four of Tony's men including big Harry stood in front of their boss eagerly awaiting his orders.

"I want you to find that cunt Jumbo and bring him to me.

Its fucking funny how he ain't turned up for work the day after we get turned over. If that wanker thinks he can take liberties with me he can fucking think again."
Nothing else was said and the men were soon on their way over to Jumbo Smith's home on Castor lane in Poplar. Jumbo had lived in the same council house for his entire life and when his parents had both died he had taken over the tenancy as was his right. It wasn't much of a place and in all honesty was worn down to the point of requiring a complete refurbishment but to Jumbo it was home and somewhere he could indulge his hobby of watching the hardest core pornography he could get his hands on.

Harry and the boys pulled up outside and hearing the noise of the car made Jumbo get out of his seat and peer from behind the grey net curtains. Seeing who it was, Jumbo could instantly feel his body begin to shake in fear but he knew there was little point in trying to hide as the men would just break down the door. As quickly as he could he opened the front door before Harry had the chance to kick it in. Jumbo didn't hang about to greet the men and instead walked back through to the front room. He was in a desperate hurry to stop the player and remove the disc before they had a chance to see what he was watching but he wasn't quick enough. The four men surrounded him with big Harry Chrome standing right in front.

"Well well well and what do we have here then? You fucking fat pervert!"
Jumbo could feel his cheeks flush with embarrassment as he glanced at a naked woman engaging in a disgusting act with a dog and which was now frozen on the screen for all to see.

"The boss wants a word."

Jumbo knew only too well what it meant when the boss wanted a word and he could feel the colour drain from his face. He began to back away from the men and as he did so stumbled over a footstool and landed heavily on the floor.

"Come on now Jumbo, you know the score and trying to get out of it ain't going to happen."

"Look Mr Chrome, I was scared that's all, scared that Mr Miller would think it was me and it wasn't. Please Mr Chrome; give me a break I ain't done nothing wrong honest I ain't."

Harry totally ignored the man as if Jumbo hadn't even spoken. Glancing around the room the distaste was evident on his face.

"Fuck me Jumbo however can you live in a shit tip like this?"

True the furnishings and decor were old but it wasn't just that, there was an unwashed smell about the place and Harry didn't know if it was coming from the carpet or from Jumbo himself. Now terrified, Jumbo Smith scrambled to his feet.

"Please Mr Chrome don't make me go, I don't know anything. I went to the yard as usual this morning and when I saw the state the dogs were in and that the door to Mr Millers office was open, well I got a bit scared and came back home again."

Harry Chrome walked over to where Jumbo was standing and placed his hand onto the man's shoulder.

"That may well be the case sunshine but I've had orders to take you back with me and I ain't leaving this shit hole without you. Now we can do this the fucking hard way or the easy way, the choice is yours?"

Over in Soho Macy Langham was just waking up. Her shift at the Admiral Duncan hadn't finished until late and by the time she'd got home she was worn out and had gone straight to bed. The pay was good but it wasn't like Delphine's and she'd had a heavy heart as she walked home in the early hours of the morning. Macy hadn't seen Anna but hearing her now singing away to the radio in the kitchen she decided to get up and have a bit of breakfast.

"Morning love, it's nice to hear you're a bit chirpier. See I told you it would all work out for the best and that you'd soon be happy and back on track, didn't I honey?"

"Yes you did and I am thanks Macy. Take a seat sweetheart and I'll make you a cuppa, I've got so much to tell you."

Macy was now intrigued as she wondered what had put her flatmate in such a good mood. It crossed her mind that maybe Anna had got back with Tony Miller but she prayed that wasn't the case. She watched Anna closely as the girl prepared the tea but there was something odd about her, she had a strange look in her eyes that Macy had never seen before.

"So what have you got to tell me?"

Anna placed two mugs onto the table and then took a seat. Bending into her bag she removed the ledger and placed it onto the table. Macy could only stare on but Anna laid the flat of her palm over the cover, an indication to Macy that it was not for her eyes just yet.

"I went out yesterday and got revenge for both of us."

Suddenly Macy could feel her stomach begin to churn at the thought of what she was about to hear. This could be a dangerous place to live if you upset the wrong people and personally she liked it here. Macy had lived in Soho for years without too many problems, well at least not until now. The idea that the apple cart might well and truly have been upset because of something her flatmate

had done didn't bear thinking about.
"How?"
"Well firstly I went over to that Delphine's place and sprayed acid in your boss's face, Macy you should have heard him scream. I do hope I got the right one but now I'm not so sure as when he looked up he seemed older and not as pretty as you had described. I don't suppose it really matters; I mean they will both suffer because of it."
Macy jumped up from her seat and as she did so her cup of tea went flying across the kitchen.
"Oh my god, oh my dear god in heaven, Anna what have you done you stupid little bitch!"
"Wait, wait, you haven't heard the best of it yet. Last night I went to Tony's yard, drugged the dogs and broke into his office. This is what I found, well not in the office but in some old caravan but that's beside the point."
Anna Hillman tapped the ledger with her index finger.
Macy was struggling to stay calm but she had to find out just how far the stupid girl had gone.
"What is it?"
"This, my dear sweet friend, is what will put that wanker Tony Miller in jail for a very long time."
Macy reached out her hand and Anna passed over the tatty looking book. Macy opened it up and scanned the pages, it didn't take long for her to realise what it was and the colour drained from her face as she looked up at her friend.
"Anna you have to take this back."
"No way!"
"You really don't understand what you've done do you? If you don't return this love, then Tony Miller will hunt you down."
"He doesn't know it was me and by all accounts, after reading this, it's obvious that someone else has written it

so he couldn't possibly know it exists."

"It's not bloody rocket science love and he will seek out anyone that's been to his office uninvited or who has pissed him off. When he's had time to think and has put the feelers out he will realise that it was someone who wants revenge and you are at the top of the list my girl." Anna Hillman snatched up the book and hugged it to her chest. She looked angry and Macy realised that she really didn't know the young woman at all.

"As long as you keep your trap shut I won't have anything to worry about now will I?"

With that Anna stormed off to her room leaving a frightened Macy standing in the kitchen with her mouth wide open. She mulled over in her mind everything she'd learnt in the last few minutes. Whatever had the silly little bitch done and just who had she hurt at the restaurant? Grabbing her coat Macy ran from the flat and headed in the direction of Delphine's, hoping and praying as she went that it hadn't been Dougie who had borne the brunt of Anna's anger.

Over in Limehouse Harry, Joe and Terry stepped from the car. Jumbo remained seated and for a second refused to get out but he soon changed his mind when Terry Hanson pulled out a flick knife from his jacket pocket and released the blade.

"Please Harry! I ain't done nothing honest."

"Get in there you fucking tart and stop acting like a bleeding baby."

Harry grabbed hold of Jumbo's shoulder and shoved him forward into the cabin, Joe and Terry silently followed behind while Gazza drove the car around the back and out of sight. As the four men entered the office Tony was seated behind his desk but there was no warm greeting and Jumbo almost ran over to the desk and began to plead

236

with the man before him.

"Please Mr Miller I ain't done nothing wrong, like I told Harry, I got here early and when I saw the place had been broken into I went home again, honest I did."

"So why didn't you contact me or one of the lads you fucking low life?"

"I was scared Mr Miller, scared you would think it was me and honest to god on my old mums grave it wasn't. You've got to believe me Mr Miller please!!!!!!!"

"Oh I believe you Jumbo, you ain't that good a fucking actor but what I do want to know is what you had stashed away in that scummy old van of yours?"

Jumbo's Smiths face was instantly ashen when he suddenly remembered the ledger. Sweat began to form on his forehead and as Tony studied the man's every changing expression he knew that Jumbo was hiding something.

"Nothing Mr Miller, honestly there's nothing, nothing!"

"You seem to have developed a fucking stutter Jumbo!" Tony was now on his feet and fast losing his patience. It was obvious that the tow rag was lying and Tony new that harsher tactics were called for.

"Have no doubt that whoever the fucking cunt was, that had the cheek to try and fucking screw me over, will be found and dealt with. Now you have a choice sunshine, spill your guts and tell me what the fuck has been going on or my man here will spill your fucking guts for real, right here on this office floor. The choice is yours?"

Jumbo's legs began to tremble and suddenly he felt his bladder release. It didn't go unnoticed by Tony but he made no comment, he was more interested in getting to the bottom of things.

"Well?"

Jumbo Smith bit down nervously on the inside of his

mouth. He knew that to keep quiet would ultimately result in his death but to tell the man what he wanted to know would cause him to get a merciless beating, the likes of which he'd never received before. When it came down to it he really had Hobson's choice in the matter. "Look Mr Miller, it's like this, when the boys used the crusher, a few years back now it was, well I found some human remains in the cube and it scared me shitless. I was worried that if the Old Bill ever came sniffing about that I would get the blame."

He didn't continue and Tony was starting to get a bad feeling about all of this.

"And?"

"Well I started to keep a kind of book."

"A fucking book!! What kind of book you cunt!!!!!!"

"It was just a kind of safe guard, that's all."

The malice in Tony's voice was terrifying and it even surprised Harry Chrome. Harry had seen his boss get mad on many occasions over the years but even he could see that this went way and beyond normal anger.

"I just jotted down the comings and goings of this place; you know dates and times and if anything was brought into the yard, that sort of thing. I'm sure there ain't anything in the book that can cause you any aggro Mr Miller."

Tony began to pull at his bottom lip with his thumb and index finger. He thought of all the jobs he'd carried out over the last few years, all the unsavoury characters that had been involved and who had called at the yard regularly. There were even the bodies to contemplate, bodies that had been crushed and disposed of and he knew that with a good forensic team pulling the yard apart they were bound to find enough evidence to put him away for life.

238

"So who did you tell about this little fucking book?"

"No one Mr Miller, I swear no one except me knew about it."

"Take him away Harry; I've heard enough of his fucking snivelling."

Harry Chrome pushed Jumbo towards the door where Joe and Terry each grabbed one of Jumbo's arms and led him into the front reception. Harry turned to face his boss, no words were exchanged but when Tony drew his index finger across his throat Harry knew exactly what he was being told to do. Outside in the yard he held out his hand and demanded the keys to the crusher from Jumbo. When they weren't given freely Terry and Joe held Jumbo firmly and Harry delved into the man's pocket and removed the single key that would ultimately end Jumbo's life. Switching on the crushing machine Harry then climbed into the cab of the grabber and as he turned on the engine the beast spluttered and then burst into life.

"Please Mr Chrome please!!!!!!"

Jumbo's pleading fell on deaf ears and as he realised what was about to happen he started to cry like a baby. Terry and Joe grabbed hold of Jumbo and frog marched him over to a damaged ford focus that had been brought into the yard a few days ago. Opening the door they pushed him in head first and slammed the door just as the grabber hit the cars roof and the claws burst through the window showering Jumbo with broken glass. He knew what his fate was going to be and desperately tried to open the door but the metal beast was clamped tight and he didn't have a hope of escape. Slowly the car was lifted into the air and as the grabber swung round it placed the vehicle sideways into the crusher. The massive compression plate began to move downwards and even though Jumbo Smith was screaming for help, his voice was drowned out by the noise of the machinery. The sound of creaking metal could be heard as the plate made contact with the cars roof and slowly pushed down to begin the crushing process. The last thing Terry Maynard saw was a spurt of blood that shot out of the broken window and then Jumbo Smith was history. The men made their way back to the office where Tony had been wracking his brains trying to think who the intruder could have been. As yet all he'd come up with was a big fat zero.

"Harry I want you and the boys to hit the streets. Find any of the scum that owe me a favour. Someone must know something about this and I need to find out who and fast!"

CHAPTER TWENTY FOUR

As Macy Langham neared Delphine's she could feel her heart begin to race. The street was unusually quiet and as she reached her former place of employment she could see a sign that had been posted on the door. Forgetting to bring her glasses she strained her eyes and was just able to read the note, but apart from a telephone number in case of emergencies it didn't really reveal anything. Pulling out her mobile phone Macy tapped in the number and wondered just who would answer her call. When Stella had telephoned her son late last night she'd asked Stevie if he would place a note at the bar early the next day just in case anyone needed to get in touch and luckily for once he had done what she'd asked. She hadn't been up long and was sitting in the front room eating a slice of toast when her phone began to ring. Stella snatched it up from the coffee table, Daisy was still asleep and she didn't want to wake her. Yesterday had taken its toll on her mother and Stella knew that at her age the more rest her mother could get the better.

"Hello?"

"Oh hello, this is Macy Langham and I'm a friend of the owners of Delphine's."

"Hello Macy love this is Stella."

As soon as Macy realised who it was she felt a lump begin to form in her throat. The only reason that Stella would have left her number as contact, was if the person that had been hurt was Dougie.

"Oh Stella, whatever has happened?"

Luckily for Macy Stella was tired and stressed so she didn't think anything of the question, didn't wonder how Macy knew that something had happened.

"I really don't know Macy love; some bastard went to the restaurant and threw acid in my brother's face. The poor sod ain't ever hurt a soul in his life so why would anyonc do that to him Macy, why?"

Feeling more guilt than she'd ever felt in her life before Macy just wanted to sob but holding her composure as only an aging pro knew how to do, she spoke calmly and gently to Stella.

"I ain't got a clue babe, Old Bill any help?"

"Whatever are you saying Macy, you know as well as I do that we don't involve the coppers in family business, any business come to that. They did come to the hospital as a matter of course but Dougie was in no fit state to speak to them and even if he had have been, well it goes without saying that he would keep his trap shut no matter how much pain he was in. I suppose they will be back at some point but they won't get a peep out of me or mine."

Macy felt relief wash over her, at least for the moment Anna was safe but at the same time she had felt stupid asking the question, she just hoped that it wouldn't come back to bite her in the arse.

"Of course I know that, it was a silly thing to say but I suppose it's just the shock. What hospital is he in?"

"University College but I don't know if they will let you see him. When we were there last night it was family only but I'll tell him you called. Macy I need a favour if it ain't too much trouble?"

"You only have to ask sweetheart, you only have to ask."

"Can you meet me at the restaurant in say two hours? The keys are being held by someone called Billy at the local newsagents."

"Of course I can love."

"See you there later then, oh and thanks for ringing."

With Stella being so nice, Macy felt even more guilt and

she didn't like the feeling one bit. After hanging up Stella was about to take another bite of her now cold toast when there was a knock at the door. She was in the hall in an instant as she desperately didn't want them to knock again and wake Daisy. Opening up she was more that surprised when she saw who her caller was.

"You've got a fucking cheek!"

"Just let me in Stella so we can talk about things, please!" She didn't invite him in but as she silently walked back into the front room it was a message that told Tony Miller she was up for listening. It was years since he'd been in the flat and he smiled at the realisation that nothing had changed, god even the decor was the same. Stella was once again seated on the sofa and continuing with her breakfast she tried her best to act as if things were normal but they both knew that things were far from normal. She didn't have a scrap of makeup on but for once it didn't bother her, as far as Stella was concerned he could take her or leave her because right at this moment she really couldn't stand the sight of him.

"I ain't here to say I'm sorry, because whether you believe me or not I ain't got nothing to be sorry about. What I am here for is to try and find out what the hell has been going on. Now if you want me to leave I will, but believe me Stella, neither I nor any of my blokes laid a fucking hand on your brother nor would we. When you came to me and asked for help I didn't hesitate and took on board all that you asked of me so why would I go back on my word?"

Stella studied his face, a face she had loved for more years than she cared to remember.

"Well?"

"Then tell me who did do this to Dougie, who the fuck threw acid in his face? My poor innocent brother has

243

never hurt anyone in his life so why would someone, if not you, do this too him?"

Tony Miller took a seat beside the woman that in such a short time had made a huge impact on his life, a woman that he wanted to spend eternity with but who was now looking at him as if he was the scum of the earth.

"Think about it girl, what reason would I have to do such a thing? Fuck me Stella, I'm the first person to admit that I ain't a saint but what could I possibly gain from doing this. Dougie was, after a little threat, more than happy to accommodate my wishes, well your wishes actually, so I had no reason whatsoever to hurt him. You're barking up the wrong fucking tree love, and though it might not be of any interest to you, my office was broken into last night."

"So?"

"Well I'm hoping they didn't find anything that could cause me bother but I really don't fucking know and to top it all off I've now got my bird blaming me for all fucking sorts that I ain't guilty of. As much as you're hurting Stella, I really don't need this extra fucking aggro."

Again Stella studied his face, she liked being called his bird and god was he handsome. She looked deep into his eyes and something told her he wasn't lying but if he was telling the truth, then who had hurt Dougie and why. This had all got so out of hand and she just wished that she could turn the clock back a couple of weeks.

"Ok I believe you Tony and I'm sorry for accusing you. So what do we do now?"

"I've got my men out on the street asking questions but you know as well as I do that when shit happens everyone clams up. I ain't going to let this rest Stella, I promise you that I will do all that I can to find out who did this to your brother, even if it kills me I promise I will

244

get you some answers."

Tony Miller stood up and walked from the flat without a goodbye and Stella slowly shook her head. This was all getting insane. About to return to her breakfast for the third time, she was stopped again when a bleary eyed Daisy appeared in the hallway.

"What's all the bleeding noise about? I was having a lovely kip and some bloke's loud voice woke me up. Who was it Stella, what did he want? Was it to do with Dougie, is he alright"

"Dougie is fine mum, well as fine as he can be under the circumstances. If you must know it was Tony."

"Tony bleeding Miller has been in my flat! Fuck me girl are you nuts?"

"Yes he has mum and yes I probably am nuts but for the life of me I don't know why you're making such a big deal about it. I'm going to get dressed now and for once you can sort your own bloody breakfast out."

As Stella headed towards her bedroom she could hear Daisy chuntering away to herself in the kitchen and she couldn't help but smile. Thirty minutes later and Stella was washed, dressed and on her way to the underground station. Arriving in Soho strangely felt normal and she no longer had to seek out directions as she was now so used to coming here that she felt she could have made the journey with her eyes closed. Reaching Delphine's Stella was greeted by a warm smile and a loving embrace from Macy Langham. The women didn't know each other that well but since the first day they had met there had been an instant connection. Stella unlocked the door and the two went inside. The area behind the bar was still wet from where James and the paramedics had tried to neutralise Dougie's acid burns and without being asked Macy retrieved her faithful old mop and began to clean up the floor but she talked as she worked.

"You do know James sacked me don't you?"

"No I didn't but that's all water under the bridge now love."

Stella smiled, she really couldn't understand why they had got rid of the woman, she was a hard worker and just what any business needed. Ten minutes later and with the bar area now sorted out Stella made them both a coffee and together they took a seat at one of the tables. Stella turned to Macy and her face was deadly serious.

"How do you fancy running this place?"

"Pardon?"

"Look my brother won't be back here for a very long time and the last thing I want is for him to lose his business. Now I know that you are more than capable so what do you say?"

Macy Langham couldn't believe what she was hearing and grabbing Stella's hand she lifted it to her lips and kissed it.

"Oh stop that you silly sod, now I need to ask you something else. Macy I know you love my brother and I wondered if you had any idea who he or James might have upset or got on the wrong side of, I mean people don't do things like this for no reason do they."

Macy looked down at the floor and Stella instantly knew she was hiding something.

"Macy if you know anything I would really fucking appreciate you sharing it with me."

Macy Langham rested her elbow on the table and held her forehead with her hand as she desperately wracked her brains trying to think of something to say. She didn't want to drop Anna in the shit but she also knew that there was a whole lot of trouble brewing which she could innocently get caught up in. Self preservation suddenly

246

filled her, true she liked Anna but the girl seemed to be going a bit nutty, and at her age Macy didn't want to be a casualty of the fall out.

"I will Stella but only if you swear not to tell a soul?" Stella Nicholson didn't like liars, she also knew that she might not be able to keep the promise she was about to make which made her feel bad but not bad enough to not want the truth. Macy was a nice woman but blood was thicker than water and right at this moment all she cared about was getting justice for her brother.

"Whatever are you on about Macy? This is my brother we're talking about, a kind sweet man who for no reason has had acid thrown in his face. I might also add, a man that has only ever shown you kindness, now start spilling your guts Mrs!"

Macy inhaled deeply; betrayal didn't sit well with her but if what she said was never repeated she reasoned that it would be alright to confide in Stella.

"I share a flat with a young woman named Anna Hillman. She was in a relationship with Tony Miller, have you heard of him?"

Stella nodded her head and at the same time she had a sinking feeling that she wasn't going to like what she was about to hear.

"She hadn't been seeing him for long but you know what young women are like, the silly cows will insist on confusing bloody lust for love. Anyway, he dumped her and it broke her bleeding heart Stella. Seems he found himself another woman and a lot older than Anna I might add. Honest to God, I ain't ever seen anyone in so much pain over a bloke. Well when James sacked me and I told her she just lost the fucking plot, swore revenge on them all. I only found out today what she'd done. The stupid bitch muddled Dougie for James and that's how

you brother got hurt. She also broke into Millers yard
and pinched some kind of book that contained enough
evidence to send that wanker down for years."
Stella tapped lightly on the table top as she thought of
what to do next.
"And where is this Anna now?"
"At home I think."
"Well I need to get down the hospital but thanks for
sharing that Macy, not that it makes me feel any better or
changes anything."
When Stella had locked up the restaurant and the women
were about to head off in different directions Macy gently
grabbed Stella's arm
"Remember you promised!"
Stella could only nod her head and smile. A few minutes
later she hailed a cab and asked the driver to take her over
to Limehouse, she'd called Tony all the names under the
sun and now she had to help him as a means of making
amends. The journey took longer than usual as the traffic
was heavy and as Stella sat back in the taxi she went over
in her mind all that Macy had confided. If she told Tony
what she knew then there was no telling what he would
do but on the other hand if she did nothing then he would
go to prison for god only knew how long. By the time
the cab pulled into the scrap yard she had come to a
decision.
Before she had chance to close the cab door big Harry
Chrome walked out of the cabin door. Stella asked the
driver to wait for her and then turned and smiled at the
giant of a man who was obviously blocking her way to
Tony.
"Can I help?"
"I need to see Tony."
"I'm afraid the Boss is busy but if you want I can give

him a message."

"Just tell him Stella is here, he'll see me I'm sure."

Harry disappeared into the cabin but was back within a minute and was now eagerly inviting her inside. Entering the office she saw Tony sitting behind his desk with a broad grin on his face.

"You just can't keep away from me can you?"

Stella pulled up a chair and then took a seat opposite him but ignored his remark.

"I've got something important to tell you. It was told to me in confidence and I promised the person that I wouldn't reveal what was said but what I'm about to tell you has and will have, a big impact on both of our lives."

He could see that she was troubled and that this was serious so he instantly stopped grinning.

"Do you know a young woman by the name of Anna Hillman?"

"Why?"

"You hurt her, she had a crush on you and Dougie, well Dougie was mistaken for someone else."

For a second Tony's brow furrowed deeply, he didn't have the foggiest idea how Stella could know about the girl but he was too interested in hearing what was to come next that he nodded his head.

"She was the woman that threw acid in my Dougie's face and she was also the one that broke into your office. Apparently she has some sort of ledger that could land you in a shit load of trouble. I'm only telling you this because I don't want you to go to prison."

Tony Miller smiled in her direction but Stella could see and feel the underlying fear and anger. She hoped he would go easy on the girl but that was out of her hands and in all honesty and after what the girl had done to her brother, Stella didn't really care. Knowing that he would obviously be keen to sort the matter out she said her goodbyes and climbed back into the cab and asked to be taken to the hospital. Tony immediately called Harry Chrome into the office.

"What's up Boss?"

"I think you and those other Muppets that work for me are losing your fucking touch."

"How so Boss?"

"How fucking so? I sent you cunts to find out who had fucking robbed me and you came back empty handed, now within a few minutes I know all I need too. Fetch the Cleaner and go over to Soho and pick up that thieving little bitch Anna Hillman. Don't bring her back here; use the railway arch lock up. When you've got her give me a call before you arrive and if Alan Mendham gives you any trouble, tell him to come and see me but I don't think he will, she only works for him and he knows better than to interfere in my business."

The Cleaner as he was known, real name George Vennimore, was a specialist in removing people. George would carry out anything required of him and was adept at disposing of victims without leaving a trace.

"But the Cleaner Boss? I mean, she's only a fucking kid!"

"Are you fucking questioning me? Be very careful my old son!"

"No boss, never!"

"Just make sure it stays that way, now fuck off and do as I told you."

Tony didn't continue further but the glare in his eye was enough to tell Harry Chrome that he was deadly serious. Without another word Harry walked from the office, grabbed the keys to the white Transit van and went to collect George Vennimore. Harry hated the man with a vengeance; he was a complete bastard, had no moral code whatsoever and would resort to anything for money. That said there had been deeds carried out over the years that even Harry would have walked away from, so he supposed it was good that George was always available at a moment's notice but only god knew what the boss wanted done. Harry had a bad feeling and just hoped that the girl gave Tony what he wanted or it didn't bear thinking what would happen to her. As he drove away the big man began to chastise himself for being soft. If the little bitch had caused his boss aggravation then she deserved everything that was coming to her.

CHAPTER TWENTY FIVE

As soon as Macy had left to go to Delphine's Anna emerged from her bedroom with the ledger already wrapped in brown paper. Slipping out of the flat she made her way over to the post office on Poland Street. There were queues of people and she continually glanced over her shoulder, of course no one knew what the parcel contained but after Macy's words of warning Anna was starting to get scared but still not scared enough to stop what she was about to do. Handing over the package, she asked if it could be sent first class. It was addressed to a Detective Peter Connors at Charing Cross police station. Anna had come to know the detective while living on the streets and she just hoped that he was still working there. Tony Miller had some friends in high places and if the package ended up in the wrong hands it could easily disappear but as Anna couldn't risk physically delivering it herself she didn't have much choice. Now back outside on Poland Street Anna wore a wide grin on her face as she walked along. Hopefully by morning the shit would have hit the fan and Tony Miller would be experiencing some really bad trouble that even he wouldn't be able to get out of. Glancing at her watch Anna saw that it was already eleven thirty so she headed straight for 'Take A Look' as her shift was due to start at twelve. Harry Chrome and George Vennimore were already waiting for her in Alan Mendham's office and the man had been given strict instructions that he wasn't to forewarn the girl.

"Come on Harry, she's only a fucking kid!"

"Sorry Al but those are the boss's orders, unless you want to give him a call yourself?"

He wasn't happy about the situation and had done his best for her but Alan knew it was futile to argue further. Having known Tony Miller for years, even spent a good few nights out and had a right laugh with the bloke, he had learned early on that Tony would turn in an instant and a friend could become an enemy in the blink of an eye. He hoped that whatever the silly little bitch had been up too wasn't so bad that it couldn't be sorted out; the only problem was the fact that he knew the services of George Vennimore weren't called upon unless it was really serious and he now had a sick feeling in the pit of his stomach. Glancing at his watch he accepted defeat when he realised that she would be here at any moment. He would have given anything to have been able to have warned her but that wasn't going to happen. After hanging up her coat Anna took a seat in the cubicle and waited for the first punters to appear. Sam McKenna was the doorman for the day so when Alan called the internal telephone and asked Anna to pop up to his office, she got the Scotsman to hold the fort for her.

"I won't be long Sam but watch out for the foreigners; Alan said there's a group of eastern Europeans that have been causing a few problems around here in the last couple of days. Most of them are robbing bastards so just stay on your toes ok?"

The Scotsman nodded his understanding and Anna, unaware of what was about to happen, closed the cubicle door and merrily trotted up to the first floor office. Tapping lightly she walked straight in but stopped dead in her tracks when she saw George Vennimore standing beside her boss. As she took a step forward Harry Chrome moved behind her and closed the door. Hearing this Anna spun round and when she saw the man, a man she had seen before at Tony's yard, she knew that the

253

game was up.

"Hello there Anna girl. Tony would like a word with you and I think you know what it's about."

Looking towards Alan her eyes were pleading for help and as much as his heart went out to her, all he could do was slowly shake his head from side to side. Her eyes were beginning to fill with tears and turning back towards Harry she tried to push past him but she was no match for the giant of a man and with one hand he gave her a shove and she stumbled backwards.

"Don't be fucking stupid you silly little girl!"

"I ain't got the foggiest idea what you're on about now let me out of here before I scream the place down and the whole of Soho comes running to find out what's going on."

"Now we all know that ain't going to happen sweetheart, so why don't you save yourself a whole lot of grief and be a good girl. If you come quietly this will all be over a lot quicker."

Anna Hillman didn't hear anything else and as George's fist made contact with the side of her face she immediately fell to the floor. Everyone in the room heard the crack as her jaw broke.

"Fuck me! That's a bit bleeding harsh ain't it?"

Harry glared at Alan who was now just as scared as his employee had been a few seconds earlier.

"If you know what's good for you Alan you'll keep your fucking nose out of Tony's business. I know you two go back a long way but believe you me, where this is concerned friendship counts for nothing. If anyone comes asking about the girl you tell them you haven't seen her and that goes for the gorilla on the front door as well. Got it?"

"What's going to happen to her?"

254

"Best you don't know sunshine, best you don't fucking know."

Anna was unconscious as George grabbed her arms and hauling her up, flung her petite body over his shoulder in a fireman's lift. A few minutes later the men had exited though the fire escape, Anna Hillman had been chucked into the back of the van and Harry proceeded to phone his boss and inform Tony that they were on their way. Staring from the upper floor window, Alan was now in no doubt that he wouldn't be seeing the girl again but there was little he could do about it. This was the side of Soho that Alan Mendham hated, the ugly cruel side that the hoards of tourist who frequented the area on a daily bases never got to see. In the last few months it had begun to cross his mind that maybe it was time to think about retiring. The thought was now on his mind again, he was too old and too weary for this kind of life style. Slowly walking down the stairs he relayed to Sam all that had occurred and warned the man to keep his trap shut or the same fate would befall him. The archway lockup that Tony had referred to was situated at the rear of Kings Cross station on Camley Street. Tony had leased it for several years though it was hardly ever used. When the van pulled up with Harry, George and Anna onboard, the roller shutter was instantly raised. Harry drove inside and the shutter was dropped within seconds. With the flick of a switch the cold empty space was now illuminated by a row of five metal industrial lights that hung from the ceiling on chains and cast bright discs of light down onto the concrete floor. The two men climbed out and walked over to Tony who was now at the rear of the building standing in front of a strategically placed office chair, the swivel kind that could be easily moved about without much effort.

"Everything go ok?"

Harry was about to reply but had no time to answer before the noise from the overhead trains drowned him out, it was annoying when you were trying to talk but at the same time it was handy if there were screams coming from inside the lock up.

"Sweet as a nut Boss! I don't think Alan was too pleased though."

"Well he wouldn't be but the blokes too much of a fucking coward to try and do anything about it."

"You want me to fetch her, she's in the back and has been as quiet as a fucking lamb, though I doubt that will be the case when we get her out."

"Well let's see shall we, George do the honours will you."

Walking over to the transits rear doors George Vennimore pulled on the lock and a second later was staring at a very frightened Anna Hillman. As he went to grab her arm to pull her out Anna kicked his hand with as much force as she could muster and then pushed her body to the rear of the van. Her heel had caught George squarely on the wrist and he rubbed at the bone with the palm of his hand.

"Why you little bitch!"

Climbing inside he roughly grabbed her and as he hauled her to her feet she smacked the side of her face on his shoulder. The pain from her broken jaw was intense and she screamed out.

"Shut your fucking trap or I'll rip your head off right here and now."

George pushed her forward and she fell into Harry's arms but the big man felt no pity as he carried her over to his Boss.

"For fucks sake sit her down then!"

256

Anna stared up into Tony's eyes but they were cold and hard and she couldn't believe that just a short while ago she had thought she was in love with him, had given her body freely to someone that was now about to hurt her. Just as she was studying him, Tony was staring back at her and wondering why on earth he had been so interested in the first place. True her face was now badly swollen but looking beyond her injuries, she wasn't that much of a looker; the only thing she really had on her side was youth.

"Right you little cunt! Where's that fucking book you thieved from that nonce's caravan?"

"I don't know what you're talking about Tony, please this is stupid."

Anna's voice sounded strange and she was having trouble speaking with her jaw causing so much pain but she had to plead, plead for her life in fact. Attempting to stand, she was immediately pushed back down onto the chair and the look in Harry's eyes told her not to try again.

"Look! I ain't fucking wasting my time arguing, I know you took it so best you tell me where it is or you are going to suffer more than you ever thought possible."

Anna began to cry, if she said nothing he would hurt her and if she told the truth he would also hurt her. Maybe it would be best all round if she just confessed, at least it would soon be over and she prayed that they would take her to the hospital afterwards.

"I haven't got it honest. Tony you broke my heart and I wanted you to suffer like you'd made me suffer."

"I ain't got time for this, now where is the fucking book!"

His voice was filled with rage and the look on his face scared Anna so much that she began to pitifully plead with the man standing before her.

"Please Tony, I told you I don't have it, please let me

go!!!!!"

"This is the last time I'm going to ask you Anna before I let this animal loose on you, so start fucking talking now!"

Tony made eye contact with George and Anna followed his gaze. George's expression was menacing and as she looked down she could see that he was holding some kind of hook like blade.

"I posted it this morning. It's safe that's all I'm saying but if you let me go I'll get it back."

"George, make her talk! Harry hold the little bitch down!"

Harry Chrome pushed down on Anna's shoulders and at the same time George moved towards her with the vicious looking blade.

"Ok ok! I posted it to the police

Tony Miller couldn't believe what he'd just heard and he began to pace up and down in an agitated manner as he tried to think of what to do. He had some contacts on the force, maybe they could help him out. After continually running his hand through his hair with frustration he suddenly stopped dead in front of her and leaning in he began to shout.

"What station and to whom?"

The tears were now falling thick and fast and Anna swallowed hard.

"Charing Cross, Detective Peter Connors but he won't get it until tomorrow so I can still get it back, I'll say I made it all up. Please Tony pleeeeease!"

Totally ignoring her last words Tony was trying to recall the coppers name. Nothing came to mind but luckily for him he did have a contact at that particular nick.

Sergeant Munroe had been on the payroll ever since Tony had returned to London. Several times over the last few years he had been very useful and was well worth a good bung every month. The policeman was near to retirement and he was also a compulsive gambler. Monroe sailed close to the wind and was always racking up debts which seemed to accumulate heavily at the end of every month when his salary was due to be paid. The man was continually in a dilemma, pay his wife's housekeeping or clear his debts, either way he would be made to suffer if he didn't cough up and it was then that he would call Tony for help. There were just two days until the coppers top up was due so Tony hoped that if he bunged the twat an extra grand he could grab the ledger before it ended up in the wrong hands.

"Right, I'm off. Harry you can drive George back after he's finished. George, a word in your ear mate."

George Vennimore walked over towards Tony and when he reached the man, leant in close so that no one else could hear what was about to be said.

"Make the little bitch suffer."

George didn't add any comment but a sickening grin spread across his face. With that Tony pulled up the shutter, walked outside and got into his car. Harry, as hard as he was, didn't want to watch George at work so climbing into the van he drove outside and then closed the shutter sealing Anna's fate. He would be ready to leave when it was all over and he also wouldn't have to look the young girl in the face as she died. Switching on the radio he began to hum away to Tom Jones as the singer belted out 'It's not unusual'. George Vennimore walked over to the back wall and slowly shone his torch so that the old whitewashed brickwork became illuminated. Anna could clearly see blood stains from previous tortures and she began to scream but now due to rush hour the overhead trains were running constantly and drowned out any chance of her being heard. Making his way over to the girl, whose eyes were now wide open with fear, George grabbed a large handful of Anna's hair, and roughly hauled her up from the chair and began to drag her towards the wall. A set of heavy chains had been drilled into the brickwork about a metre and a half apart and as he secured a shackle to each wrist Anna knew that her life would soon be over. Removing a roll of tape, her assailant proceeded to slap a large piece over Anna's mouth. It wasn't because of any noise she was making but purely the fact that it was something the Cleaner liked to see. He enjoyed torturing people and none more so than women. A sadist from a young age, the man had liked to hurt people for as long as he could remember. Anna's eyes were dazzled by the light but she was still able to see the glint from the hooks blade as he approached her. When her crisp white blouse was sliced open from chest to waist her tears flowed freely. George ran the tip of the hook down her exposed skin and as the cold steel opened up her pale white flesh she passed out but seconds later the pain she felt from her broken jaw being slapped soon woke her. Anna studied the man's face but all she could see were his cold cruel eyes. Her skirt was now crimson with blood and as he cut her again only this time a lot deeper, she felt a whoosh as her intestines dropped from her body. This couldn't be happening, she was still alive for god's sake and where was the pain, there was no pain! Staring into the brutal eyes, down to the floor and then back up to her executioner Anna tried to speak, cry out, plead for her life but no sound emerged. George slowly tilted his head from side to side as he studied every changing expression on his victim's pretty face. Lifting the blade he took his time as he gradually drew it across her neck.

The pressure was great and when the blade cut through her jugular vein he took a step to the left to avoid the jet of blood that shot out from Anna Hillman's body. Walking towards the roller shutter George Vennimore glanced back for one last look, his victims entrails were still steaming on the concrete floor but her head was now slumped down onto her chest and he knew it was a job well done. Deciding to return later to clean up George stepped from the lockup with a broad smile on his face. After he'd returned to his car, Tony Miller had removed his mobile and dialled Burt Munroe's number. It only rang twice before it was answered and as was the usual practice, no words were exchanged. It was a code that told the sergeant that Tony needed to see him and ten minutes later when his break was due Burt headed off to Bev's greasy spoon on Villiers Street. He wore a long overcoat to cover his uniform and as he entered Tony was already seated at the back. Taking a chair on the opposite side of the table there were no niceties, it was straight down to business.

"So what's up Tony?"

Tony Miller proceeded to tell the sergeant all that had happened, well everything apart from what the ledger contained and what was happening to Anna Hillman right as they spoke but then that really wasn't important and also none of the coppers business.

"Fuck me Tony you really have slipped up big time. I can't promise you that I'll sort it I ....."

Tony Miller slammed his hand onto the table and at the sound three other customers in the cafe all turned around to look. Continuing in a hushed tone, Tony leant forward so that no one heard his words apart from Burt Monroe.

"Listen to me you cunt! I don't fucking pay you hundreds a month for you not to help me out when I need

261

it, now fucking grab the post as soon as it comes in! If this doesn't get sorted I'm looking at a lengthy fucking stretch and your bank of fucking handouts will instantly dry up."

"So whose name am I looking for?"

"Detective Connors."

"Fuck me Tony, he ain't just a detective he's an Inspector!"

"So?"

With that Tony stood up and throwing a five pound note down onto the table to cover the two cups of tea he marched outside. Burt puffed out his cheeks; this was going to be difficult as Debbie Pearson, the civvy post lady, guarded her mail as if it was the crown jewels. Well he would do his best but at the end of the day Tony Miller had nothing on him so he didn't have too much to worry about. He was retiring soon and if Miller just happened to go away for a stretch, would it really matter? Still, it had to be seen that he was doing his best in the eyes of Tony's cronies but at the same time protecting his pension was paramount. When all was said and done, none of this sat well with Burt and he wanted the next morning to come as quickly as possible.

CHAPTER TWENTY SIX

Stella had arrived at the restaurant bright and early after arranging to meet Macy at nine am as they were interviewing waitresses. After convincing Dougie that opening the place up as soon as possible was a good idea she had thrown herself into making sure everything went smoothly. Macy was already waiting outside Delphine's when Stella arrived and the woman's face was as white as a sheet, almost as if she had seen a ghost. Knowing never to ask questions or talk openly in the street Stella pushed on the door and the two women made their way inside and into the rear kitchen. With the kettle on Stella at last turned to her new partner.

"So are you going to tell me what's wrong Macy? Only you look terrible darling."

Macy Langham was street wise, had experienced and seen more atrocities than most people would ever know yet standing in the kitchen of Delphine's and about to begin a whole new and probably the best chapter in her sorry life so far, she had tears in her eyes.

"Anna didn't come home last night and I'm worried sick that something has happened to her. Oh Stella please tell me you did keep your promise?"

Without thinking Stella nodded her head and Macy managed a weak smile. Stella hated telling lies and she prayed that the girl was fine and that Tony hadn't been involved in her disappearance. Deep down she knew that it probably wasn't the case but if you lived by the sword then you had to be prepared to die by it. As soon as that thought entered her head Stella felt ashamed for even thinking it. Normally the idea of someone getting hurt would have played heavily on her mind but it seemed that since her brother had been so terribly injured and added to the fact that Anna Hillman was to blame, then really Stella didn't give two hoots what happened to her.

"I'm sure she's just off somewhere having a good time and will be back home before you know it, young girls can be bloody thoughtless at times. Right, we have a lot of work to do if we're going to reopen this place on Saturday. Now how many applicants did you manage to rustle up?"

Macys face coloured red with embarrassment.

"Only one."

"One!"

"Yeah and to be honest she ain't a lot of cop, I worked with her a few years back and her personal hygiene ain't the best."

As hard as she tried Stella still couldn't stop herself from laughing. Pulling out her phone she began to dial a number and was still giggling when her daughter answered.

"Hello Mum, what's so funny?"

"Oh nothing love. Listen Ronnie, I need your help."

Within a few minutes Ronnie and Jane had agreed to help out on the opening night and Stevie had offered up the services of Jo and Bianca although they weren't yet aware of that fact. Macy Langham couldn't believe how quick Stella sorted out a problem and she had no doubt that the reopening would be a resounding success and that the place would probably be even more profitable than it had been in the past.

At Charing Cross police station Burt Monroe had arrived an hour earlier than his shift required. He hadn't got a wink of sleep all night and was now pacing the main foyer in a nervous manner that didn't go unnoticed by his colleagues but for once Burt didn't care.

Continually glancing at his watch he was willing Gavin the postman not to be late but what Burt wasn't privy to, was the fact that Gavin Johnson was away on holiday. Gary Wilcox the man's replacement, who was only a temp, was at this moment in time sitting in a cafe across the road eating an all day breakfast special and not caring that everyone on his route was waiting for their post. Forty five minutes later he patted his large stomach, swigged the last of his tea, wiped his mouth and then pulled his mail trolley back out and onto the street. Just as he approached the station, Burt Monroe was called through to the custody suite to book in an arrest. Glancing at his watch one more time he slowly shook his head as he walked through the internal double doors. A few seconds later and Debbie Pearson entered the reception and was handed a vast amount of letters of all different shapes and sizes. After she'd signed for anything important she made her way to the post room to begin sorting the mail. Over the course of the morning Burt Monroe entered the post room several times but Debbie was always in residence and had been watching him like a hawk. Debbie took her role as chief of mail very seriously and she trusted no one. With a heavy heart Burt took an early morning break and headed outside with his mobile phone. Knowing Tony would hit the roof made him reluctant to make the call but he couldn't put it off forever so the sooner he faced up to the gangster the better, the only problem was or would be, Burt Monroe didn't have a clue that his name was also written in the ledger.

"Yes?"

"Hi Tony, it's me."

"Are you fucking crazy?"

"Calm down, it's fine, this is my own mobile and it's a

265

pay as you go so it's untraceable. Listen, I wasn't able to get the post."

"You cunt!"

"No, please listen. I still don't know if it was delivered so I'm going to keep trying but I just wanted to warn you."

"Fucking warn me you wanker! For your sake you had better sort this."

There was no further conversation and Tony Miller instantly hung up. Back in the station and slowly pushing her steel trolley along the corridors Debbie began to deliver the letters to the various offices. For some strange reason there had been an exceptionally large amount today and she stopped for a second and removed her shoe, the corn on the side of her foot was throbbing and she was now looking forward to a sit down and a nice cup of tea. Her last port of call was the custody suite and when he saw her enter Burt Monroe's heart sank in his chest. Debbie handed over the post and was about to walk away when Burt, someone that never normally gave her the time of day, asked a question.

"Was there any post for DI Connors today?"

"I beg your pardon?"

"I said was there any post, anything like a book sort of thing that you took to the Inspector?"

Debbie Pearson was devoted to her job and her boss. Her eyes narrowed as she studied the policeman for several seconds before she spoke.

"If I did Sergeant, it's none of your business."

With that she quickly pushed her trolley back out into the corridor and her manner told Burt in no uncertain terms that there was no way she would ever reveal anything that didn't directly concern him. He contemplated phoning Tony again but then thought better of it, either the shit would hit the fan or it wouldn't but either way, whatever happened was now out of his hands.

After pressing in his code, Detective Inspector Peter Connors pushed open the rear door to the station. A well respected and liked Boss he was met with friendly greetings as he passed other officers of all ranks. Peter had signed up at the age of eighteen and to begin with had climbed the career ladder slowly but in the last five years he had received promotion after promotion. Now an Inspector, he was being viewed by the powers that be for the post of Superintendent of homicide at New Scotland Yard. He didn't like to think that it was anything to do with the weekly golf games he had with the Assistant Commissioner but in reality he knew it was, still if it meant doing a good job for the country then he was happy to accept a helping hand along the way. The position came with a hefty pay rise and it had been Peters dream rank for as long as he could remember so he was more than happy to take advantage of the old boys' network if it helped him advance his career. Entering his office he closed the door and relished the peace and quiet that he knew would only last a few minutes. Taking a seat behind the desk he sifted through the mountain of post that had been strategically placed to face him. Nothing caught his eye until he saw the larger than average package wrapped neatly in brown paper. Peter looked it over for only a few seconds before his inquisitive nature got the better of him and he was compelled to unwrap it. The first thing he saw was the hand written letter from Anna.

Dear Peter

We met several years ago but I doubt you would remember me. I think you will find the enclosed ledger of interest and hopefully you will act on it when you see that the pages contain very damning evidence and also that there is police corruption involved.

Regards

An old friend

Peter Connors wracked his brains but no old friend came to mind. That said it didn't stop him reading the enclosed book and when he saw the name of Tony Miller roughly scribbled on the front, his curiosity suddenly grew tenfold. Miller had been of interest to the Met for a very long time but so far they hadn't been able to pin so much as a parking ticket on the man. Detective Inspector Connors had a strange feeling that was all about to change. It did cross his mind for a second that this could well be some sort of test but as he read further and compared the notes with criminal activities on the same dates, Peter knew it was the genuine article. Jumbo Smith had listed many names, some of which the Inspector recognised and it was clear to see that there was corruption right up to the highest level. This caused a problem for Peter and he gave some serious thought as to how he should progress with the information. If he handed it over to his team he was in no doubt that somewhere along the line it would disappear, the only thing for it was to pay a visit to the Assistant Commissioner. Ron Kiddle had been his mentor back when Peter was a young cadet and Ron was still an Inspector and the two men were extremely close. Inspector Connors made a telephone call and a few minutes later he pulled on his coat, pushed the ledger into his briefcase and left the station. He had been to the Met headquarters several times recently but he still got a thrill every time he walked past the iconic sign. The building was vast but Peter knew exactly where he was going and shortly after entering trough the large glass front doors he was knocking on the door of the Assistant Commissioners office. Ron Kiddle was seated behind a large modern desk but stood up and walked towards Peter when his visitor entered the room.

"Good morning Peter, you sounded very ominous on the telephone?"

"Well to tell you the truth Ron, something worrying has come to my attention and I would like your advice on the best way to handle it."

"You need my advice!"

The two men laughed but Ron could still see that his colleague and friend was troubled.

"Take a seat and tell me more."

Peter Connors did as he was asked and as he sat down he slid the ledger across the desk. The room was silent as the Assistant Commissioner scanned through the book. Peter didn't think the man was taking things seriously because of the speed at which he looked at the pages but nothing could have been further from the truth. When Ron Kiddle came to the last page he closed up the book and then studied his friends face.

"This is explosive stuff Peter."

"I know, that's why I've come to you"

Ron had seen several high ranking names but he was also a stickler for truth and honesty and as far as he was concerned, the old boy network meant nothing when it came down to corruption. It was one thing to use it as a step up the ladder but quite the opposite when it came down to bent coppers.

"Let me take this to the next level. Now I really don't know which way he will want to proceed but whatever happens, you have my word that it will be thoroughly looked into and the guilty culprits will be brought to book one way or another."

Detective Inspector Connors thanked the man and thcn headed back to Charing Cross police station. In all honesty he was relieved that he was no longer connected as he knew that when Ron took things further and he had no doubt that was exactly what the man would do, then the shit would well and truly hit the fan. With the door to his office closed Ron Kiddle again studied the ledger but this time it was more in depth, this time he was looking for his own name. It had only happened once and it was years ago when he was a young recruit and struggling financially that he had taken a small bribe. Afterwards he had felt so bad about his dishonesty that he had sworn to himself it would never happen again. Ten minutes later and when he was content that he hadn't been mentioned personally, he made his way up to the Commissioner's office. Lesley Hardbrook held the office that Ron had set his heart on and he knew that if the man swept this under the carpet and it ever got found out that he'd hidden evidence, it would be a free for all to gain Lesley's position. Ron hoped that if the Commissioner did what he hoped then very soon he could be looking at a high promotion. Knocking on the door he waited to be summoned and was soon seated opposite his Boss.

"What can I do for you Ron?"

For the second time in only a few minutes the ledger was slid across the desk. This time the Commissioner took his time, the man had nothing to fear but where Ron had hoped that loyalty and honour to his colleagues would far out way right, he was to be sorely disappointed.

"Well this certainly makes for interesting reading."

"So what do we do?"

"The only thing we can, bring the bastards down."

"But some of those named have been in the force for years and are well respected not to mention well connected."

"That statement surprises me Ron, I thought better of you. I might be a lot of things but bent I am not."

"I didn't for one moment think that you were."

"But you did assume that I might cover for others and that is just as bad in my book."

Ron Kiddle could feel his face flush with embarrassment. "Leave it with me; I need to get a tight team together so that nothing gets leaked. Thank you Ron, it will be a feather in your cap for being so honest, something that is obviously lacking in a lot of other Met officers if this is anything to go by."

Ron Kiddle returned to his office, this was all going to turn out badly and he was just thankful that he hadn't been named. Whenever police corruption was brought to the public's attention there had to be a face to blame, a scapegoat that more often than not was innocent but then that was the MET for you and Ron wondered which unlucky sod it would be this time. Burt Monroe finally finished his shift and as soon as he was a safe enough distance away from the police station he telephoned Tony. To begin with there was no reply but just one ring away from it going to voice mail his call was at last answered.

"Yes?"

"It's me and ...."

"I fucking know who it is; now just say what you have to."

"I didn't get it but on the plus side nothings been mentioned so it either hasn't arrived yet or it's being swept under the carpet. I will keep my eyes peeled again

271

tomorrow."

"I'm warning you, if you don't sort this you will be joining me in the dock you cunt!"

Tony slammed his phone down and barked at Harry to fetch the car. It would turn out to be a nerve wracking night spent pacing the floor of his apartment. He had not one ounce of remorse for what had happened to Anna Hillman, it was now all down to self preservation and he just hoped that he had greased enough palms over the years to see this mess buried and with no come backs. As he walked through the front door of his home Burt Munroe felt physically sick and Tony's last words were playing heavily on his mind. Jean would soon be asking her husband what was wrong and if a miracle didn't happen he would have to tell her everything within the next few days. He could cope with his marriage ending but the idea of going to prison at his age let alone the fact that he was a bent copper was terrifying and there was absolutely nothing he could do about it.

CHAPTER TWENTY SEVEN

Harry had been instructed to collect Tony early that morning. They didn't normally work on a Saturday but then the circumstances of the last few days had been anything but normal. Tony Miller was waiting in the front foyer as Harry Chrome pulled the car up to the kerb. Harry was shocked to see his boss, it was highly unusual and he suddenly had a bad feeling in his gut. Tony always liked the porter to phone up to the apartment and only then would he come down stairs but for some reason today he was in a hurry, and that was never a good sign. Harry nervously cleared his throat as Tony climbed into the cars passenger seat.

"Morning Boss, good night?"

Harry glanced out of the corner of his eye and couldn't be off noticing Tony's steely glare.

"No it fucking wasn't now just drive!"

Neither of the men noticed the black Omega pull away from the street at the same time. Tony was too deep in thought and Harry was concentrating on his driving, not wanting to get on the wrong side of his boss again. As they neared Limehouse a second unmarked police car pulled out in front of them and it was all done smoothly and effortlessly so as not to cause any interest from the vehicle behind. As the car approached the yard Tony instantly saw that the gates were open and that there were several police cars and vans inside, he also couldn't be off noticing the two blue tents that had been set up and which could only be there for one reason.

"Fuck it! Drive Harry, get us fucking out of here now!"

"I can't Tony, that wanker in front is slowing down. Come on you cunt move!"

The road on this part of the estate was narrow and with the car in front blocking their exit, there wasn't anywhere to overtake. Suddenly there was a screech of tyres as the car slammed on its breaks causing Harry to do the same. Looking out of the rear window Tony saw that the Omega was now only inches away from the rear bumper and he knew it was game over.

"Here we fucking go!"

Stepping from the car he straightened his tie and smoothed down his jacket.

"Keep your fucking trap shut Harry, you got that?"

Harry Chrome nodded his head, he was a Londoner through and through and the Old Bill would stand more chance of getting shit from a rocking horse than they would of getting anything out of him. From out of nowhere they were surrounded by armed police and when Tony and Harry were ordered to stretch out their hands and place them onto the car, they both instantly obliged. Within seconds they were handcuffed, read their rights, placed into a van and then driven over to New Scotland Yard. To begin with it had just been a standard operation but when human body parts started to appear it had swiftly escalated to the highest level. Tony realised what was to come but he just hoped Harry wouldn't turn grass, the man knew too much and just what he was and wasn't prepared to say was all down to him and out of Tony's hands. The one small consolation for Tony was the fact that if Harry disclosed too much about their business, then his own fate would be sealed regardless of whether Tony was locked up or not. No one tolerated a grass whether it was on the street or somewhere spent in one of her majesty's finest. When the duty solicitor entered the interview room Tony sneered back his lips in distaste but as it would take a while for his own brief to arrive, for now he would just have to go along with standard procedure. Tony Miller was under no illusion that he was going to walk away from this, the best he could hope for was damage limitation but even that was clutching at straws.

It was the day of the restaurants reopening and by eight that morning Stella Nicholson was already on her way to the premises. There was a delivery of fresh fruit and veg to check in, not to mention a special order from Thomas's the butchers. Stella had telephoned Tony the previous night and invited him to the opening but she wasn't sure if he would come. She knew he was having problems but not to what degree and when he was non committal and a bit vague, she just said the offer was there and it was up to him. It was fair to say that Stella was more than a bit narked and when she abruptly ended the call and Tony was left holding the telephone to his ear, he had instantly got the message. Today Stella wasn't about to let Tony Miller or anyone else spoil her excitement, the sun was shining brightly and she wanted to do the best for her brother and make him proud. Macy was already inside giving the place a spruce up but as Stella walked past the large glass window she noticed the sad expression on her new friends face. She guessed it had to do with this Anna woman but even though Stella was anything but uncompassionate, today of all days she just didn't have time to listen to someone else's problems. Dougie was banking on everything going right with tonight's opening, it had taken several days to talk him around but once he agreed he had been giving orders left right and centre from his hospital bed. Her brother was very demanding but Stella Nicholson didn't mind in the least, anything that took his mind away from the horrendous injuries he had suffered was fine by her. By five pm they were nearly ready; the girls had arrived and had been instructed by Macy what to do and even Daisy had been put to work folding napkins. The place shone like a new pin and as Stella surveyed all that her brother had built up, she couldn't help but feel proud. When Daisy called out, Stella's happiness immediately dropped away.

"Stella, I want a word."

"Yes Mum, what's the matter?"

"Have you invited Micky Mackerson tonight?"

With all that had been happening she hadn't given poor old Micky a second thought and now she felt guilty. For a second she considered calling him but then it could turn into a nightmare if Tony did decide to turn up.

"No Mum I didn't, I will have enough on my plate worrying about this place tonight."

As Daisy rolled her eyes and shook her head it didn't go unnoticed by her daughter but for once Stella let it drop. At six thirty on the dot Macy propped opened the front doors and it wasn't more than a few minutes before the first guests of the evening arrived. The night was a roaring success and when the doors were finally closed at midnight, a very tired but satisfied group of women treated themselves to a nightcap. Stevie had arrived an hour earlier to ferry them all home and realising that his mother was now a restaurateur for good, he offered to find and interview professional waitresses for her. The till was bulging with money and Stella couldn't wait for the morning to come so that she could go down to the hospital and tell Dougie all about it. There was only one thing to mar her success and that was the no show from a certain Mr Miller but she was sure he would eventually surface in the next few days. Gathering her children she asked them all to take a seat.

"Right you lot, I have some good news for once.

276

The shops are now finally in my possession."
Stella looked in her son's direction for some kind of response but there was nothing.

"Stevie nothing is going to change for you and your family love. You can carry on paying the same amount of rent as you've always done; I think that's only fair. That money will then be split between Ronnie, Jane and Ray."

Ronnie was over the moon that she would have a little extra income each month and Ray was yet to learn of the windfall but Jane was none too pleased although she didn't voice her opinion.

"If Stevie should ever decide to retire then the properties will be sold and the proceeds divided up between the four of you. Now I don't want any arguments and after all that's happened I hope you are happy with the outcome, I mean, after what's gone on we could have been sitting here with nothing."

Stevie Nicholson was the first to stand and as he began to clap his eyes filled with tears. He was soon joined by Ronnie, Jane and then to Stella's surprise her mother joined in.

Tony Miller had been interviewed twice; the first with a duty solicitor present and the second with Jeremy Blyth, his own brief who had represented Tony for the last ten years. Both interviews were exactly the same and were concluded within an hour as the only response was 'no comment'. At the same time Harry Chrome was also being questioned and even though he knew he was up to his neck in it, Harry also refused to speak. When the police requested an extension both Tony and Jeremy Blyth knew it was the end. Privy to some of the evidence that had been gathered, Jeremy advised his client to answer any questions honestly but Tony wasn't having any of it. If the Old Bill had him bang to rights, then it was down to them to prove it, the only problem was, for years Tony had buried guns, bodies and anything else he had wanted hidden and he didn't know exactly what they had unearthed. That said, he was willing to take a punt, either he would go down for the rest of his life or receive a few years and he was content to just sit tight and see how things panned out. He didn't have to wait long as thirty six hours later he was formerly charged with the murder of Luke Gray. Luke had been an unassuming young man whose opinion just happened to differ from Tony's. On a night when he was out and in a bad mood, Tony had taken an instant dislike to Luke. Cross words had been exchanged between the two men and after downing several whisky's Tony Miller had followed Luke Gray into the back alley of one of the clubs he often frequented and then stabbed the man in a frenzied and unprovoked attack. Because of the circumstances Tony had chosen to dispose of the body himself and in the early hours of the following morning had started up a JCB in his yard to dig the young man's grave. After excavating the hole eight feet deep he had hauled Luke's body from the boot of his car and thrown it into the murky pit along with the murder weapon complete with fingerprints. It might have been due to his intake of alcohol that had caused Tony to be so careless but that act of carelessness would seal his fate for the future. Luke Gray's parents had reported their son missing, but after eighteen months and when the police were no nearer locating the man the case had gone cold. When the scrap yard was raided, helicopters had been brought in and ground-penetrating radar was used to detect previous soil movement. It didn't take long to pin point a body that would later be identified as that of twenty five year old

Luke Gray. Five more sites were eventually located and Tony Miller was charged with six murders' in total. A special night court was held and Tony was placed on remand. Harry Chrome was brought back in and also charged with being an accessory to murder. Two days later and Stella was still unaware of anything that had happened but when Macy Langham came running into the restaurant; Stella wasn't expecting to hear what the woman had to say.

"You're in a happy mood Macy?"

"Yes I am, to tell the truth I'm fucking ecstatic."

Stella laughed, it was nice to see people in a good mood and happy staff was also good for business.

"Why is that?"

"That cunt Tony Miller has finally got what he deserved."

Stella instantly felt her stomach begin to churn. Macy wasn't aware of Stella's connection to Tony yet and even though she wasn't about to spill the beans, she was still desperate to find out what had happened.

"Tony Miller?"

"Yeah, you know that gangster I told you about, the one that was shagging Anna. He's been arrested and charged with murder, the wanker won't see the light of day for a very long time and as far as I'm concerned it's good fucking riddance. I don't care what anyone says; he had something to do with Anna's disappearance, I just know it."

Stella felt hot; the back of her neck was sticky and clammy and as she reached up to wipe her neck, she could feel the tension beginning to form.

"Will you be alright if I pop out for a bit Macy?"

"Yeah sure, take as long as you want."

Stella almost ran from the restaurant, the only trouble was, she didn't have a clue where she was running to.

Her head was swimming and at the same time her heart was breaking. Was it all her fault, if she hadn't told Tony about Anna would he still be a free man? She needed to speak to him, if only for a minute she needed to know that he was alright. Maybe Macy was exaggerating, maybe it was all a lie and he was carrying out his business as usual and would laugh when she told him but either way she had to find out. Hailing a cab she asked to be taken over to Limehouse and for the entire journey she felt as if her heart was in her mouth. When the cab came to a stop at the yard and she saw all the police activity she asked the driver to wait. Stepping onto the tarmac Stella made her way to the main gate but realised she wouldn't be allowed any further when a young constable walked over to her.

"Can I help you?"

"I'm trying to find a friend of mine, Tony Miller?"

The look on the constable's face was enough to tell her that things were really serious.

"Wait here and I'll see what I can find out."

Ten minutes later and when Stella was just about ready to give up hope the constable returned.

"All I can tell you is that Mr Miller is being questioned at New Scotland Yard."

Stella thanked the young man and then getting back into the cab she asked the driver to take her over to Victoria. All the events of the last few weeks were swimming about in her head, was she doing the right thing, had she treated poor old Micky in the right way. Looking up at the sky she cursed her father for all that he had brought down upon the family. Her life had been simple but good and her family had been happy but now in just a short space of time everything was a mess and she wondered just where it would all end. Paying the fair, which had risen to forty pounds due to the earlier waiting time, she entered the building and walked up to the secure reception area. The woman sitting behind the glass screen looked Stella up and down and for the first time in years Stella Nicholson felt self-conscious. When informed that Tony Miller had been remanded to Belmarsh Prison her heart sank to the pit of her stomach. Once again Stella hailed a cab and asked to be taken to Western Way. As the taxi approached its destination the building loomed heavily and Stella could feel her knees begin to shake. Paying the driver she then made her way to the visitors centre and asked if she could make a visit. The large lady seated behind the reception desk wasn't overly friendly when she informed Stella that remand visiting wasn't until two o'clock. Stella glanced at her watch, it was only twelve thirty but she decided to wait. There was little point in returning home or to the restaurant as by the time she got there it would be time to come back again. Flicking through some old magazines she was quickly bored but when a short while later the usual visitors began to arrive, things suddenly became more interesting. Women with snotty nosed kids in tow and prostitutes with their trademark clothes and looks began to fill up the area. There were arguments with staff and amongst themselves and she knew that there was no way she could live this kind of life. At two thirty her name was finally called and after making her way through the rigorous cheeks, Stella was at last sitting in the visiting room. It was totally alien to her and all of a sudden she felt nervous, as if she was seeing Tony for the first time. Gone were her memories of the intimacy that they had recently shared and she didn't like how she was now feeling. When the door at the far end of the room opened and the prisoners were led out, Stella realised she

281

had made a big mistake in coming here. Even though Tony approached her with a wide grin on his face and a cheeky glint in his eye, it didn't make Stella fccl any better.

"Hello girl! Nice to see you babe."

"You alright Tony?"

"You know me darling, it goes with the territory."

"I can't do this Tony."

"Do what?"

"I can't spend the next god knows how many years, visiting you once a fortnight."

Tony Miller grabbed hold of Stella's hand and lifting it up, smothered it with kisses.

"I wouldn't expect you to babe, I'm just grateful that you're here today. I've always been a firm believer of the old saying 'you should never go back'. We gave it a try love but look what happened?"

"Are you blaming me for all of this?"

"Oh sweetheart, never in a million years would I ever blame you. There's only one person to blame for this and that's me. I should never have left you in the first place, I didn't realise what I had until it was too late. Babe I want you to make a fresh start, and that begins with no more visits to this shit hole. Tell that boy of ours that all I have is now his and I'll make all the arrangements. I have a couple of properties that are legit so even if the law decides to seize my assets he'll at least get something, god knows I won't have any use for it and if I ever get out of this shit hole, which is highly unlikely, then the only thing I'm going to need is a Zimmer frame and an old people's home."

Stella began to cry and Tony tenderly lifted her chin so that she was facing him.

"Please don't babe. Look sweetheart, this ain't no place

for a lady so go now, live your life and never come back here."

Standing up Tony quickly leaned forward and kissed her on the lips.

"Go and remember, don't have any regrets."

As the guards led him away he continued to look back at her over his shoulder smiling. Stella wearily made her way outside and once in the open air she let it all out, let every ounce of the emotion she was feeling exit her body. When there were no more tears left she began the very long walk back to Roy Street, the restaurant would just have to manage without her tonight. All Stella could think of doing was to go home, crawl into bed and pull the covers over her head and shut out the world.

CHAPTER TWENTY EIGHT
Eight months later

The restaurant was going from strength to strength and with the shops once again secure, things finally seemed to be back on track, business wise at least. Stevie had tried to replace the waitresses for professional girls who weren't family but the Nicholson women were having none of it. Jane had given up her job to join Stella full time and mother and daughter were actually beginning to like each other. Dougie was now out of hospital but even though he was back at work, he never left the kitchen for fear of ridicule regarding his looks. He was slowly coming to terms with the idea of a life without James and even though he had many more operations ahead of him, he was still hopeful of a happy future. Stella had even managed to get Daisy on board, it was only a couple of nights a week folding napkins but at least she was involved although recently she had been demoted to the rear of the restaurant after insulting a customer who was rude to her; you could never take the East End out of a woman like Daisy Nicholson so it was best not to even try. All in all things were good but Tony's court case was fast approaching and it always seemed to be on Stella's mind. She hadn't seen the man since her initial visit to the prison but that hadn't stopped her constantly thinking about him. Now that a date had been set Stella was adamant that she would be attending, she had to see him, had to see his beautiful smile just a few more times before it would be gone forever. The only person aware of her true feelings was her son and his heart went out to his mother. Shortly after his arrest, Tony had asked Stevie to come to the prison for a visit. The meeting had gone well but after he had given his son instructions regarding his properties and money, Tony had told Stevie the same as he told Stella 'live your life and don't come back here again'. As he walked away from the prison Stevie couldn't believe how he'd felt. Deep down he knew that if he had been given the chance to have a relationship with his father then they might well have hit it off, which even to him sounded a little absurd as the man was a murderer. Life was a bitch and then it was over, his dear old mum deserved better and even though she had never complained, Stevie knew that her life, for the most part anyway, had been shit but he was now hopeful that with her new found business skills she would soon be earning a pretty penny, enough to at least treat herself to some of the finer things in life. After selling off Tony's two properties Stevie really didn't need to work again but there was something in him, something that pushed him on to continue making his own living. The shops were as busy as ever and going in to work each morning still thrilled him as much as it had on his very first day and he hoped he would never lose that feeling. Now the day of judgement had arrived and sitting in the public gallery of a very packed court at the Old Bailey, Stella Nicholson glanced all around her. She studied the jurors one by one and could easily see that they were ordinary people just like her; she could also see that several of them were here under duress and she prayed that it wouldn't affect them giving Tony a fair trial even if they were desperate to get out of this place and return to their normal lives. There were five women and seven men of varying ages and Stella wished with all her heart that she could speak to each of them in turn. She wanted to tell them that no matter what they were about to hear regarding the man soon to be standing in the dock, he

285

hadn't always been that way. She wanted to say how kind he was, how generous he was and that he would help people out even when there was nothing in it for him but she couldn't, all she could do was plead with her eyes even though she knew it would make no difference whatsoever. At exactly ten o'clock that morning proceedings got under way. The gallery was full to capacity but glancing around Stella didn't recognise anyone. Most were men and by their dress it was obvious they were from London's gangster fraternity but whether they were here to support Tony Miller or to cheer when he was sentenced was anyone's guess. The world in which he had lived was alien to her, it was one she could never have imagined living herself and the thought that it could easily have come down to a choice scared her. Stella Nicholson liked life to be simple with no complications, just day to day run of the mill and where it might have seemed boring to most; to Stella it was all she craved. When she saw Tony emerge from below the courtroom and led into the dock it made her feel physically sick but when he looked in her direction and smiled, she couldn't stop herself from grinning back and blowing him a kiss. Everyone in the room was told to stand for the right honourable Judge Fergus McGiven and as he took his seat Stella tried to study his face for any sign that he was caring and would be sympathetic but with the white wig and robes he just looked solemn. No one in the East End had any time for the law and judicial system, they had all seen loved ones or knew of someone that had or was serving time for a crime they supposedly didn't commit and Stella wondered just how fair this trial would be. As the charges were slowly read out Stella began to have a change of heart. All along she had chosen to believe that even though Tony wasn't as white

286

as the driven, to her at least, he was still a good man. Now listening to all that he was being accused of Stella couldn't believe what she was hearing and when she stared in Tony's direction his head was bowed and as hard as she wished him to, he wouldn't or couldn't look in her direction. The man she had silently loved for over thirty years was disappearing before her very eyes. Had it all been a lie, how could she ever have loved someone capable of such terrible crimes? With every statement, every cruel account of the pain he had inflicted, it was like a knife being plunged deeper and deeper into Stella's heart. Suddenly she saw him for what he was, a mean sadistic human being and his refusal to look at her told Stella that he knew what was coming, knew that they had him bang to rights and he was guilty. As the prosecution began to reveal further evidence there was no mention of Anna Hillman but there had been several other bodies discovered at the yard along with numerous weapons. When it was time for the pathologist to read out his report, a woman member of the jury gasped out loud. It was very detailed and stated that two of the bodies had been horrifically tortured prior to death. Tony Miller was called into the witness stand but still he wouldn't look in Stella's direction. The trial had been listed to last a week but it was almost concluded after two days as Tony had refused to answer any of the prosecutors questions. The only noticeable reaction from him was when Harry Chrome's name was called out. Harry's own trial had ended a week earlier and he was now serving a ten year stretch in Pentonville prison. As he walked into the witness box Tony did a double take, his right hand man had changed so much in the last few months that he was now hardly recognisable. Harry's weight had dropped considerably, his hair had begun to go grey at the sides

287

and he appeared to have a stoop. Only once did he look in Tony's direction but there was no recognition between the two men and Tony had been convinced that Harry was about to grass. Nothing was further from the truth and with each question that was asked, his only reply was 'I can't remember'. The Judge soon became angry and threatened Harry with contempt but there was nothing that would ever make him squeal and it wasn't anything to do with loyalty to Tony Miller. Self preservation was his only priority and Harry knew that if he played his cards right and if the two men should ever happen to find themselves in the same nick, then Harry would have a soft ride and be well looked after. Before long it was time for the summing up but there really wasn't much that Tony's barrister could put forward in his defence as the evidence had been so overwhelming and damning. Jumbo Smith's ledger had tied everything together perfectly and there was no room for any doubt. Stella had attended the trial every day, desperately praying that something would be produced to prove that this was all wrong, that her man was innocent but after hearing what Tony was capable of she realised that she really didn't know him at all. Each evening she had relayed all that had happened to her son and on the final day Stevie had accompanied her to hear the verdict. Now they were anxiously sitting in the public gallery and Stella could feel the perspiration on the palms of her hands. How was it possible to despise someone, hate their very existence but still love them at the same time, Stella Nicholson wasn't able to answer her own question and for that she felt ashamed of herself. All the dubious men that had attended on the first day were back again for the last. To Stella it felt like they saw it as a day of entertainment, a day when they would see one of their own thrown to the lions like in the times of ancient Rome, the only difference was her Tony wasn't a gladiator and there was no prize to be won. Would Tony Miller crumble upon hearing his sentence or would he stand tall and take his punishment like a man.

"You alright mum?"

Her son's voice snapped Stella from her daydream and turning in her seat, even though her heart was breaking, she smiled at Stevie as she squeezed his hand.

"Yeah I'm fine love, I just can't get my head around what he did, how can you do those things to people Stevie?"

Stevie Nicholson could only shrug his shoulders, he hated to see his mother in so much turmoil and not be able to do anything to help her.

"I'm never going to see him again."

"You don't know that mum; he could be out in a few years and ..."

Stella stopped her boy's sentence by placing her hand up. "Please don't try and make me feel better with worthless words love, we both know that Tony is going down for a very long time. Now you might not have noticed, but your old mum ain't no spring chicken and if he is ever released which I very much doubt, then I will probably be long gone or at best I'll be dribbling in a nursing home somewhere. I wonder what made him become so cold son, what could turn a nice man into an evil animal?"

Stevie didn't reply or try to add anything more to his mother's statement and instead he leaned over and gently placed a kiss onto her cheek. Suddenly they were all told to rise as the honourable Judge McGiven entered. No time was wasted and the foreman of the jury was asked to stand and give the verdict of them all. You could have heard a pin drop and most of the public gallery were now sitting forwards on the edge of their seat.

"Guilty on all counts your honour."

The strange men that Stella now realised had known Tony well, began to shout and jeer and it was obvious that they had been here for support all along. Judge McGiven slammed down his gavel and ordered silence but it still took several minutes before he would allow the proceedings to continue. When order was at last restored and before Stella knew what was happening, Tony was told to stand and face the judge.

"We have listened to some compelling evidence, some of which is the worst that has ever been brought before me and you have been found guilty of the most heinous of crimes. It is clear to me that you are a very real danger to our society Mr Miller. You may have felt that you were above the law and for that misguided belief you will now pay the consequence. I pass down a sentence of twenty five years with my personal recommendation that you should serve a minimum of twenty two years before you are even considered for parole. Take him down."

As Tony was led down the stairs to the holding cells below the room was again in uproar but this time Fergus McGiven didn't try to maintain order and instead he quickly disappeared through a rear door that led into the Judges chamber. Stevie placed his arm around Stella's shoulder but as soon as she had wiped her tears away, tears that were as much for her as they were for Tony Miller; she stood up and gathered herself.

"I'm fine son, come on let's get out of here."

"Do you want to go for a quiet drink somewhere?"

"And what good would that do!"

Her reply was sharp and as soon as the words left her mouth she wished she could have taken them back. True he didn't really know his father but at the end of the day Tony was still that, his father. As much as she had lost

290

the man she loved, her boy had lost any chance of getting to know the man who had given him life.

"I'm sorry love, that was out of order but I don't want to dwell on things or mope about. Tony Miller is now out of my life, just like he was when he disappeared all those years ago and deep down I know that it's for the best because eventually I would have found out what he was really like. Now I have to get on and start to live my life again without him. Let's go back to the flat and tell your Nan, I can guarantee she won't shed a tear when she hears what has happened."

"Why did Nan never like him Mum?"

As mother and son walked down the stone steps of the court Stella took a moment to think before she answered. "Because of the way he treated me I suppose, you know your Nan, well maybe you don't actually. She wasn't allowed to voice her opinion, she was far too scared of the old man for that but all the same, I know she felt my pain. You know something son, I have never been able to forgive Tony for leaving me and I probably never will but it didn't stop me loving him. Even after all I've heard in this place, I still love him, sounds a bit sick doesn't it?"

"No it doesn't Mum! For every villain or murderer in this world, well they all have someone who loved them at some point in their lives. The heart is a strange thing when it comes down to feelings and you can't just switch them off no matter how hard you might want to darling."

Stevie hugged his mother to him as they walked along but he didn't continue with the conversation, there was no point. Stella was hurting and anything he said would only add to her pain. Back at the flat Daisy had just sat down with a cup of tea when Stella walked in. Hearing the front door close she called out.

"Kettles hot!"

Stevie had dropped his mum off before heading home, even though he hardly knew the man he didn't have the stomach to listen to his Nan's ravings today, at least not when it concerned his father. Stella walked into the front room and flopped down onto the sofa. She waited for Daisy to start but not a word left her mother's lips. After a couple of minutes Stella couldn't contain herself and had to ask, in all honesty she was so uptight regarding what had happened that she was spoiling for a row.
"Well?"
"Well what?"
"Don't play silly buggers mum; I know you're dying to find out what he got."
"Well it's nice to know what you think of me Stella! For your information I knew it wasn't going to be good news, well at least not as far as you were concerned. So no, I am not as you put it 'dying to know what Tony Miller got' thank you very much!"
"I'm sorry then ok?"
"So what did he get?"
Stella rolled her eyes up towards the ceiling; she had always been able to read her mother like a book.
"Twenty five."
"As long as that? Oh well that's life."
The conversation stopped there, Daisy wanted to watch the telly and Stella now didn't want to argue. She was tired not to mention depressed and as it was her only night off from the restaurant she decided to turn in. Tomorrow was another day and hopefully things would be better, because how she was feeling right at this minute, things couldn't get any worse.

CHAPTER TWENTY NINE

The following year passed without event, the restaurant was doing better than ever and Dougie's wounds were healing as well as could be expected. Although he would never look the same, he was now at a point where he felt able to pop into the dining room if forced. He had managed to obtain a quick divorce due to James's desertion and even though he was lonely and would only admit it to himself, he was far happier living on his own than he had been when married. Dougie's days and evenings had become busier than he'd ever known so when the restaurant closed he relished the peace and quiet. Ronnie, Jane, Macy and Jo were still waitressing and loving every moment of it. They all took pride in the place and it showed in the till receipts each night. Macy was finally aware of Stella's involvement with Tony Miller but she didn't hold it against the woman, when Stella had explained everything and when she swore that she didn't know anything about Anna's disappearance, Macy decided to put the matter to the back of her mind but just a small piece of her was still hopeful that the girl would one day surface. Macy saw Stella Nicholson as a good sort and the two were now firm friends which was something Macy treasured above all else. On the evenings when Daisy was on napkin duty she was continually studying her daughter and she couldn't be off noticing how quiet Stella was. In the past her girl had been the life and soul of the place but now, for the last couple of months at least, it seemed as if she was running on auto pilot. She treated the staff and her customers well, was the full on party provider when it was called for but somewhere along the line she had lost her spark and it broke Daisy's heart. On a quiet night and as Stella made her way across the restaurant to the kitchen her mother grabbed her hand.

"What's wrong love?"

Stella had a quizzical look on her face, almost as if she didn't have a clue what her mother was talking about but deep down she wasn't kidding anyone.

"What do you mean mum?"

"Don't try kidding a kidder girl, your old mum knows you better than you know yourself."

Stella tenderly stroked her mother's hand.

"Oh I don't know sweetheart, sometimes I just feel that life is passing me by I suppose."

"Don't be so bleeding daft; you're still a spring chicken, well at least you are compared to me."

"It's not that, you know when you were a little kid and you had all those hopes and dreams for the future?"

Daisy looked at her daughter in a confused way but deep down she knew exactly what Stella meant.

"Well my hopes and dreams never came to anything did they? I feel like the only thing I have to look forward to is running this place, don't get me wrong I do love it here but it doesn't keep me warm at nights does it?"

"Well then do something about it girl, I didn't raise you to be a bleeding quitter."

"No you didn't sweetheart but you know something mum? I really don't have the energy anymore. I'm so tired and I think the last few months have drained me more than I ever thought possible."

"So it's not because of that wanker Miller then?"

"Mum!"

"Well is it?"

"No love it isn't, I suppose, and as reluctant as I am to admit it, I'm just getting old."

Stella kissed her mother on the cheek and then continued through to the kitchen. There and then Daisy Nicholson decided to take matters into her own hands, if her daughter didn't know what was good for her, couldn't see what was blatantly staring her in the face, then her old mum most certainly could.

The next morning after Stella had left the flat to check in the deliveries, Daisy pulled on her overcoat, grabbed her handbag and stepped from the flat. She never normally went out without a member of her family to escort her and she knew that if they found out there would be murders but what they didn't know about wouldn't hurt them. Reaching the bottom step she began to cross the tarmac square when Raymond approached her.

"Hello there Nan, what you up to girl?"

"Just going for a walk. Have you been alright Raymond, only I ain't seen you for ages and you know how much your mum worries about you?"

"I'm fine doll, you know me, been busy ducking and diving with a bit of this and a bit of that. My Mum would still worry if she saw me every day; it's just the way she is. Since Stevie started giving me rent money I'm starting to do alright, you know, getting my shit together?"

"Never did understand you youngsters saying that, in my day shit was what you left behind in the bleeding khazi and nothing else. I need to get off now; you can keep me company if you like?""

The invite was strange to say the least, Ray wasn't stupid and he knew that normally the old woman wouldn't give him the time of day. Maybe she was softening, maybe she had an ulterior motive but one thing was for sure, he wasn't going to miss an opportunity to get back into the family fold. Ray nodded his head and gently taking his

295

grandmothers arm they set off down Roy Street. At the end and instead of turning right like she usually did, Daisy steered her grandson left in the direction of Ford Road. Raymond didn't question his Nan but even he was astute enough to know that she obviously had a particular destination in mind. Thirty minutes later and when they reached the Dundee Arms Ray was grinning from ear to ear.

"What are you up to you crafty old cow?"

Daisy fished about in her handbag and retrieved two pound coins that had long since been rolling about in the bottom.

"Never you mind you nosy little bugger, now here's a couple of quid for a drink. When you've been served go and sit down, what I have to say is private and not for your ears."

Ray pushed open the main door and the unlikely duo stepped inside just as Micky Mackerson looked up from his newspaper. The pub wasn't open yet and he was about to say 'we're closed' but stopped and smiled when he saw who his visitors were.

"Hello there Daisy girl, long time no see you been keeping alright sweetheart?"

"Too bleeding long if you ask me and yes, I'm good thanks love. My arthritis gives me jip but I suppose at my age I ain't got any right to complain. Get this one a drink will you and then we can have a chat."

"What you having son?"

"Just a half of Fosters please Micky."

Raymond picked up his larger and took a seat at the far end of the pub just as he'd been asked. He would have liked to have known what was being said but he knew better than to cross his Nan. Daisy Nicholson had suffered terribly at the hands of her husband but when it came down to her kids and grandkids she was a force to be reckoned with.

"So Daisy, what can I do for you?"

"It's not what you can do for me but what you can do for my girl."

"But she's with...."

"I know very well who she was with and I do emphasise was and as you well know, Tony Miller won't be seeing the light of day for a very long time. My girl is a silly little fucker at times and she's also headstrong, though lord above knows where she gets that from."

Micky tried his best to stifle the laugh that was desperately fighting to escape. Stella was so much like her mother and it was something he loved about the woman.

"We both know that you two had a good thing going but her head was turned by that evil bastard. Obviously you're aware that he's been sent down and to tell you the truth Micky, my girl is a changed woman, lost her spark if you know what I mean but it ain't because of him, believe you me that's well and truly over. Oh for fucks sake Micky, you ain't making this easy for me, what I'm trying to say is why don't you give it another shot?"

He couldn't believe what he was hearing, he had missed Stella like crazy and now that there might be another chance a wide grin spread across his face. For the next twenty minutes the unlikely pair were huddled in deep conversation and when Daisy finally nodded in her grandson's direction indicating that it was time to go, he was desperate to know what had happened. They began the slow walk back to Roy Street and for the first couple of minutes he kept quiet but when it was obvious that his Nan wasn't about to spill the beans, he couldn't hold his tongue any longer.

297

"Well!"

"Well what?"

"You know fine well what I'm on about Nan, so what was said?"

"You mind your own bleeding business and if a word of this gets back to your mum I'll know where it's come from. For once boy, do the right thing."

Nothing more was said and when he'd seen Daisy safely into the flat, Raymond Nicholson set off up the road. Suddenly he felt the need for a little something to lift his spirits and as usual when Raymond Nicholson felt the need, all thoughts of what his Nan or anyone else was up to swiftly disappeared from his mind.

Two nights later and just as Stella was about to pull her coat on to go to work Daisy made her way into the hall and looking her daughter up and down from head to foot she frowned

"You're not wearing that are you?"

Turning from side to side Stella inspected the black dress in the hall mirror.

"What's wrong with it?"

"Nothing if you're going to a bleeding funeral. I know you're a bit down in the dumps love but there's no need to let yourself go. You'll never meet someone if you don't put in a bit of bleeding effort."

Her mother's words were not intended to upset her but all the same Stella now felt self-conscious. Placing her handbag onto the floor she walked through to the bedroom and opened up her wardrobe. Selecting a cream suit she'd had for Ronnie's wedding she was about to pull it out when she heard her mother speak.

"Oh not that one love, it makes you look so old not to mention fat!"

Stella took a deep breath, Daisy was starting to piss her

298

off big time and she knew that any minute she would snap and let rip.

"Bloody hell mum, it ain't a fucking fashion show you know. Look you pick something for me, anything to keep you bleeding happy but hurry up or I'm going to be late for work."

With a wide grin on her face Daisy Nicholson walked over and pulled out a cerise and blue patterned shift dress. She had always thought how much it suited her daughter and showed off her figure, which for someone in their mid fifties, was still pretty good. Seeing her mother's choice Stella slowly shook her head and smiled.

"Alright alright, well go on then, outside so I can get changed."

"You ain't got nothing I ain't seen before; remember I gave birth to you."

"How could I ever forget, but that was many moons ago so if you don't mind I would like a bit of privacy."

A few minutes later Stella walked into the hallway and Daisy did a quick inspection.

"That's much better."

"Well I'm glad it meets with your approval, now I really must get off. See you later and make sure you lock this door when I'm gone mum."

Stella headed out, but before the front door had fully closed Daisy was already on the telephone making sure that the final pieces of her plan were being put into place. Reaching the restaurant Stella's brow furrowed and she did a double take when she saw the closed sign hanging in the window. If Macy hadn't turned up for her shift there would be hell to pay but then again, where was Dougie, surely he would have opened up. Pushing on the front door she found it locked and began to mutter under her breath 'what the fuck is going on'. Fishing about in

299

her handbag she finally retrieved her keys and let herself inside. The place was in darkness except for a dim light shining from under the kitchen door. Stella called out but there was no answer so she made her way to the back of the room. Pushing on the swing door she gasped at what greeted her. Micky Mackerson sat suited and booted at a table which had been set to perfection and candles were romantically burning. Stella began to cry and standing up Micky walked over and took her in his arms. No words passed between them but as she held him tightly she wondered why he was giving her a second chance. Micky was strong, honest and had treated her well but for some stupid reason she had walked away from him. It was only now that she realised it never would have worked with Tony; you couldn't and shouldn't ever go back. Tilting her head upwards Micky kissed her tenderly and Stella knew she finally had what she always wanted, someone who would love her forever. It really was strange how life had a way of working itself out and how you never realised what you had until after it had gone.

"Why?"

"Why what?"

"Why are you giving me a second chance?"

Micky slowly planted kisses all down her neck but at the same time he spoke in a hushed tone.

"I would have given you a million chances girl!"

An hour later and when they had eaten the delicious meal prepared by Dougie, the couple chatted over a brandy and Micky revealed that everything had been set up by Daisy. Stella couldn't believe what she was hearing and now more than anything she wanted to go home and hug her mother. Micky ordered a taxi and dropped her off at Roy Street, there would be no sex that night as this time they had decided to take things slowly, this time it would be a proper relationship. Running up the stairs like a youngster Stella eagerly placed her key into the lock and opened up the door. Sure that her mother would be asleep, she tip toed along the hallway and entered Daisy's bedroom.

"Mum? Mum are you awake darling?"

When there was no usual sarky comment Stella walked over intending to gently kiss her mum on the forehead but as soon as her lips touched Daisy's cold skin Stella knew that she would never get the chance to say thank you.

"No no no, oh please don't leave me mum!!!!"

It was far too late to get help and laying down beside the only woman who knew her inside out, knew what made her tick and what made her angry, Stella Nicholson cradled her mother in her arms and cried like a baby for the one person who could never be replaced. Life had indeed changed, some of it had turned out for the better but this, this was a loss so great so heartbreaking that Stella knew she would never get over it. Daisy Nicholson had spent her entire life making sure that everyone around her was happy and had what they needed, even in her final act she had made sure that her beloved daughter would never be alone again.

THE END

Printed in Great Britain
by Amazon